LANCELOT
AND THE SWORD
THE NEW EDITION

Mirador Publishing
10 Greenbrook Terrace
Taunton
Somerset
UK
TA1 1UT

THE KNIGHTS OF CAMELOT
Book 2

LANCELOT
AND THE SWORD
THE NEW EDITION

SARAH LUDDINGTON

Also available through Mirador Publishing:

The Prophecy
Vampire
Seelie
Unforbidden: A Queer Collection

The Knights of Camelot Series:
Lancelot and the King
Lancelot and the Sword
Lancelot and the Grail

Lancelot's Challenge
Lancelot's Burden
Lancelot's Curse

Betrayal Of Lancelot
Passion Of Lancelot
Revenge Of Lancelot

Lancelot The Lost Years: The Spear

Sons of Camelot Series:
The Pendragon Legacy
The Du Lac Legacy

The Rock and Roll Mysteries:
Chords for the Dead

As always my love and gratitude to my knight.

CHAPTER ONE

"WELL, THERE SHE IS," Arthur said as he leaned on the pommel of his saddle. "My curse."

We had crested the hills that peered down over Camelot. Rain started to spit from the sky and we were all cold and tired. We'd been riding hard since just before dawn and we'd missed lunch.

"That's a fine way of talking about your home, Arthur," Merlin snapped. They hadn't managed a civilised conversation for some time.

"Do you blame me? I have a wife who hates me and might just be responsible for trying to kill me. I have enemies who I counted as friends. I have the possibility of war hanging over my head. And you want me to give up my one consolation."

"He just asked you to be cautious with what we have between us, Arthur," I said. I'd grown weary of this conversation over the last ten days of travel. I ached all over, my hand hurt in the splints and bandages Merlin fashioned to hold it still and nightmares dogged my sleep.

"So, you too are ashamed of what we have?" he asked. We'd had this exchange at least once a day on the journey to Camelot. I closed my eyes and begged for patience. I think he actually feared his own shame and confusion over our love, rather than mine, but Arthur reflected our anxiety into the light.

"You know the answer to that. I am not ashamed, Arthur, but I am aware of other people's opinions. You have a wife and crown to save," I said.

His eyes swivelled to take in the city swarming down toward the river and the sea. "I know, Wolf, but I don't want it."

There we had the final confession.

Arthur Pendragon, King of Camelot and England, wanted to throw his crown into the sea. When the messenger arrived in Avalon to say we had trouble brewing at home and Kay needed help, I watched Arthur close down before my eyes. When it had just been the two of us in the Abbey, we'd grown so close and we were so happy, we'd both forgotten the real world waited to close its jaws on us once more.

"They need you, Arthur," I said gesturing to the city and meaning the people.

"I know but I need you," he whispered.

"I will always be at your side, my King," I said, laying a hand on his bowed head.

He nodded and pushed Willow forward. Merlin clucked his shaggy mountain horse, Daisy, into a walk, and I gave Ash his head. If I were honest, I didn't want to return to Camelot any more than Arthur did but that was not my decision. Where my King went I followed, always would.

As we rode into the city, during the busy afternoon rush in the markets and around the inns, Arthur kept his ears open. We walked a circuitous route and he maintained his anonymity. Merlin watched and listened just as hard. He'd not been in the city for more than five years. I rode behind them; hand on my sword, ready. I knew how restless and unhappy Camelot had grown over the months. Even having been in prison for almost a year, then banished, it didn't make me ignorant of the problems we faced. The evidence of Arthur's neglect lay everywhere.

The city guard were not guarding, they were chattering with whores. The women in question offered themselves on the streets, rather than quietly in the houses, which made ignoring them impossible. Litter, mud and shit covered the paved roads and we heard endless arguments about prices and guilds taking advantage of the power vacuum. There were more beggars, more obvious hunger, more poor. We found an area of the city which didn't even have houses, just shacks thrown up against each other, streets too narrow to ride through. We witnessed crime, cutpurses, the illegal sale of narcotics, unlicensed alcohol, and theft. Merlin bought some of the drugs we found and almost choked on the foul smell.

"It's fly agaric and poppy. It'll kill in these doses if someone doesn't know what they're doing," he said.

"I had no idea it had become this bad," Arthur said.

"I told you, if the king is sick the land is sick and Camelot is the first place to turn bad when the king is bad," Merlin lectured for the hundredth time.

"It wasn't exactly my fault," Arthur snapped.

"You didn't have to drink the poison, Arthur," the old wizard snapped back.

"It seemed like a fine idea after I almost killed my –" he paused and bit back the word he wanted to use to describe me. "What do I do to fix it?" he asked instead.

"Rule, bring leadership back to Camelot. Stop the fey from poisoning our people, in mind and body. These people would welcome Stephen taking the throne from you if he promised them health, wealth and happiness. So, you need to give it to them but make them proud of it, make them work for it. Don't just hand over money to the churches to care for them in their sickness. Make them proud to belong to Camelot by forcing them to invest in their city, in you. They are your greatest defence against Stephen and the fey. Use them, Arthur. Woo them. You know how to do it, you've just lost the common touch because you've been in pain for too long. Now, you are free of that pain, so help them help themselves." Merlin's grey eyes shone as he guided Arthur. I remembered watching almost exactly the same scene when Arthur had just gained the throne all those years before. Merlin had told him the same thing to help him become the great king I loved.

"We need to start with the guard. We give them back their pride, give them something worthy of the uniform," I said. "Give them a reason to police their city."

Arthur nodded and I knew as we walked through the city to the great keep, he already had a list of orders a mile long to give us all. He'd always held to the law and maintained a tight rein on the detail of his government. I had the feeling any slack which may have occurred would be banished.

The walls to the entrance of the keep could be seen at the end of the road we rode up. Arthur stopped. We stopped. Merlin looked at him.

"What is it?" the wizard asked in that voice I'd grown wary of over the years. It meant Arthur tapped into a part of himself connected to another world.

I watched as Camelot's King drew in a deep breath and closed his eyes. "There's something wrong in there," he said. He turned to me. "We go in there armed and we stake our claim to my city." His blue eyes shone with an inner power.

I grinned. "Yes, Sire." My right hand groused that fighting didn't seem a sensible idea, I ignored it.

The three of us turned the horses and rode back to a nearby inn we'd all been drunk in at one time or another. I slipped off Ash and entered through a discreet door at the back. I spoke with the innkeeper. He came out, bowed briefly before Willow and Arthur and took us to a small set of private rooms he kept for his more illustrious patrons, when they were doing something they shouldn't.

We piled into the rooms and I found myself alone with Arthur for a moment. I looked around. "I should keep these rooms on retainer for our private enjoyment," I said.

Arthur tried to scowl but gave up and laughed. "Think I'm becoming your whore?" he asked.

I frowned, considered and said, "More like mistress." Then Merlin walked in.

"You are quite correct, Arthur." His presence dominated the room. No mean feat with two huge warriors in there as well, "Camelot is sick and the sickness is at her core. We are going to have problems, my friend."

Arthur, his moment of jovial silliness fleeing before the wizards unhappiness, said, "Tell me."

"There have been countless arrests throughout the city. Men are being held without charge and decent women are avoiding the keep. Those that work in the keep but live in the city are scared. There is foulness in the stones."

"I haven't been gone that long," Arthur complained. "How can things be as bad as that?"

"Your spirit has been gone from Camelot for a very long time," Merlin stated.

Arthur glanced at me. "My spirit almost died in Camelot," he spoke with such emotion, my own heart ached in sympathy for the golden young man who had to become king.

"Well," I said, trying to control Arthur's anguish, "it doesn't make much of a difference what kind of malaise is in Camelot's walls, we have to stop it." I grabbed my breastplate and began buckling it on. "If we are facing an enemy in Camelot, whether it can be defeated with a sword or with our spirits we need to put on a display of victory and that means looking shiny and fierce."

To be honest I had no idea if I was right but I'd far rather face anything with a sword in my hand than complicated politics. Displays of strength I understood. In the end, Arthur helped me into the armour, the fingers of my right hand too damaged. I worried I'd never be able to function as a warrior again, but Merlin seemed convinced I'd heal given time. Something of a luxury.

When Arthur finished dressing he turned to me. "What do I do about Guinevere?"

The question came from nowhere and I had nowhere to hide. My heart rate shot up. We'd not spoken of Guinevere for weeks. I'd shied away from thinking about her and the consequences of caving into Arthur's desire. Correction, our desire, I couldn't blame Arthur for this mess.

"I'm not certain I'm the person to ask," I said, hedging around the subject.

Arthur's eyes narrowed. "I want your opinion not a tactful withdraw from the field," his tone hardened.

"Arthur..." I tried to escape but the look in his eyes gave me no retreat. I puffed air out and stared at the beams in the ceiling looking for inspiration. "Alright, if you want my honest opinion here it is, don't fight her. Find out what she wants. Find out why she is so angry. Talking, not screaming or fighting. One day at a time and give her space to be angry with you." I grabbed Arthur's steel shoulders. "You need to try to save your marriage, Arthur. You loved her once."

His gaze dropped. "Now I love you," he said.

"We share something different," I spoke to the top of his head, "but you still need a Queen, a wife and an heir."

He nodded and turned away, burying whatever conflict he suffered under the armour of a king. Wearing my own armour made me feel invincible. When Merlin returned, in his formal black cloak rather than riding leathers, the three of us walked from the inn and I revelled in the feeling of being at home with my King at my side.

I'd buckled my sword onto my right hip, ensuring I'd have a clean draw with my left, but it made an untidy remount of Ash. He danced and pranced around the inn's yard, the armour and Willow's company making him think we were in for a fight.

Arthur grinned at me. "I have the best at my side once more, Wolf."

"I will always be at your side, Sire." I smiled in return.

We clomped from the yard and into the streets of Camelot. All three of us had our heads bare, no great helm or coif. Each of us recognisable in our own way. As one unit, we returned to the curtain wall of the castle and followed it around toward the main gate.

The sun sat low and squat in the western sky on the short winter day but people began to realise their sun rode the streets. Arthur sat, straight, strong, proud and the epitome of knighthood. Damn it felt good to be home.

News of Arthur's appearance in the city spread more swiftly than fire, water, or air. People filled the streets in moments and the cheering started. With bare heads, we watched the people and they watched us. My name rushed from lip to lip as Arthur walked ahead, my coat of arms as familiar to the people as the king's because we were so close and I won the tourneys. Arthur smiled and waved to those he recognised of the traders and craftsmen. People adored him and he adored them back. A king is his people and the people are their king.

By the time we reached the keep's outer walls, a surging living tide of humanity cried out our names. Except for Merlin. Mother's invoked his name to scare their children but I felt their relief in his presence as much as my own. The old team were together, now all ills would be cured.

I only had to hope they were right. The welcoming committee at the gates made me think they might be proved wrong.

CHAPTER TWO

THE BRIDGE OVER THE deep moat leading from the main part of the city to the mighty keep itself should have two men guarding it. As we rode up, twenty men stood on the bridge and none of them in Arthur's colours of blue and gold. Merlin and I moved up and flanked him. I heard a low growl come from his throat.

The colours the men wore were also an unwelcome sight. Turquoise and yellow, far too close to Arthur's colours. They lined each side of the bridge and only one person stood in the centre.

Stephen de Clare. The man I loathed more than any other breathing in our world. I felt my teeth grind and my desire to kill translated itself to Ash. Up until that point, he'd simply enjoyed the pageantry, the old tart, but now he knew we faced an enemy. His hind quarters twisted outward and he gnashed his bit.

"Calm down, Lancelot, you aren't helping," Arthur muttered while he focused on de Clare. He knew Ash translated my own mood.

De Clare walked toward us, the crowd of Camelot hushed. I watched and realised he hadn't changed at all in the year since we had last met. Not as tall as either Arthur, or myself he nevertheless stood as stout as a tree. Older than me by ten years, his brown hair not yet touched by time. His face though, betrayed his temper as a man. A large head, flat face, small eyes, thin lips and a harshness which brooked no sentiment. I had never worked out what colour his eyes should be, they sat too far back in his head and he scowled too much of the time. De Clare did not forgive those who failed in his eyes and he punished wherever that gaze fell. When his eyes saw me, riding beside Arthur, they glowed with rage.

He bowed low. Arthur muttered, "Well, that's something." I snorted. Merlin rode forward and spoke.

"My Lord de Clare," he said loud enough for the crowd to hear. "We are well met by you having returned from our pilgrimage to reunite old friends. But this rich display of force," he swept his hand toward the bridge, "is hardly necessary to honour our King's return. You have outshone the stars in heaven by such a demonstration."

Damn, Merlin was good. I'd have gone in there and hacked his head off, which is why Arthur sent me to kill and others, usually Geraint, to negotiate with his enemies. I weakened them while Geraint talked them into final capitulation. I hadn't thought of him for days. I wished he flanked Arthur's other side. I wondered how his marriage was working out for him.

"Merlin, what a surprise, we thought you'd abandoned Camelot. Given up on your King," de Clare's voice boomed making my ears ache already. "These men are here for the protection of Camelot while the King is indisposed. They are also here to aid me in protecting my sister from any who would harm her." His eyes fell on me. For the first time I was very glad we had Else safely tucked away in Tintagel.

Merlin paused for dramatic effect before saying, "But, my Lord, why would Camelot need protecting? The King has been gone just a few short weeks, what could have happened that the Seneschal needed armed men other than those of the King's for Camelot's defence? We saw no enemies on the plains around our fair city." The wonderful teasing tone of Merlin's words made Arthur chuckle.

"Camelot needs a noble able to defend her at a moment's notice," de Clare announced. "I feared the King had been taken from Camelot in a moment of..." he paused and shrugged so the audience could make up its own mind.

Arthur didn't let that happen, "Moment of what?" His voice rang out with the clarity of the sweetest bell. "Moment of madness, my Lord de Clare?" He laughed and slapped me on the back. "Well, if it is madness to be grateful for the return of old friends such as Merlin and Sir Lancelot du Lac, then I am sore mad indeed and still rage in my madness."

His voice invited the crowd to roar and laugh in approval, which they duly did of course because Arthur has that effect. When he talks, he controls the people around him.

"Sire," de Clare announced. "The traitor –" He never had a chance.

Arthur rode Willow forward hard, the dying light of the day catching his armour and burning it red. His golden curls morphed to flame as he turned his huge black warhorse, his back now to de Clare and the men on the bridge. I heard Willow's rear hooves hit the wooden slats and knew I couldn't reach Arthur in time to defend his back. Merlin realised the same thing and pushed forward as Arthur cried out.

"I have been on a quest. A quest for the heart of Camelot. My heart. I have been rudderless, my people. I have been lost in a mighty sea unable to save myself or you." Willow reared at this point, Arthur artfully emphasising his words. "I found my heart when I reclaimed it from my lost friend." He leaned over as I reached his side and grasped my shoulder making our armour chink. "My people, you know of the crimes my friend is supposed to have committed and you know I had him punished according to the rule of law, but I ask you this, when your heart is torn from your still living chest and sent away, how is a man suppose to survive the ensuing sickness?" he asked the crowd and a soft murmuring breathed over them.

One voice, a woman's said, "You cannot, Sire. You are our heart."

"Indeed I am," Arthur replied. "I am your heart and you are mine. My friend, my Wolf, my Champion," a nice way to announce my new title, "protects that heart and I would not be parted from him. Not when he rode to save my heart despite my blind stupidity." He paused. "Yes, my people, even a king can be stupid," his rueful tone brought laughter. "How could I not forgive such bravery? We are sick, Camelot. We are weak. We have been torn asunder, you," he swept his arm over the crowd, "and I, ripped from each other." I could feel their sadness. "But now," his voice rose, "Now, we are strong. We have sought forgiveness and we have gained it. We have managed to heal the broken heart and we will become strong again, together for all time. You and I are Camelot," he told the crowd. They roared. Willow reared and screamed a challenge to the sky.

He looked magnificent and he bloody knew it. As they quietened, he modified his tone, making it intimate. "Go home, people of Camelot. Go to your loved ones and heal the wounds that might lie in your hearts. For tomorrow we will celebrate the new life of Camelot. We will feast and holiday. Then we will begin our world again and make it stronger than ever."

The crowd roared once more. Arthur turned Willow and galloped over the bridge with the two of us half a pace behind. Stephen de Clare flung himself into his own men to avoid being trampled to death.

We raced through the killing fields behind the curtain wall, through the mighty gate and into the inner courtyard. Once there, Arthur pulled Willow up and began laughing.

"Oh, that was fun. I really enjoyed it." His eyes shone with tears as he laughed.

Stable boys appeared and we slid off our warhorses congratulating ourselves. I chuckled but Merlin sat on his scraggy mountain horse, pensive.

"Arthur," Merlin said. "Wait." His voice sounded as though it came from a wisp of wind travelling over death on a battlefield. We both stopped and turned toward him. He crouched like a bird of carnage on the back of the mare.

"What is it, Merlin?" asked Arthur, walking to the wizard's horse. Merlin's green eyes shone in the dying light like old copper pennies.

"Feel your home, Arthur. A single speech is not going to force the darkness from these walls. It wants your blood." Merlin peered around him as though the golem were living in our halls.

The horses were led away. Arthur paused and closed his eyes. I heard de Clare and his men walking back over the drawbridge and through the killing fields. Arthur's eyes snapped open and his face paled. I thought he would faint, so I moved toward him when I heard him whisper, "Guinevere."

He turned without seeing me and raced for the steps.

Merlin looked at me, "Don't just stand there. He needs his Wolf by his side."

I didn't need telling twice, I raced after Arthur.

CHAPTER THREE

THE CASTLE, WHICH SHOULD be alive to the sounds of preparations for the evening, seemed eerily quiet. Or maybe the noise of two men in full armour sprinting up stone stairways drowned out everything else. Arthur, having been training against Geraint and I for weeks on the road had hardened, his fitness increasing to the point we both bounded two steps at a time without effort. Servants flinched and hurried away or stared at us as we rushed past, there were no guards except a pair in Stephen's colours on Guinevere's door.

Her suite of rooms were next door to Arthur's. Mine had been the other side of hers with Kay's also on the same floor. Geraint, when he came to Camelot shared with me. Guinevere's suite had one door from the main hall of entry. A door also linked her rooms to Arthur's and mine, both of which became an open secret. With the main keep being a huge square structure, Arthur and half of Guinevere's rooms looked over the river and hills of Camelot. While the other half of her rooms and mine, looked over the largest proportion of the city. Arthur and I could both see into the inner and outer baileys from different perspectives.

When we saw the men on her door, Arthur froze. I did not. I had no idea what they were doing there, but Guinevere lay behind that door and Arthur knew something was wrong. They were not heavily armoured but they had heard us coming. When they recognised Arthur, they looked confused which gave me the opening I needed.

I back fisted one with the mailed side of my left hand. Smashing his face, but making certain I didn't break anything obvious. The other moved his halberd to stop me entering the apartment but nowhere near fast or firm enough. I knocked the weapon aside and punched him in the guts. He wore mail under his tabard and I'm never certain if that's worse because of the metal or helps because of the protection. Regardless he doubled and dropped as intended.

Arthur strode forward and tried to open the door. I heard noise and turned to the end of the corridor, Kay rushed toward us and Merlin appeared from the same direction we had taken. The door didn't move, someone had locked it.

The King stepped back and aimed a kick at the lock. It didn't give, so he did it again, the sound of his armoured foot connecting with the metal and wood of the door sent shivers of fear through me. I remembered seeing Guinevere dead on the antlers of the white hart in my dream.

The lock smashed and the door flew open. Various young women squealed and dashed around the large anteroom like startled chickens. Arthur strode through the room. I walked at his heel.

The door to Guinevere's bedchamber opened. Elaine, Kay's wife stood there. A small round matron, who could fight like a vole when trapped by a cat. She would howl the place down before giving into the inevitable. She'd provided Kay with five children in the time they'd been married. Just a year longer than Arthur and Guinevere. Her black hair now contained streams of grey, while her round face had wrinkles which didn't detract from her inner beauty. I'd always liked Elaine but the Queen never favoured her as a lady in waiting. I often wished Guinevere had more sense. Elaine would have been a calming influence.

"Arthur," she gasped in shock. Then she dropped to a curtsy still in the doorway and said, "Sire."

"Guinevere," Arthur said and tried to push past.

"Sire, wait." Elaine didn't move an inch despite being over a foot shorter than Arthur.

Kay rushed into the anteroom. "Everyone out," he ordered. I peered at him and realised he'd aged in just the few weeks since we'd last met. He looked so thin and worn, like a misspelled word scraped off a piece of vellum. The young women all babbled.

"Out, now," I bellowed. Women vanished. De Clare's guards vanished with them, doubtless to report our arrival.

"Arthur, Sire," Kay said in a rush. "Please wait, we need to talk. I need to tell you what has happened since you've left."

Merlin placed a hand on Kay's arm. I watched the tension and stress in him dissolve but the sadness remained. Arthur stared at Elaine until she moved. He walked like a wooden man into Guinevere's bedchamber. I followed, drawn by his pain and so many memories.

The large bed, which sat central to one wall, lay crumpled with sheets of linen, fur pelts and wool blankets. The colours were bright, almost garish in the dying light of the day. They contrasted with the heavy wooden bed and its four great posts. Everywhere lay cushions and pillows. Where Arthur's rooms were simple, these were opulent and dressed in tapestries and rugs. Small tables and chests, with delicate chairs sat against the walls, somehow looking forlorn in the firelight. There were candles too, as though Guinevere ordered the sun to remain in the sky.

Our star, the star of Camelot, which ruled our world, both Arthur's and mine for so long, sat in the centre of the bed. Her long blonde hair lay in a tangled mass around her body. Her ice blue eyes were huge as they peered at us from dark circles on her pale skin. The long fingers, once elegant, looked skeletal as they plucked at the cloth on the bed. She sat in a simple shift of pale cream silk and rocked backward and forward, staring at us. I saw her mouth move but no words, just a whisper of sound. Arthur stepped toward the bed.

His jaw moved and I saw him try to speak, but he seemed as stuck dumb as Guinevere. Her eyes focused on him for the first time.

"Arthur," she whispered and I watched huge scalding tears fill her eyes, only to fall like drops of mercury on the blankets.

He whimpered, stepped to the bed and in one fluid movement swept her into his arms. She made no sound but clung to his chest, her eyes wide and staring at the floor over his shoulder. The pain deep in my guts flowered like a poisonous black rose. I was too horrified for rage, too shocked to think about vengeance.

"Lancelot," Arthur said his voice as fragile as the creature in his arms.

"Sire," I managed.

"Everyone out," he said. They too were stupefied with shock. Elaine moved first, shaking herself and turning to herd people out. Merlin had tears coursing down his cheeks, as did poor Elaine. Kay took his wife by the shoulders and led her out. They returned to the anteroom. I found my legs still functioned in this strange new world, so walked after them.

"No," Arthur said. "I need your help." The words flowed as they would for a dying man giving his final speech. I moved to the bed. Whatever orders Arthur gave I would complete with gladness in my heart.

His blue eyes were dark, rage filling them. "I don't know how to deal with her," he said.

She whimpered like a puppy.

"Just love her, Sire," I said, confused by his anguish. I wouldn't need to ask how to feel or what to do to help. Hold Guinevere safe, then slaughter everyone involved in her pain.

His arms flinched and I feared he would crush his Queen. I reached out my hand and he released her, I sat on the bed and pulled her against my chest, the armour hard against both our bodies. Guinevere curled up into my lap.

I now heard the words she'd been whispering. An old nursery rhyme. I held her close. I rocked her like a mother with a babe. She had no weight and a scent of sickness came from her but I kissed her bowed head and whispered soft words. The cooing noises calmed her while Arthur just sat beside me, staring into the distance as night claimed day.

Time stretched and I realised I needed to prompt him. "Arthur, you need to take off the armour. You have to be softer. She needs you to be kind with her."

"She is my Queen, how could this happen? Who could do this?" he turned toward me.

"Those are questions which can wait." Though I knew exactly who had hurt Guinevere. I just needed confirmation, "Your priority now is helping your wife survive this horror."

He moved, rising to strip his armour. Guinevere cried out at the sudden shift. "Lancelot, help me," she said, acknowledging me for the first time. "I need my Champion. I've been hurt," her voice a quiver of fear.

I grunted as though she'd felled me with a mighty blow. When I could draw breath and speak I said, "I am here, my Queen. I will protect you. I will keep you safe, my dear." The endearment was a reflex habit but it brought a wave of grief from Guinevere. Arthur turned at the sound, his armour and mail stripped from him in moments. He moved toward me, his focus only on his wife and I stood. I held her in my arms and passed her toward him, a broken doll. She wept, great heaving wails, as she turned toward Arthur and buried herself in his sweaty shirt. I relinquished control. He held her, turning to a window seat and sitting. I watched them for a moment and then unable to deal with their private grief, I left the room, closing the door.

"Lancelot?" Merlin asked, as though checking I was still me when I walked into the antechamber.

"They are together," I said. My fists were clenching and releasing. My shoulders felt as though they had been welded to my armour as a solid mass. "How did this happen?" I asked, my head swinging toward Kay and Elaine.

Kay rose. "Lancelot, I know you are anxious, but I should speak with Arthur first."

I growled low in my chest, "How did this happen? It is my duty to protect the King and Queen. I am King's Champion, Kay, how did this happen?" I stepped toward him. Kay blanched and backed off. Elaine stood and stepped calmly before me.

"Lancelot," she said placing both palms on my armoured chest. "The Queen has suffered quite enough for the moment, she doesn't need your rage flattening her as well. There is nothing any of us could have done."

"And you know that do you?" I snarled into her face. Right then I could have ripped her head off just for breathing Guinevere's name.

"Sadly, yes, I do," Elaine said. She sighed and stared at the door to Guinevere's bedchamber. "If I don't tell you, you'll do something stupid won't you?" she asked but didn't really seem to need an answer. Elaine just kept talking while we all listened. She turned from me and returned to the fire. Merlin began removing my armour, in the hope I think I might not kill anyone if I weren't dressed so aggressively.

"It began as soon as de Clare arrived," Elaine told us. "He was furious that Eleanor had vanished into the night with the three of you to go on this pilgrimage." She made it plain in her tone she also thought it a stupid idea. "But Kay managed to deal with him and said Arthur would explain on his return. The days rolled by and no Arthur, no message. We sent people to look for you, but they didn't find any sign. Stephen began spreading poison through the court and the factions became restless. It doesn't take long. Then the Queen decided to have some fun. She decided to make much of your return to favour, Lancelot. The factions started to grumble about slack leadership and Arthur's grip on reality. When Stephen and the Queen sided against Arthur using you as the weapon of choice, they found fertile ground." She paused and sipped some wine. "They met in private. Kay did all he could to stop them, but Guinevere and Stephen between them outrank him too much. Without Arthur we couldn't do much." She paused once more.

Merlin, now sat in the corner, said, "Speak the words, Elaine. If you speak them they cease to have power over you."

A tear slid down her round cheek. "The night of the last full moon," she said and I felt my heart squeeze tight in shock. That night I'd dreamt of Guinevere standing, knife in hand, ready to kill the white hart. I had killed her instead. I forced myself to focus on Elaine. "They met in private. In the morning Kay came to her rooms to ask her to attend to some household matter he needed her advice on, or at least that was the story. He really wanted to check de Clare had left her apartment. He found her, on the floor of her chambers, bloody. Beaten everywhere but her face and hands. The rape clear."

It was the first time any of us had used the word. We all flinched. Elaine continued, "He called for me. We knew how difficult it would be if others knew so we kept the circle small, but when she woke it became clear the Queen's mind had been affected. She's does eat or sleep. Sometimes she is lucid and that's how we found out what happened. But most of the time she is elsewhere, waiting for you and Arthur to come home."

"De Clare's men were on the door when we arrived," I said.

Kay said, "I couldn't stop him. He hasn't been back but he's made his intentions clear. When he destroys Arthur, he's taking the Queen as his wife and his men were here to ensure she didn't leave. Because of her state of mind and the huge quantity of men he has, I couldn't declare what he'd done to her. Not without Arthur. It would have caused a war, which I can't declare. So, Elaine agreed to stay with the Queen and keep her safe. We haven't left her alone for a moment and we haven't allowed anyone else to see her but Arthur's steward."

"So," I said, "de Clare has been running Camelot? Usurping you?"

Kay hung his head, "Pathetic aren't I? Arthur trusted me with his wife and Camelot and I've lost him both. You've only been gone five weeks."

It felt like years to me so much had happened. Then I realised I had a focus for my anger. I'd listened to all this and missed the point. De Clare had raped Guinevere. I moved without thinking. I picked up my sword, which Merlin had just removed from my hip and walked to the door. I knew how to solve this, I knew how to end Guinevere's pain and Arthur's. I knew how to protect him. Kill Stephen de Clare.

CHAPTER FOUR

I STRODE ACROSS THE room before anyone thought to stop me, except Merlin. He didn't move from his chair, just said, "Hold, Wolf. You are not exacting Arthur's revenge."

I turned toward him, the darkness welcomed Merlin, his white hair and green eyes the only clear thing I could see. "I am the King's Champion. I am the King's Wolf, not yours." I spoke as though this point made it bloody obvious I should be the one to slaughter the second most powerful man in the country. Me, an outcast until weeks before, still penniless and landless.

Merlin moved and the shadows dropped away from him, "No, Wolf. You will go where your King asks you to go, not where you wish to go. At this moment, Arthur needs you here. Stephen cannot be killed. You cut off the hydra's head and two more will grow in its place. We need to do this right."

My need was to ease the pain in my heart with bloodshed, lots of bloodshed. The pain stopped me breathing. I turned toward Merlin. He raised his hand and touched my head. "Easy, my Wolf. Easy. Your time will come, Lancelot. Give me your pain." He took a mighty breath in and I felt the top of my head dissolve as if he reached in and stole my rage through my brainpan.

The red mist dissipated and for the first time since we walked into her rooms, I felt myself once more. Able to think and function as a man, not a weapon of destruction.

Merlin smiled. "I know this is hard for you, Lancelot. But Arthur will need you to help him think and blood is not the path, not yet. We need to destroy Stephen de Clare by unpicking his power and those with whom he is allied."

I stared at the door for a long time. Part of me wanted to find de Clare and part of me wanted to run back to the wildwood so we didn't have to deal with this horror. Frustrated, thwarted, my stomach a sour mass of unspent anger, I finally relented and turned away. I went to the window and watched Camelot light herself against the night.

None of us spoke. We all just sat or stood and contemplated what Arthur must do to control this monster in our court. We contemplated the civil war it would bring and the death, which would be inevitable. I could see de Clare's men in the killing fields, some talking with those in Arthur's colours. I realised the rot in Camelot could be as deep as the foundation stones. If Arthur couldn't trust his own guard what hope did we have?

The night wound on, we waited. I thought about Else. Out there, in Tintagel, with Geraint protecting her. Would he be enough to ensure her safety against her brother? If Stephen had done this to Guinevere, the Queen of England, what would he do to his adopted sister? Then the sickening realisation hit me that Stephen would doubtless welcome Geraint as a brother-in-law, even try to persuade him to change sides. Not that I thought Geraint capable of betraying Arthur for one moment, but it did put my life into perspective. If I were Eleanor's husband, her life would be in danger. I had no lands or title with which to protect her from Stephen de Clare.

I also thought about my life with Guinevere, touching memories I had been avoiding for months. I remembered how loving and giving she could be, I remembered her wedding day to Arthur. I had stood by his shoulder as he declared his love, while my own split in two. One half for him, the other for her. At that memory, the tears came and I wept for their pain, the ruin of the love I saw in them both that day. With youth our companion we saw a world full of hope and light. Now we were older, darker, infinitely sadder.

Long into the night the door opened and Arthur stepped through. His eyes were haunted and red rimmed. Kay rose, his hands trembling and I saw he would sacrifice himself for Guinevere's shame. I didn't think it would be enough, I wanted to scream at him and beat him.

"How is she?" Merlin asked, stepping toward Arthur.

The King sighed. "Sleeping at last." He turned to Elaine. "My Lady, can I ask you to sit with her? Call me if she wakes?"

Elaine glanced at her husband, wanting to remain to support him. Kay nodded. Elaine bobbed a curtsey and left the room. Arthur took her seat and took her wine in his hands. I moved to stop him drinking, but he shocked me by setting the glass down.

"I need Camelot's cellars emptied. All the wine is to be destroyed. We'll buy wine from the merchants in the city. Someone will be happy with me at least."

I didn't understand why we were talking about the wine which had poisoned him, we had more important issues to deal with, "Arthur, we need –" He held his hand up to stem my demands.

"No, Lancelot, we need to stop. Rest. Think. Don't push me, please. I cannot afford to just react, I have to think." He looked as fragile as Guinevere.

I moved to beg him to let me go, to let me fight, when Merlin lay his hand on my chest. "Don't, Lancelot, he's suffering enough."

"Sire," Kay said. His voice trembled and he dropped to his knees, "I beg your forgiveness before you declare your judgment over me." His scalp showed through his thin hair, glowing in the candlelight. Arthur reached out, his hand steady and grasped Kay's shoulder.

"My dear friend, there is nothing to forgive. Guinevere has told me how you tried to protect her, how she allowed de Clare into her rooms and what you have done to preserve her dignity. She is deeply wounded but she knows she owes you and Elaine a great deal."

I heard Kay sob. "Thank you, Sire."

Arthur looked up at me and I saw something inside him I'd never witnessed before, fury. Deep, burning, powerful but so controlled. His dark blue eyes flashed violet as he growled, "I need guards I can trust. We are going to have a change of policy in my home. Lancelot, you are one of my best generals, I will have you personally in charge of protection for myself and the Queen."

"Yes, Sire," I said, remaining formal. His anger shook me. I understood it, mirrored it, but I am just one man, Arthur is a King with an army for his vengeance. What I'd seen as fragile confusion was my King trying to control his desire for blood. He wanted to use his brain before using his sword. Another example of why I followed him.

He stared into the fire as he spoke, pulling plans together from the air. "I need a personal guard for Guinevere and myself, a show of military strength. I want you to find men you trust. You know them best and they respond well to your leadership. Kay, I need to meet with you and Merlin to discuss the damage that has been done and the factions I need to unite or destroy. I want Geraint summoned from Tintagel. I want him here using that gin trap of a mind he possesses to find the faults in my court. I want the weaknesses destroyed, carved out, the cancer torn from my city," his voice hardened. Arthur paused, fighting to control the stampeding thoughts. He won and continued, "Lancelot, this personal guard. I want them to look hard, different to the others. I want a very personal army I can trust."

"The militarisation of Camelot might be a mistake," Merlin said.

"I will not have de Clare thinking he can sweep through my life and take everything without a fight," Arthur growled. Countering his orders was not a good idea. "Lancelot, I also need you to write down that damned dream. All the men you saw and which side they appeared to be supporting, give it to Merlin."

I had already written it down, at the Abbey. "I will find the list as soon as possible, Sire." The thought of Geraint returning to Camelot with his new wife, my wife, started a babble of noise in my head. One too many straws during a night of horrible shocks. I stamped on the turmoil. Arthur's pain came before my own.

Arthur nodded, he rose and said, "Right, to work gentlemen. And, Lancelot." He looked directly at me with the eyes of a King. "De Clare's head stays where it is until I give you the order. Am I clear?"

All my instincts told me he was making a mistake, but I said, "Yes, Sire. I am not to kill de Clare."

He left with Kay and Merlin. I moved to take up position outside Guinevere's doors.

I stood, a soldier following orders, staring at a white wall. Nothing inside my mind but my job.

An instant later my breath came sharp and I stared at blood on the wooden floor beneath my feet. It dripped from my left hand and the right hand's bandages were in disarray, the fingers twisted once more.

"Why is it always the women who pay the price of our fight for dominance?" I asked aloud. The question had rattled around in my head unformed for years. The blood didn't answer. More plaster fell off the wall where holes now existed.

I never desired the fear and terror involved in bedding an unwilling woman. They were too precious to me, even those I paid for and never met again.

"Because you can hurt your enemy in a very personal way. If we cannot protect our women, we are weak," my internal voice informed me.

I groaned and lay my palms flat on the wall, head pressed into the cold stone, my back tight and my throat closed with the desire to scream and rage my helplessness.

"Lancelot?" Arthur's voice shot through my torment. I forced the emotion down and turned to face him, only then feeling the pain in my hands. He glanced down at them. His blue eyes filled with pity.

I watched his own hands flex. He stepped toward me, then stopped and shook his head, "I can't." The words came out strangled and his eyes became haunted. "We can't."

I realised he needed me and the pain of separation overlaid Guinevere's horror, adding a harsh gloss. My feet though would not move. We were trapped within walls that would condemn us.

Arthur shifted pace. His back straightened and I watched the gates close on his outpouring of anguish. "The time will come for us to fight, Wolf. I need you whole for our vengeance," he spoke, a chill to his words, and pointed to my right hand. He did not touch me. "This is not acceptable."

"I am sorry, Sire," I said bowing my head. The lump of fire in my chest flared and closed my throat. I ached to reach out and pull him into my arms so I could protect him.

He flinched at my use of his title. "The Queen..." he began. Once more I watched him wrestle with emotions too raw to hide. "Guinevere," he managed more softly. "She needs to be kept safe."

"I know, Arthur. You have my life at your disposal." And I meant it.

He nodded, just accepting my words as truth. "I will guard her for now. I need you to find men to help." He became fragile once more, his eyes glowing with unshed tears. The sudden shifts between one dominant emotion and the next ripped into me and left me uncertain of my role. He moved toward me again, now within arm's reach. He whispered, "I don't know how to do this."

I wanted to hold him, but servants appeared in the hallway. Instead I said, "Yes, you do, Arthur. Follow your heart, use those you love the most to lean on and seek council when you are lost."

"Don't leave me, Wolf," he said his voice so thick I barely understood him.

"I will never leave you, Arthur. You know that. I will do all I can to protect you and Guinevere."

"Do you still love her?" he asked out of nowhere. The question hit me hard in the guts and I grunted aloud.

"No, Arthur. She cost me you. I love her as my Queen and your wife. I will lay down my life for her but I do not love her as I did."

"I don't know how I feel about her," Arthur said. "But I will not have her hurt. Do you understand?" He could not meet my gaze, as if it hurt too much to see me. We had been happy and lovers, while his wife lay fighting in Stephen De Clare's arms.

"I understand, Sire," I murmured.

He nodded once more. "Good," he said. "Go to the guard house now and find my soldiers. You need sleep this night. I will stay with Guinevere but I want you in my rooms. You can reach us fastest there."

I wanted to argue with him, perceptions are so important in such a small community but tacitly it made most sense. He needed me close to hand.

Arthur released me from his personal gravity and returned to his Queen. I watched him leave with a confused rush of emotion swirling inside me.

Public displays of affection could not be allowed to happen. If we were caught, it would be the ruin of Arthur. I knew that, just as I knew returning would end our affair. It had taken so long for me to consent to his desire and now I felt it dissolving in the acid filling Camelot's halls and it hurt. He needed Camelot to love him and he needed an heir. I focused on my task and forced away all griefs, both old and new. He was right Camelot was a curse. A curse on both our souls.

An image of Guinevere's tear streaked face coalesced inside my mind. A whimper escaped my control. What kind of hellish selfish monster am I, if all I can think about is my love for Arthur? Guinevere needed to be the centre of his world and mine. We would protect her and see de Clare dead for this suffering.

I gathered my scattered resources together and left the hallway to seek out the first members of our new guard. I strode through the keep, surprising people as I went. I circled down and out to the guard's quarters at the back of the main building, near the stable. I was on the hunt for a particular man.

CHAPTER FIVE

I MANAGED TO GRAB a cloth from one of the servants who happened to pass me at some point and walked to the guardhouse wrapping my knuckles. The barracks were a series of long low buildings where the single men shared their lives. When I'd arrived in Camelot they had been wooden and simple, but Arthur changed all that. He'd had them built of stone, with a good tiled roof and a stone floor. He kept it covered in clean rushes and gave the guards the best food and drink. They were all well paid.

As I walked into the barracks, I saw de Clare's colours on men as well as Arthur's. I stood, the struggle not to kill becoming powerful enough to cause me to forget my task.

"My Lord?" a man asked in Arthur's colours. The guard had just changed and men were undressing, preparing for the evening, eating, playing dice, a silence began to descend.

"I am looking for Sergeant Moran," I said not hiding my distain of the scene.

"Yes, sir. He'll be in the guardhouse on the main gate. He has duties tonight," the man spoke with an eye on the crowded room. "I can take you to him, Sir Lancelot."

At the sound of my name, being used in the familiar made me turn toward the speaker. A young man, strong, dark, with intelligent eyes. I searched my memory and realised I looked at someone who had begged to become my squire just weeks before my arrest.

"Tancred, right?" I asked.

He stood to attention. "Yes, sir," he said.

"You joined the guard?"

"The only place I could go considering," he said tactfully.

I half smiled. "It's a plan, I suppose. Good, then take me to the Sergeant."

He glanced at de Clare's men and almost slinked from the barracks. I logged all this away and realised I'd be able to use Tancred for my special guard.

We walked across the yard and I saw other colours among the soldiers wandering around. Arthur had an enemy army camped inside Camelot.

The guardhouse in the bottom of the large circular tower, protecting the main gate into the city, appeared to be quiet. A single candle burned in the room where the men received their orders, kept some equipment and took their rest periods. Tancred knocked on the door and entered.

"Sir," he said, "you have a visitor."

Moran looked up from a small leather bound book. His fingers were covered in ink stains. The man could both read and write. He had been the one to recognise me as the black knight only a few short lifetimes ago. He sat in the near dark completely alone. The candlelight woke the old deep scars on his face and made them dance. His shirtsleeves were rolled up, his hands scarred and calloused, his arms whip thin and corded with muscle.

When his eyes focused on me, they widened. "My Lord du Lac," he said.

"Yes, and more or less in one piece," I said shocked at the relief I witnessed on the older man's weathered face.

"I thank, God, for it. My prayers have been answered," he muttered and his head sank toward his chest.

I stepped into the room. "Sergeant, what's wrong? Other than the obvious."

"You noticed the change of colours then," Moran said, rubbing his eyes in exhaustion.

I glanced at Tancred. He said, "Those of us who are unhappy with the Lord de Clare's actions have taken it upon ourselves to take double guard duty where we can to monitor the other soldiers. There have been incidences in the town which the King would find unworthy of his men."

I didn't need them to explain, I'd been around armies often enough when they occupied enemy territory. "Don't tell me," I said. "You've hardly slept since they've arrived?"

"Forgive me, my Lord, I don't mean to be rude," Moran struggled to his feet. I waved him down.

"It's fine," I said sitting. "We are back and we will rout de Clare. In the meantime the King needs men like you." I paused trying to think of a positive way of stating what would be obvious to the men who became personal guards of the King and Queen. "There have been problems in the royal household while we were away."

"I know what happened to the Queen," Moran said. I could see his grief.

I paused, "How?" I wanted to protect Guinevere's reputation because it was the only duty I had left.

"His guards were outside the doors that night and I heard them laughing about it. I tried to challenge them but this young pup," he jerked his head toward Tancred, "stopped me. He said I was no use to the King if I were dead. Which I would be if de Clare found out I knew."

I glanced at both men. They seemed to feel the Queen's pain almost as much as me. "I see. I hope it hasn't become the gossip of the barracks."

"No, my Lord, the guards were sworn to hold the secret and I've heard not another word of the dishonour since. There have been times I've thought I imagined it and I haven't been able to reach the Queen to tell if she is safe, but word has not spread," Moran stated.

"At least it saves me from explaining."

"I've been maintaining a record as best I can, though I'm no scholar, so the King can bring men to justice. It's all I can do. De Clare keeps trying to root out and sack those of us who cause trouble at his presence. In a few short weeks he's caused havoc."

"Well, I've been chosen for a new task," I said, trying to lighten the mood. "I am the King's Champion once more and given the duty of creating a guard capable of protecting their Majesties at all times. Arthur wants a personal guard. Their own uniform, training, weapons, horses. The works. You report to me and we keep them safe." I smiled.

"Who will be in charge? You need a good captain," Moran said, his face showing signs of life for the first time.

I grinned, my decision made. "I will need a good captain and I'm looking at him."

Tancred laughed. "Congratulations, Captain Moran."

I wished I could have held the image of Moran's face clear in my memory forever. I have never seen a man swell with such honest pride as the news filtered through layers of despair and exhaustion. The three of us talked for some time about the preliminaries of our personal guard. Moran also had a list of men he wanted reinstated or taken from other duties. We came up with a simple change in uniform from blue and gold to black and silver. Each man, there would be sixty in all, broken down into teams of four with one leader, would have their own horse and new weapons. I wanted these soldiers to be a shining example of type. Men would fight to become a part of the elite. Captain

Moran had more ideas than I knew what to do with and I realised I'd chosen well. I left him and his new Sergeant mulling over who should be sent to relieve me from guard duty.

I did not see Stephen de Clare as I returned to my post. I did however find Arthur's steward, Roger of Halse, another competent and trusted person, outside Arthur's rooms. Men like him, who could organise a castle the size of Camelot, were more terrifying than a general with an army of fifty thousand knights. He was arguing with Kay who looked defeated.

"You don't need the King to sign off on this, Roger, just pour the damned stuff away." Kay sounded exhausted, as though he'd been having this argument for some time.

"But there is so much and it's so valuable," Roger said, his bald head bobbed in stress. He actually wrung his hands and his watery eyes looked more watery than usual.

I put a hand on Kay's shoulder and he looked to me for support. Roger glanced at me in surprise. "Lancelot, I mean, my Lord."

I smiled. "Lancelot is fine, Roger and do as Kay says. Really, the King wants it gone and we have our reasons. Most of them to do with the King's temper over the last few months." I laid a heavy emphasis on my words and Roger's eyes widened.

"Oh, right. Well. Considering. Um, now then?" he asked.

"Yes, now, and I want it supervised by someone you trust with the lives of your children and I want a list of all the people who have access to that cellar. All the key holders and all those who serve the wine to his Majesty."

"May I ask why?"

"Because the Queen is not the only one to be made a victim of certain horrors and I intend to avenge the Pendragon family," I said. My role in Arthur's life began to solidify; it made me feel complete.

The steward nodded, muttered and walked off with a mission to fulfil. Kay smiled. "Thank you, brother, I was drowning under the weight of that man."

I hushed him, uncomfortable with his company considering what happened under his charge. Arthur might be able to forgive but I wasn't certain I could.

The rest of the evening passed without event as I stood outside Guinevere's door and I found myself relieved by two guards I knew, men sent from Captain Moran. I ached to slump into my own bed. Geraint told me he'd kept it in good order over my incarceration and exile. Instead, I went to Arthur's rooms and checked everything I could to ensure nothing lay in waiting for him as a gift from Stephen. I then stripped off, washed down, found a clean shirt and half dressed again just in case. I ate on the move and when I finished I lay down with a knife under the pillow and my sword by my left hand.

It felt odd to be in Arthur's bed, so much had changed since the last time I'd slept in this room. I considered those changes and my fears over Else becoming another victim to Stephen until I slept.

The dream evolved slowly. A dark swirling mist surrounded the Wolf, confusing me, stopping me from finding my path. I turned full circle searching for the White Hart and the doe. Nothing, nothing but dark mists which smelt foul. I walked forward and my paws felt sharp stones under my pads. My claws bit into shale and it hurt to move. I whined. I did not like to be alone. Noises came after the stench of rotting and mould, a distant sound of screaming, both animal and human, male and female. It rushed on the wind as faint as the beat of an owl's wing. I couldn't discern the direction but I knew I should move. I didn't want to be found by my enemies.

I walked forward and whimpered as the stones dug, then cut my poor feet. For the first time in my dreams, I wished I was as small as a mouse and lighter than a feather. The muscle I used to race the wind weighed heavily on my paws. My walk became a hobble and I barked in an attempt to find the Hart. Nothing. Onward I stumbled growing more and more fearful, wishing I could wake until, in my distress I sat on the sharp stones, raised my head and howled in anguish longing for my companions to save me from this trial.

"Lancelot, wake up for goodness sake," came a sharp voice I knew.

"God, Arthur." I rolled over and found him next to me but dressed.

"Bloody hell, what have you been doing? You're bleeding everywhere," he said holding me at arm's length.

I looked down. My shirtfront was crimson. My hands smarted in the cold dawn air. Small lacerations covered my palms and I realised, the soles of my feet. The manifestation of my dreams shook me to the core. Not only for myself but also for Guinevere's sake.

Arthur rolled off the bed and fetched me a glass of water. "You look terrible," he said.

"Thanks," I said as I realised I'd been sweating. He grabbed a rough linen cloth and made me hold it in my hands before I drank the water. "I thought you were staying with Guinevere?"

"She was asleep with Elaine holding her. Kay says she's been with her night and day for a week or more," Arthur tried for a light tone, but I heard his pain.

His eyes were hollow, he hadn't slept at all that night. I placed my water down and pulled my feet away from where he dabbed at the blood.

"We need to talk about these wounds," he said looking up at me.

"You need to sleep," I countermanded. I coaxed him into my embrace and we lay, his head nestled against my chest, my arms protective around his back. I wanted so much more but dared not ask.

"I'm scared for the future, Lancelot," he murmured.

"Whatever it holds, you will not be alone," I said, stroking his hair with my makeshift bandage.

"I fear that more than anything. I would be lost without my Wolf."

My dream rushed over me and I shivered, Arthur held me as I held him and soon we were safe and asleep.

CHAPTER SIX

WHEN I WOKE, I woke alone and the day shone through the windows. I did hear him next door, which meant he'd left the door to Guinevere's apartment open. I rose, with the sun glinting on the sea in the distance and the sky cloudless overhead.

"For pities sake, Guinevere, I need you to do this," my friend was trying very hard not to yell.

I flung back the blankets and struggled into my hose and doublet. I stuffed my sore feet into boots and pulled gloves onto my hands. Still lacing my clothing, I walked into Guinevere's apartment. She sat, cross legged on the bed, her face set in stubborn lines. Arthur paced the length of the room.

"I need you in court, as my Queen. I know it won't be easy, but that is your job. Please, Guinevere. I need a show of support and I need your people on my side. They will follow you, or do you want de Clare to win the throne and string me up?" Arthur asked his tone too brusque to make the joke work.

Guinevere's eyes filled with tears. I stepped between them. "Arthur, I think you are being a little harsh," I said.

He whirled, he hadn't heard me walk in, his face flushed. Guinevere looked at me and then at Arthur.

"I'm sorry," she said tearful and for once, genuine. "I simply cannot attend court. I don't mean to be difficult."

I sat on the edge of the bed and looked at her, she appeared to have slept at least but the large dark circles under her eyes still dominated her face. Fear haunted this woman and would for the rest of her life if we didn't prove she could care for herself.

"Guinevere, you are my Queen, you always have been," I said, taking her hand in mine and patting it. "But Arthur is my King and he needs us. He needs our strength."

Her lower lip wobbled. "I have no strength."

Female psychology is not my strong suit but I do know something about war and we were going to war.

I took both her hands in mine and gazed into her ice blue eyes. "My Queen, you are the greatest of warriors. Just because you do not wear a steel breastplate, not that you wouldn't look lovely," she smiled, "it does not make you weak."

"I am so scared, Lancelot, you can't know what it is like."

"No, my Queen, I can't. I can never know and for that I am sorry." I meant it too. "But I do know war and make no mistake, Guinevere we are at war and you are a part of that battlefield. If we show Stephen we are divided he will have already won. We are a family and we need to stand together."

"Is that why you returned?"

I paused and managed not to glance at Arthur. "Yes. Arthur was threatened and I had to save him. I did not know of your vulnerability or I would never have let him leave."

"You didn't abandon me, I know that. This is my own fault," Guinevere said so quietly I could hardly hear her. She raised her eyes to mine. "You will be there?"

"I will be there forever." I now glanced at Arthur hoping he'd say something appropriate to help us out.

"Lancelot is in charge of our personal guard, Guinevere. He will be near to us until we are safe from all our enemies." He approached. "Please, please, help me with this. You need never be present at Court again, just please, help me today."

Her nails dug into my skin, which hurt because of the lacerations I'd suffered. "You promise you won't leave me alone?"

"I promise."

A long pause followed, before, "Alright, I'll do it."

Arthur sighed and in moments we were in the centre of a whirlwind. I found myself being whisked off to be washed, shaved and dressed in a new livery. My old heraldry no longer existed. Arthur changed my emblem to the silver Wolf I'd used when I'd challenged as the black knight. The wolf's head sat in a blue field, the same colour as Arthur's. There was no doubt I was Arthur's man. If I ever had children, they would be close to the Pendragon line. The thought made me proud as I stroked the new doublet's soft fabric and traced the embroidery of the wolf's head on my left breast. I found a quiet corner in the castle and stood alone for the first time since waking. I relished the quiet. Life spun faster in Camelot than on a battlefield sometimes. My sword hung from my right hip, a great comfort and my favourite knife sat at the front of my left hip, the hilt covering my lower stomach. My draw would be a little slower but if I ever drew a blade in Court we really would be in trouble.

"Well, don't you look lovely," Arthur came into the small room. A place we used for meeting before presenting at Court. A stuffy, overdressed cage but it was quiet inside the chaos of a castle preparing for a banquet.

I smiled, feeling bashful. I hadn't been in Court for over a year and I rarely found it necessary to dress up but Arthur wanted a show.

"Thank you for the new livery, Arthur," I said.

He stepped toward me and fussed with some laces making them even. "Blue suits you."

"It's your colour, Arthur." I sudden fear hit me, would he think I had a right to his colours after everything the fey queen had told me?

He smiled. "You are my man." His eyes were the same colour as my doublet and his own.

In one short breath we were kissing. I grasped Arthur's neck and lower back, pulling him into my body, plundering his mouth like a starving man. Arthur's fingers tangled into my still damp hair. With our skin freshly shaved it felt odd, different, softer. He smelt of lavender and sandalwood. A noise outside the room made us break, panting and still hungry. The pain of the separation brought a cry from both our lips. I realised the new fashion of my coat didn't quite hide my frustration. Guinevere walked in with Elaine and Kay. Arthur and I both bowed low, as far from each other as we could be in the small room. Guinevere curtsied and I marvelled at the woman's beauty.

Her hair lay simply over her shoulders, a golden cloak. A fine net sat over the back covered in gems. Her dress was a pale cream, almost white and hugged her figure to spill over her hips. It swept along the floor, trailing at the back. Pearls and gems shimmered as she moved. The sleeves were tight to her slim arms and pointed over her fingers. The neckline sat high and tight to her throat, no flesh showed. This was as close to a suit of armour as Guinevere could manage. The dark circles under her eyes were gone and the face of a Queen hid the fear in her clear blue eyes. She examined us as closely as we both examined her.

"My, God," she whispered. "I've never seen anything as perfect as you two." She glided to Arthur and kissed his mouth, before drifting to me and kissing my cheek. "Your new colours suit you, my Lord."

"Thank you and you as always are devastating in your splendour, a warrior indeed." I kissed her hand as I bowed over it. She brushed my head, I realised her fingers trembled. I took her hand and passed it to Arthur.

"My Lady, you have once more made me proud to be your husband." There were tears in his eyes. I realised then that Arthur still loved his Queen. I had no idea what kind of love but something remained of their marriage. It made me glad for them both despite the pain.

"Well, everything is pottering along nicely," Merlin said as he breezed in. He looked at me. "Good, the wolf, I like it." He nodded and poked my chest.

"I'm pleased you approve," I said bemused by his chirpy attitude.

He rubbed his hands together. "I can't wait for this."

Arthur grunted, his face becoming stony at the thought. "I suppose we should prepare ourselves."

He held Guinevere on his left arm. I stood behind her left shoulder. She looked at me, the fear poking through. I smiled and said, "We will not leave you alone."

"We will all be with you," Elaine said. The older woman smiled gently and I felt Guinevere square her shoulders, standing just a little straighter. She dragged a half smile up for Elaine. Both women turned to the door, a determined look in their eyes. I suppressed my own smile. These women were fine examples of their kind, strong, independent, powerful in their spheres of influence. A wash of pride made my chest swell and I nodded to Arthur.

Arthur rapped on the door and a squire opened it from the other side. His eyes widened as he looked at us and we walked forward. A mass of determined muscle surrounding our fragile Queen.

The noise of the court died, the expectant buzz cut off as though Arthur swung an axe over someone's neck. I focused on not falling over as we walked up onto a dais, which sat in front of the stone throne. Arthur used this set up when presentations to foreign courts were necessary. We were making a point to our own people. The hush brought with it an atmosphere of tense expectation. We rose onto the dais moving as one organism. Arthur stood before the grand wooden thrones both he and Guinevere used for joint presentations and everyone genuflected.

Arthur smiled, he held the moment, then said, "Friends, please, stand, there is to be no formality among my family of Camelot. Not today," his words were generous, but it was not lost on me that he took their display of honour to a hair's breadth of being the correct time regardless of his words.

Cloth rustled as everyone straightened. A shimmer of sound filled the vast hall, the politics of our presentation drove Arthur's point home. He gave them a moment before continuing his charm offensive.

He gently kissed Guinevere's hand, she bowed her head in acknowledgment and to my surprise, he gave her hand to me. I stepped up to her side. Arthur stepped forward. "Friends," he gestured to encompass us all. "We have been through terrible times. I have been sick and my friend, my brother, risked everything including his life to save me." Arthur looked at me for a long time. "There have been many words spoken against my Lord Lancelot du Lac but no more. He has saved your King more times than I can remember. Any past sins are paid for and we, the Queen and I, owe him everything." Arthur squeezed a huge amount of emotion into his words. "That is the first announcement I need to make. My King's Champion has returned. The second is harder for me and does not fill me with the joy I've known in Lancelot's homecoming. There is a serpent in our midst, a sickness. My city is weak and the people unhappy. I have not been the King you deserve but no more. My love for you, for our land, for my family," he smiled at Guinevere who smiled shyly in return, "has been tortured almost to breaking point, both in myself and in your faith of me."

He stepped down off the dais. I flinched. I couldn't go after him with Guinevere on my arm. She flashed her eyes knowing Arthur hobbled my ability to protect him. I shot a look at Kay who shook his head the smallest amount. He would not follow the King. My gaze raked over the heads in the hall, we were raised only two feet over everyone else and then I saw it, the dark head of Stephen de Clare. Guinevere's fingers dug into my hand, her eyes found him in the same instant.

Arthur spoke projecting a thoughtful persona, "I have been poisoned against my own family. I have been hunted by monsters." The crowd could take this any way they chose, metaphor or reality. Only those who were guilty would know we knew of their acts of treachery. "I have been brought low and only the love of my friends saved me. But no more, the serpent within Camelot's walls will be hunted and destroyed. I will drive the sickness from our home and from England," his voice rose as it had with the crowd in the streets. "I love England. I am England. And I will keep her safe even if it costs my life to do so." He drew parallel with Stephen de Clare. Arthur stared at him. "This is my country, given to me by God and I will drive the sickness out, carving it from the heart of my land." He paused. I saw the tension in his shoulders. His hands itched to kill the bastard de Clare. Arthur turned suddenly and Stephen flinched. "But now, now we celebrate our return to health. We celebrate the return of our friend, Lancelot. We celebrate the love I have for you and for my Queen." Arthur raced up the dais, swept Guinevere into his arms, she yipped in shock and he kissed her. Deeply and thoroughly. Guinevere wrapped her arms around him and kissed back.

Merlin raised his voice, "Three cheers for the safe return of our King." We all joined the chorus of yells. Arthur placed Guinevere back on my arm with a soft thank you. She smiled and even managed a wink.

Once the cheering ended, the crowd began to break up and we stepped from the dais to circulate. Kay shadowed Guinevere and I stayed on her left side.

De Clare walked towards us, Arthur intercepted him. I watched de Clare bow, it was just within the bounds of politeness. "Sire," he managed.

"Stephen, how interesting to see you," Arthur said with perfect civility.

I watched Stephen's brain run through any number of options. In the end he said, "I had hoped my sister would be returning with," he looked at me, "the traitor. I hoped we would be able to put an end to their association."

Arthur laughed, a harsh sound. "The traitor?" He glanced back at me. Guinevere released my arm so I could reach Arthur in a heartbeat. "I don't think Lancelot has ever been the traitor in my court, do you, Stephen?" Arthur vibrated with controlled rage and I watched his hand flex on his sword hilt. The pressure inside him pushed against the barriers he'd created in order to function as a king and not just a man.

"I want my sister returned to me, Arthur."

"I am your King, de Clare, kindly remember your place," Arthur said, his eyes dead. "As for your sister, Eleanor is busy learning to be a wife to my Lord Fitzwilliam. Quite a woman that one. But I am certain her husband will speak with you about her life since she went missing all those years ago, when they return to court in a few days."

I stepped beside my King. I couldn't speak, the anger, the need to kill, overwhelmed me. Arthur remained a poised courtier but I felt the snake within him waiting to strike.

Stephen stared at me with contempt. Arthur lay a hand on mine to stop me moving forward. He gave me an order to be still. I knew how to follow orders.

Stephen laughed. "So once more your woman has chosen someone else to wed, du Lac. I wonder what that says about you as a man? Perhaps they didn't enjoy you sharing your bed with others. It's a shame the first one didn't understand, but I suppose she was so young." The fool looked at Arthur.

Was he planning on making an open declaration about Arthur's sexuality? How did he know? This would cause civil war for certain, especially as Arthur didn't have an heir. His reference to Guinevere made my blood boil but his insinuations about Arthur and I made my soul grow cold. I did not want to be the reason Arthur had to fight for his throne.

"And as for my sister." He shrugged. "If Fitzwilliam is foolish enough to marry a woman who's been in the wilderness for years," again that sneer of contempt, "I wish him luck."

Arthur shifted but managed to play the game, "They are married, Stephen. Lancelot returned Eleanor to our court as a maid and because of her skills she helped us find Merlin. She is a brave woman, Lancelot wanted to protect her honour so offered himself as her suitor. Geraint though finally found his match, so Lancelot surrendered his position in her life. It is all legal and sanctified. I have seen to it myself."

I felt sick with the need to see de Clare's blood on my hands. I wanted to eat his liver. The thought surged through me along with a howl. The Wolf stirred. I shook, Guinevere's hand clamped down on my arm. This man wanted harm to members of my pack. I would not allow this to happen.

"Du Lac's return to court is the thing which concerns us the most. Your need for him to be close is disconcerting to us all," Stephen sneered, looking at me.

Arthur's eyes narrowed. "Sir Lancelot's return to court has been well earned. He at least I can trust to care for Camelot and my wife." He ignored Stephen's insult and delivered his own.

Stephen didn't miss a beat and would not be deflected from using me as the target. "You think his pedigree will leave him content to stand at your shoulder and not on your back?" Did he know about Nimue's desire to see me on the throne of Camelot?

Arthur sighed in a huff of air. "My Lord de Clare, I think you need to understand I have returned and my family is complete. I will not have it split asunder and you have to have a reason to force a new trial. Lancelot is not the problem."

Arthur's calm demure enraged Stephen. His temper began to fray. An interesting phenomenon. His face grew redder and the slight purpling of his nose darkened. His small eyes vanished into the folds of his face. I almost laughed until I saw the effect his anger had on Guinevere. She swayed on her feet and fought tears. Kay wrapped an arm around her waist.

Arthur stepped into Stephen's personal space. A dangerous move if Stephen drew a knife. Arthur stood a good hand's width over de Clare in height and used every inch of his golden beauty.

"So, will you declare war on me for giving Geraint my blessing on his marriage? Or will it be the return of my Champion?" Arthur asked staring deeply into de Clare's face.

Stephen straightened his back and stared back just as hard, his neck bulging. I saw a wound, still healing, just at the point his neck joined his shoulder. The wound resembled a bite mark. I flexed my own hand, I'd covered the small lacerations in soft gloves and my feet were a constant reminder of my dream. One of our supposed allies, William Roth, stood nearby listening to the interchange. I looked at the back of his legs. A bandage covered his right knee as though he'd been hamstrung. He carried a stick. My eyes shifted over the crowd, all listened more intently than I to Arthur's words. Another man nearby moved in pain, his back hurt from a deep wound in one side.

"You push me too far, Arthur, my honour will not permit these words against me and my family name," Stephen almost shouted returning my attention to the argument.

"But, my Lord, I only asked you to remove your soldiers from Camelot while I reorganise my men and their quarters," Arthur said, innocence dripping from every word. How we managed to move from my return to de Clare's men occupying the castle I couldn't guess.

"You are accusing me of betraying Camelot," Stephen shouted.

Arthur laughed. "Are you telling me you are the serpent who is trying to drive the Pendragon family to destruction, taking England with it? Really, Stephen, I know you are strong but strong enough to defeat a king?"

"What?" Stephen asked, stepping back from Arthur. He glanced around himself, "I am not declaring war on you, Arthur."

"That's what it sounds like, my Lord." Arthur released his anger. It whipped out drawing a hiss of fear from those nearest us. "It sounds and looks as though you are moving against me and I need to assert my authority."

Stephen made the mistake of a lifetime. He glanced at Guinevere and licked his lips. Arthur grunted as though struck. I growled and stepped to his side, my left hand on my sword hilt. The crowd around us shrank back.

"The time of the Pendragon family is ending, Arthur. You may think you have the power and charm but the people want a real leader. One who doesn't look to the wrong arms for comfort." He meant me, we all knew it, they didn't need evidence to do damage.

"I don't think it's my sex life we need to worry about," Arthur growled. He held out his hand, his eyes begging Guinevere to help him. She drew herself out of Kay's arms and walked to Arthur's hand to stand before her attacker.

Guinevere straightened to her full height, her regal beauty acting like a suit of steel around her fine body. "Stephen de Clare," her voice rang out surprising me. "I accuse you of rape. I want you arrested and tried for crimes against myself and my husband."

CHAPTER SEVEN

ARTHUR AND I STARED at her open mouthed. Stephen went from puce to white in moments.

"Guinevere," Arthur gasped. We were manoeuvring for quiet domination before we forced Stephen into declaring war on us, not the other way around. We did not want to be the aggressor. She knew we had no evidence and her reputation would not help matters.

She turned her huge blue eyes onto her husband. "Please, Arthur." She folded. There, in the centre of the great throne room, the Queen fainted. I moved fastest and caught her long before the stone floor claimed her.

Uproar ensued. Stephen drew his sword and bellowed in rage. I turned my back to protect the bundle in my arms and watched him attack Arthur. My heart plunged but Arthur sidestepped and drew his own weapon, he parried Stephen's attack with a cold focus I'd rarely seen in any warrior. More men flew to Stephen's aid and the world slowed. Arthur, holding his shorter single handed court sword lightly, danced as he thrust the blade into an adversary. The light in Arthur's eye echoed the desire in my soul for blood, for revenge.

"To the King," a shout echoed around the great hall. A flash of a blade and I saw Arthur's young cousin, Gawain, charge into the fray on our side. He pushed me back to help protect Guinevere. I turned and thrust her inert body in Kay's arms. He retreated. I pulled my sword and knife in the same moment. Time shifted and chaos erupted.

"The wounded are our enemies," I yelled becoming a part of the circle around Arthur.

He had his sword in his hand and asked, "What are you talking about?"

"My dream, the Wolf attack, they are all injured. All those I fought to save the Hart," I managed to explain as we found ourselves fighting in the heart of Camelot.

I realised there were not many who openly supported Stephen, we were fighting his army, not his political supporters. These soldiers must have been waiting outside the doors. How had such a thing had happened? Another man's guards on the doors of Camelot's Court? Who let them into the castle? I promised myself a long chat with the man responsible. My sword caught a great overhand strike to Arthur's head. We were fighting too close, hampering our ability. Gawain, unhappy with close quarters, bellowed like an ox and pushed outward, giving us room.

"Arthur," Guinevere's cry rose over the tumult. We both turned to her voice. Stephen fought Kay and a few of our long time friends, trying to reach the Queen. We were fighting the decoy.

"Fuck," Arthur barked. "Stop him, Lancelot." Arthur hacked at my enemy.

I threw myself against the soldiers to reach the Queen. "De Clare," I yelled to distract him. Kay bled from a head wound.

Stephen took one look at me, levelled his sword and said, "I will have your head, du Lac and you will not return to power."

We came together in a great crash of steel. He might be shorter than me but he had vast stores of strength and skill.

"You will never be king," he snarled in my face, spittle covering me.

I laughed, so he had been told fey gossip. Our swords danced, the sound of steel bounced off stone. "You've been listening to the wrong people. No, I will never be king and I thank God for it, but neither will you. And I will gut you slowly like a fish for what you did to my Queen."

"You think you're the only one to who should fuck the bitch?" he asked with an evil glint.

My temper snapped and rage swept over me, welcoming me home. I drove into Stephen and delighted in the fear blooming in his eyes. People rushed away from us as we fought, back and forth over the polished dark floor of the throne room. I pressed my advantage knowing I had Stephen where I needed him for a fine dramatic finish. Then the light died.

I thought I'd fainted but sound, the sound of fear and confusion filled my head, yet my eyes were blind. I couldn't see anything.

I wanted Stephen's blood on my hands and I couldn't see him. "Silence," I roared over the crowd, but panic had them, both men and women. I would not find Stephen in this mess. I ached to become a wolf, the Wolf could scent him, track him, rip his throat out and gobble down the blood. "Fuck," I screamed at the sky. "I will devour you de Clare." The anguish of losing my prey filled me.

A wave of light swept through the room. Merlin stood on the dais, his arms outward. "Wolf, there," he pointed.

I turned and saw de Clare rushing to the great double doors of the throne room, others fleeing with him.

I smiled, all grim intent, and raced for the door. "Lancelot," Gawain's voice. The panic gave me a moment's pause. "Arthur is hurt."

The power in my legs drained in an instant and I stumbled. I looked over my shoulder, Gawain held Arthur where he lay on the ground. I glanced at Merlin.

"Bollocks," he said over the hush. "De Clare's gone. They have horses outside the keep. You would never have reached them. Go to the King." He waved at Arthur as he descended the dais.

Released from a leash Merlin held, I raced back to my King. My sword clattered to the ground, my knees hit the stone floor hard. I felt no pain because Arthur didn't move. Blood covered him, it covered the stone floor. A deathly hush surrounded us as Merlin knelt beside Gawain. I reached out a hand, it trembled. I brushed the short blonde hair.

"Arthur." His name hurt my throat. I knew I needed to find a pulse, find the wound causing the blood and save his life. Paralysis held me. "Arthur." My fingers laced into his and his eyes opened. Focused. He grinned.

"Ouch, my fucking head," he moaned. "Some bastard bashed me on the back and the lights went out."

Air rushed into my lungs and my head spun. "You..." I couldn't speak.

"What's wrong?" Arthur said as he sat up.

"We thought you were dead," Gawain replied.

Arthur looked himself over. "Oh, the blood. I caught someone across the throat. It's ruined a bloody good doublet. Where's de Clare?"

I spoke too fast the battle frenzy still surging, "He escaped during the blackout."

"And you didn't go after him?" Arthur looked at me as though I'd suddenly turned into a troll.

"We thought you were dead," I pleaded.

"Well, get after him now," Arthur insisted. "I want his head, Wolf." His eyes gleamed in the soft light filling the courtroom. My body ached with desire for the power filling him and pouring out to us all, his knights.

I did as commanded. I reached for my sword, left his side and raced for the stables, calling for Captain Moran on the way. He'd beaten me to it, I found him in the stable with Tancred and a few other men.

"I believe we have a problem," Moran stated, throwing tack on the horses.

I explained what happened in the throne room, by the time I'd finished the horses were done and we were riding through the gates of Camelot's keep. Then we stopped, people filled every street and public space. Arthur had given Camelot a day of celebration. The streets were chaos and even as we watched, the last of Stephen's men vanished toward the city gates. The only way we could have raced after them was to run people down and we saw the dangerous chaos Stephen's men were creating. We couldn't replicate Stephen's ruthlessness against the people.

I cursed in frustration. "We'll track them," I said forcing Ash through the crowd but at a measured pace. Arthur would never forgive me for hurting the people of Camelot.

"You should return to the King," Moran said. "We can see to this." I gazed after Stephen, my bones aching for revenge. "My Lord," Moran continued. "This is my job. We will not be able to engage with them, there is too many, but we can harry them north and give them something to think about."

I felt Ash under me. He didn't display his usual eagerness for the fight. We were tired. We were all tired, including Moran. I pulled Ash up. "You're right, but I only want them chased so they can't cause damage on the way out of Camelot's lands. Follow them to our border. I don't want them to make any more of Arthur's people victims."

"Yes, my Lord," Captain Moran barked orders and his men swept past me.

I turned Ash and we rode back to the stables. He looked relieved when I dismounted and handed him back to the stable boy.

I returned to the throne room while considering the implications of what happened that morning. Guinevere's secret would spread throughout Camelot in hours. Arthur faced dishonour, as did his wife and we would be going to war. I wanted to defend them and protect Else. Despite being married to someone else I felt a keen pain in my heart when I thought about her becoming another of de Clare's victims. Geraint might have her safe in Tintagel but I wanted her here, I knew I could protect her and I would lay odds on Stephen taking her through fair means or foul. If he had fey connections he knew who and what she really was and how powerful.

The chaos in the throne room made me pause at the door. There would be political manoeuvring, currying favour and bullshit by the bucket load. There would also be the questions from the rest of Arthur's closest friends about my sudden reappearance. Did I really want to face all that? The quiet of my life on the road felt like a distant memory. I sighed and walked away, heading for my room. I walked past Arthur's and Guinevere's and arrived at my door.

I entered the room and discovered one of the joys of Camelot. Servants, the true fairies of castle life, had swept through the rooms. Geraint's belongings were most obvious. As always, he had far more permanency than myself. I sat in a large wooden chair covered in cushions. It wasn't even sext yet and I was exhausted.

My head rested on the back of the chair and I closed my eyes, grateful for the sudden peace. Weariness swept through me and I noticed a fine tremor in my hands. Blood stained them. The blood of my countrymen. The blood of those who swore fealty to Arthur. I knew then, why my hands shook, when I'd turned to see Arthur lying in all that blood, his eyes closed and so pale, my world stopped. Everything inside me ceased to exist. I knew with a horrible certainty that my own life and happiness sat in Arthur's hands. A hollow feeling and a fearful dread came over me. Stephen's comments and snubs in Court made me aware of our powerful vulnerability now I'd returned. Even though the only physical love we'd ever really shared happened in Avalon, gossip, even groundless gossip would destroy all the good Arthur did in his city. His allies might well turn against him for just being my friend, never mind my lover.

I groaned and leaned forward, my elbows on my knees. "We are never going to sort this mess out," I said aloud.

I needed to leave Camelot and leave Arthur for the stories to stop grinding down his authority.

"But he needs you here, you bloody fool," I continued to myself. I ran my fingers through my thick coarse black hair.

Whether Arthur and I were lovers or not, he needed someone he trusted with his life. I promised myself I would not threaten Arthur's leadership by allowing my feelings to be obvious. For fifteen long years I'd hidden my love and I'd be able to do so again.

With that sad resolution in my mind, I sloped off to my bed for the first time in almost two years. The blood of my countrymen stained my hands and the love of my King wounded my heart.

CHAPTER EIGHT

I DIDN'T SEE ARTHUR for three days with my time swallowed up by my new guard. Arthur remained cloistered in meetings with his nobles. Leaders who were more use to him than me, they had lands and men for war. I tried to intervene when I discovered Merlin and Kay were interviewing those suspected of treachery. Gawain told me Arthur wanted to bring them back to the fold, so they remained in Camelot. Others fled the same night Stephen left. These were de Claire's true allies. I only wanted to keep them close if they were in their graves. Gawain laughed and informed me that was why I wasn't doing the questioning.

Guinevere I did see. She came to watch our training and gradually became more confident around the men. They all treated her with great care and respect, fighting with pride to prove themselves to their Queen. Her air of fragility eased into a shield the more she knew those who would surround her life. She stayed away from the Court and politics, she spoke with quiet fondness about Arthur and how he cared for her. She even began to laugh on occasion. Elaine, her only companion, ensured she never found herself alone and I escorted them as often as possible. She never touched me, or looked at me as she used to, which left me relieved.

I heard Geraint and Else were on their way, but I forced all thoughts and considerations about her from my mind. A part of me wanted to race from Camelot to meet them, so I knew they were safe from Stephen on the road and part of me never wanted to see either of them again.

"Moran," I shouted. "That dun is never going to be suitable for the guard. He's too head shy." We were in the breaking yard for the horses, trying to pick out new mounts for the recruits.

Captain Moran came back from the horse's side. "I don't understand, he was perfect a few weeks ago."

"My Lord?" said a small voice, from a mousey boy.

I looked down. A young page stood at my elbow. "What is it?"

"The King asks for your company in his rooms."

My stomach clenched and my heartbeat trebled. "Lead the way," I said. The horses and Moran were no longer relevant. My promise to protect Arthur from my desire returned full force and I thought a visit to the more progressive of Camelot's fine drinking establishment's might be necessary. Doubtless the girls had missed my coin over the last few years.

I walked behind the boy even though I knew the way perfectly well and I wanted to race to Arthur's side. I'd missed him every moment of every day and night since our return. The boy let me into Arthur's casual room. Guinevere sat near the fire, quiet and demure. Arthur stood at the window. She didn't rise or look at me as I walked in and I registered the tension in Arthur's shoulders.

"Sire?" I asked as the boy retreated.

"Lancelot," he said without turning. My name sounded flat in his mouth. This would not be a happy conversation. I wondered if he feared Guinevere's presence in my company and I realised I'd made a mistake allowing her to enjoy the companionship of my guard.

I glanced at Guinevere. She stared into the fire. Her face pale and eyes haunted. "What's wrong, Arthur?" I asked.

He sighed and his right hand rubbed his eyes. I crossed the room drawn to ease his pain. "Arthur?" I whispered his name. I reached out to touch him, but my hand froze when I turned my head to check on Guinevere. She stood and watched us. I didn't see anything but pity in her expression.

Arthur's jaw bunched and he pushed violently against the wall to move away from me. His shoulders straightened and he forced himself to relax. My King stood before me, not my lover.

"What's wrong, Sire?" I asked again the pain in my heart spreading to my limbs leaving me weak.

"I need you to escort Guinevere to Avalon." He didn't look at me as he spoke but I saw the exhaustion in his face.

Sometimes, when the dawn arrives, the sky turns to blood. Light bleeds across the sky just as it bleeds through the soil after battle. It is a torment to kill the splendour of the night sky.

The tightness in my throat left me breathless. I managed to say, "You are sending us away?"

Arthur moved back towards me, once more leaning against the window. His hand clenched against the wall where he used it to support his weight, his gaze out over Camelot. "There are factions in Camelot I cannot stand against. They will accept you in England if you are not here with me. And as for Guinevere..." he fell silent.

"As for me," she picked up stepping toward us. "I am ruined. I am barren. A liability who is unmanageable. Who helped to tear Camelot apart with my foolish words." She stood straight, proud, strong like willow is strong, but I saw the pain and regret in her eyes. "If it is what you want, Arthur, I will release you."

He turned so fast he stumbled. I reached out, my arm bracing his chest, "No," he cried, clutching my arm. "It is not what I want." Guinevere's heartfelt resolution broke him where my own words could not. He trembled against me.

Guinevere approached, I watched her, trapped by her beautiful serenity. She touched Arthur's face with tenderness. "I have been a bad wife, Arthur. It is the very least I deserve. Others paid for my stupidity time and again." No guessing who paid the highest price. "It is time I grew up and took responsibility. I have learned hard lessons these last few months, weeks. And I cost you your closest friend. Your consolation."

The use of words which mirrored Arthur's own just a few days before caught us both off guard. Arthur straightened against my body, we both neglected to step away from each other. His shoulder against my chest.

Guinevere smiled. "The two of you are so beautiful together, it makes my heart ache sometimes." Her fingers reached up to trace the line of my jaw. "I want you both to be honest with me. Please, Arthur. These last few nights we've spoken more than we have in years. Please trust me even though I have no right to ask. Are you lovers?" Her crystal blue eyes were clear, not angry or full of hate and recrimination.

Arthur flinched. "Guinevere, I..." he began. I felt his fingers brush mine and sensed his distress.

"We are not lovers," I said, hoping to rescue my King once more.

Guinevere's eyes narrowed. "Lancelot, you never have been able to lie to me, don't start now."

"What do you want me to say? I was to wed, there isn't a great deal of room for a third person in a marriage," I said.

Her eyebrow arched at the implication. "A fact I am all too familiar with, my Lord," she said. "However, somehow that's never stopped any of us pursuing what we wanted."

A silence descended over us, thick and cloying. The heat from Arthur's body seeped into me. When he moved, he moved away from me.

"You have your answer, Guinevere," he said, his voice dragged over broken glass. "Lancelot, I want you to take a handful of men and ride out through the villages of Camelot. There are reports of bandits and I need the Wolf Pack to have some practice at killing if necessary."

He might as well have taken a war axe and cleaved me in two. "Yes, Sire." I bowed.

"It is a compromise, the best I can do to protect you," he said. "Get you out of Camelot for a few days."

"Yes, Sire," I repeated. I turned away on legs made of water.

"And what of Avalon?" Guinevere asked. "I thought you needed us both gone." I heard her anger threaded through her attempt to maintain her temper.

Arthur paced and headed for the wine, it slopped over the sides of the fine glass goblet. "I don't know, but Lancelot has his orders. The Wolf Pack are to be used by me to protect Camelot. If sending him out of the Court for a few days draws its ire then perhaps things will calm."

"Arthur, please, I just want the truth," Guinevere pleaded and took his hands in her own, kissing them and removing the wine. "Lancelot, tell him to give me the truth."

"I will leave immediately," I said ignoring her.

"You promised to never leave me alone," she snapped, out of patience.

"You will not be alone, my Lady, you will have the Wolf Pack and your husband. You will be safe." I bowed and fled, to seek refuge within my task.

Arthur and I were over, in one brief moment, and I didn't have the strength right now to protect Guinevere. He was right to send me away. When I returned from this pointless mission, I would leave Court forever.

I heard Arthur's raised voice, the strain of his words muffled by the thick wooden door between my apartment and Guinevere's. Her voice I did not hear, she wasn't arguing with him, just trying to find her way through the maelstrom of his emotions. I grabbed my travel saddlebags, which I kept packed and ready under my bed, hooked my thickest cloak off its peg and my bedroll. I left my rooms for the freedom of the wildwoods around Camelot.

I moved quickly through the keep and headed for Captain Moran's office. When I reached it, I found Tancred bent over some paperwork.

"My Lord," his head jerked up at the force of my entry.

"The King wants me out there patrolling the villages around Camelot for a few days. I need ten men out there with me," I managed to say without screaming.

Tancred blinked several times, his deep brown eyes confused. "I thought..." he began. "No, never mind." Something in my face seemed to snap him to attention. "I'll see to it now." He dropped the paper in his hands. In a frighteningly small amount of time, I sat on Ash while the rest of the men mounted their own horses.

Captain Moran appeared but he didn't speak to me. He stood next to Ash, giving orders. In the end he said, "Be careful, son."

"Thank you for your help," I said, trying to keep my emotions at bay. "Keep them safe." I glanced up at Arthur's window. He stood there, covered in shadow, staring down at us leaving him. I couldn't read his expression.

Tancred led us out of the keep's vast gates and we rode over the bridge into the city. I didn't see anything around me. Camelot's Court had found a way to separate us again.

CHAPTER NINE

WHEN WE LEFT, THE weight of Camelot fell away and I began to function with some sense of normality. The voices of my Wolf Pack filtered through the screaming confusion inside my head. Tancred remained quiet as always, but his gentle humour poked fun at his comrades. I watched him within the group, they clearly admired him and valued his leadership. He was careful with the men under his command and helped to blend the different personalities. I admired his skills and realised the young man had many attributes he could teach me. Skill with people is not a natural characteristic from which I suffer.

With winter closing in on our valley at an alarming speed, none of us wanted to be away from the warming fires of the city but we pushed the horses on and I lost myself to the journey. We ambled through nearby settlements, spreading the word that we were here and able to help them with any trouble they faced. The further we rode, the more stories we heard about violent attacks and robberies. A marked increase over the last few days. Maybe, the Wolf Pack should be doing more outside the city. None of Arthur's people ought to be this vulnerable.

That night we would sleep in a village tithe barn and when we settled, I found myself sat outside near the fire with Tancred next to me. The wind murmured and the chill tried to wriggle under our clothes. We were near the edge of a cluster of houses, with a clear view of the road through the wooden stockade. With discipline tight in the group, the men chose to turn in early and leave the village girls alone. The locals left us after offering food, never fully trusting armed men. It made the entire place quiet and dark. I heard foxes barking and owls in the nearby fields.

"I wish I could live out here," I said to the stars. The fur from my cloak tickled my nose and I huffed fluff from my face.

"I don't think the King would like that very much," Tancred said in his soft voice.

I grunted, unwilling to think about what Arthur might or might not like. "Sometimes I wish I'd chosen a different path than that of a knight."

"You surprise me, you are the best of Arthur's men and he knows it," Tancred said poking at the fire.

"I am the most efficient killer he possesses, that's all." My mood turned dark.

Tancred remained silent for a while. My hackles relaxed in his company. I asked a question of my own, "Do you wish for a different path?"

His teeth shone as he smiled and chuckled. "A different path? One where I am not sat here in the cold and damp next to you? No, my Lord, I do not wish for a different path."

I didn't know if he were serious or sarcastic and felt foolish asking. "I suppose we should get some sleep. We have a long way to go tomorrow."

"Why are we doing this?" Tancred asked. "We don't need to. Villagers will always exaggerate attacks hoping for sympathy from the King. Stephen de Clare's men are not here and I don't believe there are many bandits this close to Camelot."

I sighed. "If I answer that, Sergeant, I might have to banish you. Let's just say I'm a bloody inconvenience and the Wolf Pack are a convenient way of keeping me out of trouble."

"So we stop you drinking and whoring?" Tancred asked.

His brown eyes were bright in the firelight and I felt them measure me but not in an unpleasant way.

"I suppose so," I admitted. "Weak creature that I am."

"You aren't weak, you are just in pain and it makes you behave erratically."

I coughed. "Is that your final assessment of your Commander's mental health?" I didn't know whether to be amused or horrified.

"Sometimes a real friend is one who sees your weaknesses and cares for you anyway," he said. "But you are right, it is not my place, my Lord, and for that I am sorry."

Again, I didn't understand whether he was sorry for what he'd said, or sorry for not being important enough to be my friend. I reached out and laid my hand on his back, he jumped and looked at me startled. "I value your honesty and your friendship."

"You have both for as long as you wish," he said but I couldn't see his eyes any longer.

We sat for a while and I must have dozed off under the stars.

The Wolf raised his muzzle, confused because he couldn't scent the White Hart. I stretched, my muscles tight. A yip from downwind made my ears swivel. I couldn't smell anything but I trotted off in that direction, curious. I heard something new and a smell I recognised all too well hit me. The stink of steel, then the powerful scent of man. A high pitched whine made me flinch and a furry body hit me from the side just as a dozen men appeared from nowhere, roaring their attack.

"Lancelot," a soft hiss woke me. "You're dreaming."

"Get the men up and armed," I ordered.

Tancred rose beside me and ran into the barn. I scrambled upright and drew my sword trying to see through the darkness. Our fire burned low, more like glowing embers and certainly not enough to let me see a threat. My heart beat a calm tattoo but I felt the surge of battle filling me, making me crave the possibility of a fight.

I heard a cry, out in the night. The sound of steel on steel and the grunts of fighting. The Wolf Pack filtered out of the barn, some men still dressing.

"To me," I ordered and we ran toward the sound of fighting.

Clouds broke overhead and the half moon's light spilled onto the road. There were perhaps twelve men, fully armed and one mounted knight. The men were trying to pull the knight off his horse, the knight fought to kill. For one long moment, I stood frozen and watched the knight hack through one attacker, half his head falling off his shoulders. Another fell with a deep wound in his chest. The knight was magnificent. The moonlight made his armour shine silver, etching each perfect movement against the blackness of the night.

Tancred yelled the order for attack. I watched Willow kick out, his aggression matching Arthur's. It motivated me. I need not have bothered to be honest, there were few men left by the time the Wolf Pack reached Arthur.

When my men began to dispatch the attackers, Arthur ordered, "I want one alive." He trotted Willow toward me and lifted his visor. "I told you we had problems out here."

My heart began to beat once more and air rushed into deprived lungs. "What the fuck are you doing out alone?" I snapped. "How the hell am I supposed to keep you safe if you do insane things like this?" I waved at the massacre.

He grinned at my anger. "I was lonely, thought I'd come and find you. I knew you wouldn't have gone far and to be honest I wasn't expecting an attack, despite Merlin's nagging."

"You weren't expecting an attack and yet you are wearing full armour?"

"It was the only way Guinevere would let me out of the keep without you." He looked embarrassed.

"Well, at least one of you has some fucking sense," I said, trying to modify my tone and failing.

The commotion died but for one man struggling in the arms of Tancred and William. They dragged the man toward us, blood poured from a head wound making his face a dark and bloody mask in the moon's light. They dumped him in front of Arthur, who dismounted. The man struggled to his knees but Tancred wouldn't allow him to stand.

"Who sent you?" Arthur asked. He pulled his sallet off, his golden curls were stuck to his head. An ache shot through my loins.

"No bugger, we're just looking to make some coin," the man spoke sullenly and spat blood at Arthur's feet.

I stepped forward and backhanded him across the face. "Show some respect for your King," I barked.

The man glowered at me. I saw no fear and repentance. The Wolf raised his muzzle and sniffed the air. I crouched before him and tugged at the filthy coat he wore. Under a thick layer of wool, I found a bright and well made hauberk.

I glanced up at Arthur. "These are no outlaws."

"No." He looked to the men surrounding us, expression grim. "I want the corpses stripped and I want evidence of who they belong to, then I want their bodies collected and a cart found. We are taking them back to Camelot as evidence. Someone hang this miserable worm for treason."

I blinked. "Arthur, we need a trial, surely?" I'd never seen him so angry. Since Guinevere's attack he'd been swinging between diplomat and dictator.

"Are you countering my orders, my Lord?" he asked.

"Never, Sire," I said and rose, only to bow before him. His decisive actions and demonstration of strength just kept reiterating to me why leaving him would break my heart.

"I am sick of this game," he said and turned his back on the slaughter. I watched him walk away and shrugged. Dead enemies suited me fine. The man tried to stand when the news of his immediate execution filtered through his shock. He smacked William in the guts with his elbow, Tancred and I reacted in the same moment. Tancred's sword drove through the man's guts as my knife slid over his throat. He died with air bubbling through the blood that poured down his chest.

By dawn we had the evidence we needed. Stephen de Clare's men were in the area hunting and happened to stumble over a prize worth dying for, Arthur. We loaded the bodies onto a cart and made a slow journey back to the city. Arthur remained quiet but rode at my side. When we reached Camelot we all stopped. Lining the walls near the main gate of the city were heads.

"What have you done?" I asked amazed. Not because I didn't like to see dead men used as an example but because in all the years I'd known him, Arthur had never demonstrated such a ruthless streak. This was something reminiscent of his grandfather.

"We weren't getting anywhere with finding out about de Clare. I grew impatient and felt it time I showed those around me that arguing with me or standing against me isn't always the best idea. Besides, it stops them trying to take you from my side or forcing me to remarry," he sounded so distant.

"You did this because they wanted us sent away?" I asked.

"I did this because I will not be treated like a fucking idiot. I am King here and it's about time people bloody remembered that fact. You are my right hand. I will not have it cut off by those who are jealous of your position."

"Arthur, compassion is not a weakness," I said, concern for my friend prompting me. Of course there would be changes in him after Guinevere's attack, but this felt so different.

"Compassion gets men killed," he said.

"Compassion is your greatest virtue," I replied. I thought to myself, *'and it is the reason I love you.'* I looked to Tancred who stared at the heads. The horror in his eyes spoke volumes. A king without a heart is soon a tyrant.

I was meant to be the heartless one, not Arthur. I loved his strength in battle but also his mercy. I needed him to be my antithesis, not my companion on the road to hell. Arthur nudged Willow forward and cantered into the city.

The mood of Camelot reflected the mood of her King. Grim, hard and quiet. The Wolf Pack dealt with the dead, demonstrating de Clare's colours as they stripped the corpses and hung them from the city walls. I rode with Arthur back to the keep. Everyone appeared to be on their best behaviour, bowing as Arthur passed them and muttering a great many, 'Your Majesties'.

When we reached Arthur's rooms we found Guinevere pacing. The moment we walked in, she threw herself into Arthur's arms. "I told you I'd bring him home," he murmured, softening for her alone.

Guinevere made no sound, she simply buried her face in Arthur's shoulder.

CHAPTER TEN

THE NEXT FEW WEEKS formed a strange pattern, while I waited for Geraint and Else to return to Camelot. I tried to talk to Arthur about me leaving the city for the good of his reputation but he wouldn't hear of it, couldn't bear the thought of me leaving his side even if we were not lovers. I forced my fears away and continued my work in the city.

My guard soon became known as the Wolf Pack by everyone and within weeks, they were forged into the perfect fighting team. We took pride in ourselves, our uniform and our duties. Units within the pack shadowed Arthur and Guinevere, demonstrating to the world they were not going to be easy victims.

Guinevere became a paragon. She felled her detractors with a charm offensive that left me in awe. She worked constantly in the castle and city to help repair Camelot's heart and quietly prepared us for war or siege. There were times I heard her wake screaming and I heard Arthur trying to settle her fears. On those nights, I would slip into her bedroom with my blankets. I would lay beside her tucking her under one arm, while Arthur curled around her back. She would calm and then sleep. Arthur and I would tangle our hands together, sleeping with a horrible awareness of each other but also grateful. We never spoke and I'd always be gone before dawn.

Arthur grew back into his role as our leader and won the respect of his Court. His management of the city and country never missed a beat. We spent every moment we could together. We ate meals together, hunted and fought with the Wolf Pack regularly. We never discussed our feelings for each other but we could do little about the sudden flaring of desire, which caught us by surprise. Whenever it happened, I left his company and drank until I'd grappled my lusts back under control. I could no longer seek mindless pleasure in the company of women.

Together, a strange family at last, we approached midwinter. Arthur organised celebrations for all the religions in the city, forever the diplomat.

On an unremarkable day, the sky a leaden lid over Camelot, I walked from my rooms, through Guinevere's suite and into Arthur's apartment. I wanted to inform him of changes to the guard, enabling all the men to enjoy the planned festivities. He wasn't there but I heard something from his bedroom and walked in without thinking. I found him and Guinevere. Making love. Neither saw me. I backed away, an explosion of emotion overwhelmed me. I calmly, gently, returned to my rooms. I picked up my sword and long coat.

I left and woke up in an alley with Tancred standing over me.

"You look bloody terrible," he announced, crouching beside me.

I tried to speak but my tongue stuck to the roof of my mouth. My eyes blurred and my back ached. I groaned and my hand splashed into a muddy puddle. Noxious fumes wafted upward from the stale water. I wrinkled my nose and gagged.

"Come on," he said. "Let's get you home and cleaned up, so Arthur can stop pulling the city apart trying to find you." He bent, hooked his arms under mine and hauled me to my feet. "God, you stink," he cursed.

I made it upright, lurched sideways and puked. Tancred held me with great fortitude. Once done, he slipped himself under my shoulder and we walked toward the castle. He made no comment but when we reached the great wall we peeled off to the left and he ushered me into a small house within the shadow of the keep.

"I found him," my rescuer announced. My sword stood, propped up by the fireplace and Captain Moran appeared.

He walked to me from what I supposed to be a cooking area with the smells wafting with him. He peered up at me. "Fuck boy, you look like shit. Come on, you can scrub up out here." He propelled me through the house and into a yard. "Strip, wash, then I'll feed you." He stomped off, grumbling, rubbing his naked scalp with his rough hand.

I faced a water trough. A cold water trough. I sniffed myself. "I do stink," I croaked. I peeled my clothes off, my body stiff. The fabrics were stained in substances I would never be able to identify. My torso showed bruises. "What the hell have I been doing?" I stood in the frigid air and tried to piece together the last few days. "I give up," I moaned. I didn't even know how many days I'd been drinking. The water proved cold enough not only to steal my breath and my manhood but also my remaining self respect by making me whimper, it also finished sobering me up. I found a brush and soap by the large tub. I used both vigorously.

When I emerged from the yard a shivering miserable wreck the good Captain stood waiting with a blanket. He hustled me into the living quarters and sat me before a roaring fire. I managed to take in my surroundings for the first time. The downstairs consisted of two simple rooms, the kitchen area and this, the sitting room and dining room. Its floor space would be the same as my private suite in the keep. A large clean table took up most of the room. A set of stairs vanished upward behind me. A single rug covered the wooden floor near the fire. The only other items, except for two comfortable chairs and four practical chairs were items of armour and weapons stacked in corners. There were no obvious personal effects.

I began to thaw out and my brain started to function at something of its normal efficiency. A bowl of steaming stew and a hunk of rough bread appeared under my nose. "Eat, but slowly and you'll need to stay on simple foods for the next few days. Your guts are going to be shot to hell," his rough voice sounded cross and sorry all at once.

"Thank you," I muttered. When I grasped the bowl, my hand shook. "How did you find me?"

He sat back in one of the chairs. "Tancred could find you anywhere. It took Arthur two days to work himself into enough of a frenzy to send us out after you. Tancred's been trawling the dives of Camelot ever since."

"The sword?" I muttered around a mouthful of glorious meat.

"That's what tipped Arthur over the edge. One of your lovely ladies turned up with it, she'd bought it off some man who'd won it from you in a card game. She knew the sword and brought it home."

"I lost at cards?" I asked.

"That's the part of this that worries you?" his voice cracked. I looked up. He looked angry but this time his eyes shone with real contempt. "You are a fucking idiot." He sighed, "I've been watching you, Lancelot, since you returned from Avalon and sometimes you are the perfect knight you are capable of being. Other times, I watch you fracture before my eyes, implode, then rise like a phoenix and strive for perfection once more. What is happening to you? If you keep this up you will kill yourself."

"I like a drink," I muttered. I had no intention of speaking to this man about Arthur, Guinevere or Eleanor.

We were silent for a long time. I ate, but my guts twisted, used to a more fluid diet. When I finished the food, he took the bowl from me, he returned and he stood by the fire. "You aren't the only one who's sampled from both sides of the fence," he said out of the blue.

I blinked, my brain trying to understand what the hell he meant. Fortunately, he ploughed on without me. "Under Uther Pendragon I found myself out in the wilds of many parts of this fine country. Women were not always available, so I sampled and often preferred other company."

"Oh," I managed.

He sat. "Look, I'm not good at this stuff and I never married so I don't pretend to understand women, but I've loved. I know how you feel about the King. I can see it worming around inside you. I've watched the two of you for years, torturing each other, pining after each other. Arthur watches you fight from his window."

"I'll have to tell him to stop," I growled, drinking water from a carafe Moran gave me.

"Don't play games with me, boy," he snapped.

"Sorry."

"I'm trying to be honest with you and it's not easy. I want to help before I find you dead in a ditch because Arthur's broken you."

"It's not Arthur's fault," I said, anger finally peeping over the walls around me.

"He thinks it is." Moran paused to gather his thoughts. "He came to me. In truth it's only myself and Tancred who were sent to find you. He didn't want to shame you in front of the others. I've never seen someone so hurt without actually carrying a wound."

The thought of Arthur suffering made my throat close. I remembered how beautiful he and Guinevere looked in each other's arms. How happy. That is what was right, not what I wanted.

A rough hand reached for my own. "Steady son, I didn't mean to hurt you." Moran moved to sit in front of me.

"It's wrong. He is married and the woman I was to marry couldn't live with the love I have for Arthur. It's wrong." I managed the short sentences without shaming myself.

"You're in a worse state than I thought," he said as softly as his rough voice allowed. "Lancelot, life is not that simple. You need Arthur and he needs you. It's burning inside you both and all fires need to consume something. What's stopping you? Shame?"

"No... Yes... I fear Arthur will lose Camelot because of me. Because I will make him look like a fool. I need to marry, to find a woman who can make me feel something other than this emptiness but I fear they will all feel as she did," I told his hand where it rested on my own.

"If she didn't understand you, son, then she wasn't the right woman."

"If Else isn't the right woman then I don't know who is, apart from that one flaw she was perfect and now she's married to Geraint. She's so beautiful and strong," I said.

The Captain nodded. "I know, they arrived in Camelot yesterday." Another dagger to my heart. "The trouble is you love Arthur more than any woman," Moran informed me.

"Yes," I whispered knowing it was true.

"Is that fair on any girl you meet?"

"No, but what choice do I have?" I looked up at him willing him to give me an answer. Other than Geraint's father, this was the closest I'd ever come to having a mentor in my life.

He smiled, never a comforting sight on his scarred face. "You can be the brave warrior I know you are. Tell Arthur. If you don't do something about this the King will tear you apart because he can't let you go. You need to have peace with what you want, who you want. There is nothing wrong with your passions, Lancelot."

"That's not what others tell me." I thought about Merlin.

Moran's hand tightened on mine, "Son, it doesn't matter what others think. If you find greater happiness in a man's arms then why deny yourself that happiness?"

I sighed and thought about his words. Moran was right of course. My sexuality found greater satisfaction with Arthur than it ever had with a woman and I didn't believe that was wrong. Others might condemn me but even if Arthur didn't want me or couldn't have me because of his position, maybe someone else would.

CHAPTER ELEVEN

TANCRED APPEARED SOON AFTER our chat and delivered me some clothes. He said he'd told Arthur he'd found me and the King asked if I might attend him immediately. Moran let me change in his sparse bedroom and I wondered if being unmarried would be a better life. His home, though bare, felt like a home. He seemed happy and if I ever needed companionship I knew some of the finest women in Camelot, though the thought held little appeal and I had no idea if I'd slept with any over the last few days.

Feeling warm in my clean clothes, I made a decision. I needed to be honest with Arthur. I needed to tell him what I wanted from him and beg him to release me from Camelot. The distance would help us gain some perspective and maybe rid me of this burden so I might find love somewhere else.

When I went downstairs, I squared my shoulders, feeling more like myself. Tancred now sat by the fire. "Well, you look better," he said.

"Thanks and thanks for dragging me out of that hole."

He grinned. "It's the only time I'm ever going to have the advantage over you, my Lord, and I didn't take it. Some soldier I am."

"You ought to go to the castle," Moran said bringing Tancred food. The Sergeant smiled at the Captain and I wondered what kind of relationship they shared bearing in mind Moran's confession. "Go," he ordered me.

"My clothes," I began.

"I burned them. Disgusting mess. Here's your sword. You owe me the price the woman asked me to pay for it by the way," he said.

"Invoice, Arthur, it's his fault apparently," I said, managing to grin.

Moran grunted. "I'll never see the money if I have to do that," he complained.

I left them and realised I now had two friends in that small house. Other than Geraint and Arthur I'd never become close to anyone in Camelot. It felt good to have friends who cared and understood.

I tried hard not to think too much as I walked into the castle through the large gates. I wanted to face Arthur and remain calm. I blended in with the general bustle of the castle and slipped unseen into Arthur's part of the huge keep. The door to his private room was closed. Two of my men stood either side. They saluted on my approach. I knocked and heard Arthur give me leave to enter.

He sat behind a desk, a new addition to this room since our return. He wanted somewhere quiet to work into the night when necessary but remain close to Guinevere. His golden head was bent over some document. "Just leave the food there." He waved toward the fire.

"I would if I could," I said.

His head shot up like a hound on the hunt. "Lancelot." He rose and tripped over the table leg in his haste to reach me. I reached out to catch him but he corrected his balance, ensuring we didn't touch. He straightened and said, "I have been so worried."

I smiled in apology. "I'm sorry, I'm a prick."

The distance between us felt like leagues. "You saw me with Guinevere didn't you?"

"It's not your fault, she is your wife and you love her as you should. It just..." I couldn't finish. I still didn't know why it hurt so much. "Caught me by surprise," I added lamely. "How did you know I'd seen?"

"Only you would walk into my bedroom unannounced and leave the door open."

I looked into his blue eyes. "Well, I won't be foolish enough to do it again, Sire."

"I don't want that," Arthur said. "I want you to be welcome in all of my home." He stepped forward, but still didn't touch me. I almost swayed into his body. His blue eyes were like magnets and so vivid. There'd be no arguing with him on this but I promised myself I'd be knocking more often.

"I'm just grateful you are happy with your Queen." I meant it, really I did.

Arthur looked down. "I need an heir, the sooner the better."

"It was more than just procreation, Arthur. Don't diminish the work you and Guinevere have done on your marriage. I'm proud of you both for setting aside so much grief and starting again." I smiled, then took a deep breath to tackle a new subject. "Arthur, I need to talk to you about something else."

"What's wrong?" he asked. "Whatever it is, if you owe money, don't worry. I'll cover your debts."

I laughed. "No, the only person I owe money to, as far as I've been told, is Captain Moran. I told him to invoice you."

Arthur chuckled. "Bet he was pleased."

I brought us back to the point, "I need your consent to go to Avalon." Arthur opened his mouth to argue. I held up my hand, "No, wait, please. Just hear me out. I can't do this, I can't play this dance with you. I can't share a bed with you and not take what I want. I can't live in a limbo of false chaste love. I want you, Arthur." He finally came to me on those words, as though I'd punctured a bubble around him. I put my hand on his broad chest to hold him back so I could continue. More words rushed out to fill the gap, almost angry in their determination to be heard. "But, I need to clear the way for a wife. If I travel to Avalon, I can check on things, in your outlying territories, maybe take some of the Wolf Pack and enhance their training. Ensure the loyalty of more than just your vassals here in the city."

Arthur grew pale. "I don't want you to leave."

"I know but I can't stay. We are tearing holes in each other. If we spend some time apart, maybe things will be easier. Perhaps we will hide our lusts more carefully." I watched his expression change to one of great sadness.

"I see." Arthur moved away from me. His joints stiff, his face grim. "Camelot once more wrests my consolation from my arms." He stood with his back to me at the window. His arm against the wall, the city laid out before him.

"It is for the best," I said. The agony growing deep inside my guts said different but I knew I was right. Arthur and I could not share our love and any words we'd spoken to the contrary in the past were false promises built on naïve hopes.

"Why Avalon?"

"Why not?"

He nodded. We were still and silent for a long time. He said, trying to control his voice, "When I began to notice your drinking was linked to our desire, I knew you were hurting as deeply as I am. It is a wound, a canker eating at me because I know what it is to lie in your arms and, God help me, that's what I want."

I stepped toward him but the sound made him flinch. "No, Lancelot, don't. If I can't have you, if you won't give into me here, then you are right. You should leave because staying is hurting us both beyond endurance. Just know it is my love for you that sees you leave, not the fear of discovery."

Give into him here? I'd been waiting for weeks for him to make the first move. I couldn't do it, I was nothing in this game. Arthur had to make the decisions, he was married and King. I was just a man.

He turned toward me and tried to smile. "Leave, Wolf, tomorrow. Go and see to the security of my lands and return to me when your heart is at peace. You never know, if you find a wife perhaps all this will leave us and we can know what it is to be normal."

Moran's words flitted into my head. Even if I met a woman fool enough to take me on, she'd never cope with Arthur and we were incapable of hiding our love now it had found a voice. Why did neither of us think of our love as normal? Love is a gift, it is beautiful and I wished I could accept the changes I felt in my heart.

I wanted to take back the suggestion. I wanted to remove the hurt in his eyes. I wanted to feel him in my arms but instead I turned on my heel and walked from his suite.

I managed to cover the distance to my own rooms. They were cold and dark, the servants unaware of my return to the castle. I walked to my bedroom, linked to Guinevere's and heard great racking sobs through the closed door. The sound drew me like a magnet. I expected to hear Guinevere's voice, but I would not be comforting her, not any more. The risks were too great and the desires too foolish. Instead, I heard her giving comfort. The terrible grief came from Arthur.

I bowed my head to the harsh wood standing between my heart's desire and me. I felt the roughness of the grain and the smell of the wax. I knew, one small movement and I'd be through the door.

"Fuck," I cried out, my hand on the cold iron handle. The door opened and I stared into Guinevere's large blue eyes as she held Arthur in her arms. She'd wrapped around him where he'd collapsed onto the floor.

"Help me," she said. "He can't do this alone. He needs you."

I knelt beside Arthur and placed a shaking hand on his back. "My King," I said, meaning 'my world and my heart'. Arthur, sobbing in anguish, flew into my arms and knocked me back. I held him tight against my chest. "It's alright, I won't leave. We'll manage. I won't leave you, Arthur." The words fell from my lips but they barely covered what I wanted to say.

Guinevere coaxed him with soft words of her own. She stroked Arthur's back and head, also where I held him, her long slim fingers a comfort to us both.

Arthur calmed but he still kept his head buried in my shoulder. "I know I need to let you go, but I can't."

"I don't want to go," I told him. "I just feel I should. I don't want to be a threat."

"If having you at my side loses me Camelot, I don't care."

I hushed him, his words were insane and illogical. He didn't mean them. Guinevere and I persuaded him off the floor and I managed to get him into her bed. "We'll talk tomorrow. Go somewhere nice for awhile, you and me, or all three of us and we'll sort this out, Arthur. I promise."

"Wolf, I am so sorry," he murmured.

"There is no sorry, Arthur. It just is the way it is and we will cope." I knew then that Moran understood Arthur even more than I did, my duty lay in keeping Arthur sane. If that meant negotiating the dangers of Camelot's politics and gossip then we needed to do everything possible.

The King soon fell asleep. Guinevere tried to talk to me, all she wanted was the truth but the truth lay beyond my grasp to confess. I left her, distressed and confused.

When I returned to my rooms, leaving Guinevere in charge, it took hours for me to find peace.

CHAPTER TWELVE

I RACED OVER THE damp ground, my powerful limbs covering the leagues. The willows and aspens on the Levels raced past but still I knew I'd be too late. The evil, the all encompassing foulness I'd been hounded by for months, now lurked ahead of me. Baiting me as it engulfed the Tor in its horror. I knew I'd be running into the evil. I knew it would kill me and by doing that it would kill the Hart but I had to reach the doe, I had to save her and the place she lived. Although she'd run from me to the world of men, my sense of duty and pack pushed me towards her swiftly. I reached the edge of the evil. Madness filled my mind. I fought with shadows. I snapped and snarled at whispering voices. I howled even as I bled. I lay dying, before the gates of the Abbey. The evil grew into the form of a man, an impossibly beautiful man with my eyes, he smiled and wiped the blood off his knife onto his sleeve.

"Hello, son," he said. "If you can move you will find them both dead. Your Hart and your doe. Have to see which of them dies first when I find them in your world."

"Lancelot, wake up," Arthur's voice almost screamed. No, not Arthur screaming, me screaming.

I snapped my mouth shut the moment my eyes opened but I still heard the echo in my head. Arthur knelt over me, on my bed, shaking my shoulders. "Avalon," I managed. "We need to go to Avalon, we have to stop him."

"Calm, Wolf, calm," Arthur said. He climbed off me but stayed on the bed. "Tell me what happened."

I described the dream, leaving nothing out. His eyes filled with worry and confusion. "We need to speak with Merlin."

I didn't disagree, I just wanted to stop shaking. Arthur's hand held mine. On my bed. I was naked. He, dressed only in a housecoat. Nothing but his clothing separated us.

The fact that I noticed all this after such a horrible dream told me how bloody desperate I'd become to finish what we kept starting. Arthur, distracted by my dream, flinched when I grabbed him, pushed him back on the bed and straddled his hips in one movement. I pinned his arms over his head and kissed him, ravishing his mouth, duelling with his tongue. My cock grew hard and I became more savage. Arthur struggled but only because he wanted control. I didn't give it to him. I devoured him. Our hips rocked together for a moment and he moaned to my mouth.

When I moved from his lips to his neck all I heard was, "My Wolf, yes, my Wolf," he repeated until I released his hands so I could tear his clothing off his back.

I bit him, hard. I wanted to hear him cry out my name. His fingers grabbed my naked backside and pulled me against his hips. I flattened over him, pushing my legs back and I felt his own desperation through the fabric I hadn't yet moved. The woollen fabric felt rough as I ground myself against him. He pushed me back. No woman would have been able to move me like this and I began to push for more until I felt his hand grab my balls and squeeze the most sensitive part of my body.

"Arthur," I gasped in response my limbs going weak.

"Behave, Wolf," he told me, his eyes flashing in the darkness of a full moon night. He kissed my mouth while rolling me onto my back. His hand moved to my cock and I groaned. "Tell me you belong to me, Lancelot," he demanded.

I smiled up at him. His eyes full of promise and power. "I belong to you, Arthur." It felt so good to surrender, to let go of my foolish fears and give into our desires. It didn't matter what anyone thought, this was right and good. His eyes softened as I spoke. The blue so pure and perfect. His lips formed a smile and he kissed my mouth. "Come for me, love," he said.

"I wanted more," I told him, confused.

"And you will have it, I promise," he said. "But now, I want to watch you come for me."

To be honest I couldn't have stopped the building orgasm if I tried. His hand, large, rough with calluses and holding me so tightly, worked me into a frenzy. I barely had time to scream his name. The surging power of the orgasm shook me to my core. Arthur covered my mouth with his free hand, trying to calm my noise, but his eyes never left mine and his mouth claimed my lips as soon as my body began to relax. "We have so much time now, Wolf," he said. "So much love to share."

I moved to satisfy him, but he stopped me. "I think I need to clean up first," he laughed. His hand a sticky mess.

"Hmm, the advantage of women," I muttered.

"Yep, they get to deal with the mess," he smiled as he washed his hands in my shaving water for the morning. I walked behind him and he turned with a cloth to clean my belly. He washed me as though I were the king and he the squire. The preciously intense moment made my heart fill with a love so exquisite my vision blurred.

Guinevere's voice argued with Merlin's, the sound filtered through the thick oak door separating our rooms.

"Fuck," Arthur muttered. He pulled back. "We are never going to finish this," he cursed. I grabbed my housecoat and he picked up his from the floor. We approached the noise together.

Guinevere stood before my door like an angry terrier trying to stop a wolfhound from stealing a toy. "I told you, it can wait. Lancelot was screaming and Arthur's in there helping him. He's had a terrible shock and he doesn't need you giving him grief."

"Guinevere," Arthur said mildly, trying to interrupt them.

"You have no right to stop me," Merlin barked. "He is my Wolf." The wizard towered over the Queen, his hair in disarray, his green eyes flashing with anger.

"Enough," Arthur raised his voice. The power of a King swept both into silence. "Merlin, you do not speak to my wife like that and Lancelot does not belong to you. He is my… Champion." I watched him struggle to finish the sentence before giving away our secrets. It made me smile.

"Why don't we sit and find out what's wrong rather than arguing over who owns what," I said taking Guinevere by the elbow and sitting her in my chair. She smiled up at me and stroked my cheek.

"You look so much better," she said as Merlin began arguing with Arthur. "I wanted to give the two of you time." I did not feel ready to confess to her what happened and I wondered what Arthur may have said, but I kissed her crown and moved to stand behind her.

Merlin didn't have any such qualms. He stilled in the middle of a sentence and his eyes narrowed on me. "So, you've finally given into your passion. And the Court, what are you planning on doing about the gossip?"

I glanced at Guinevere. Arthur said, "If we are careful and no one who knows talks, we should be safe enough. You once considered this a good idea." He stood as if waiting for the rest of the attack.

"Good?" Merlin said and snorted. "I thought you'd burn it out and forget it while staying close. I didn't think it would consume your every waking thought."

Arthur glanced at me, stricken by Merlin's harshness. "Just tell us what all the fuss is about," I said coldly.

"Dreams, Wolf, dreams. You didn't come to me about this dream. You would rather fuck about with Arthur than speak to me as is your duty." His anger towered over the room, finger jabbing toward me.

"The dream burned through him, Merlin, he needed peace," Arthur said. "We didn't realise we were on a timetable."

Guinevere continued to sit still and quiet.

I try to be a rational man and it is rare give way to my temper because when I do people get hurt. I forgive quickly when others hurt me if I can. I will drink myself out of emotional quagmires, but as faults go, it could be worse. Merlin however caught the backlash of the pain and my fear about the nightmare. My brief time in Arthur's arms receded.

"Listen, wizard, I am not at your beck and call. I did not ask for these dreams and I have no wish to be a part of some fey fucking conspiracy. As for any time I might spend in my King's presence, I will not have you or anyone comment on our relationship. I will not have his throne threatened by gossip and I'll appreciate it if you spoke to me with a little more fucking respect."

Merlin grinned, "There, my Wolf bites."

A sudden urge to pick up a chair and hurl it at his head overcame me. Arthur stepped to my side and lay hand on my arm. The anger dissolved. "Just tell him the dream, Lancelot."

So, I did. Guinevere said it first, "You have to go to Avalon."

Merlin sat and frowned, his eyebrows joining. "They both have to go. I feared this, more than anything I feared this."

"I can't go, my place is with Guinevere," Arthur said.

"Your place is in the soul of Camelot. I have seen de Clare riding for Avalon with great power at his back. He wants to devour the centre of your world, Arthur," Merlin said, now very serious.

"And the mysterious man?" I asked.

Merlin remained silent for a long time. He studied me. I did not flinch under his gaze. "Yes, Wolf, he is your biological father. You were bred on your mother by the fey king to counteract Arthur's birth. You were not meant to be his friend, never mind his lover. Now, you are marked for death. Nimue wanted to use your connections and your father wants them gone. Wants you gone. He misread the signs. I knew you would be Arthur's saviour, Aeddan thought he could make you enemies."

We were all stunned by the news. The fact that I was bastard born didn't surprise me, my step father hated me for just breathing, it wouldn't have mattered who spawned me. My heritage, my fey heritage, did shock us.

"So, Lancelot really does have a claim on my throne?" Arthur asked into the silence.

Merlin shrugged. "Depends on your point of view I suppose. I don't think you need to worry about Lancelot taking Camelot, Arthur. He'd sooner cut his own throat. The main trouble is my daughter and the hidden power of Avalon, Camelot's soul. He might even find a way of using Eleanor's connection to the fey throne, through her mother. I think because of these dreams we can consider Stephen as Aeddan's puppet."

"He will never gain enough political power to take my throne," Arthur stated.

Merlin shrugged again. "The ways of men and politics are many. Think about the power he already has, Arthur and what he can use his money for, regardless he'll have your throne one way or another. Especially if he gains power over Avalon. There is power there. Aeddan will have control over the most potent of Nimue's fey channels into this world. He'll be able to force armies through the Tor gateway. Nimue will not give him access from Albion, but he can take it via our world, by controlling de Clare and Avalon while forcing Nimue back."

Arthur and I exchanged a long look. We knew the magic under Avalon's Tor. With Aeddan's power, Stephen would drive a hole into Albion allowing armies to move in both directions, dominating both worlds.

I shrugged, the politics mattered little to me, I needed to stop an army and I was not going to consider Aeddan my father. I focused on the threat I understood. "I can be there in a few days if I take one of the small ships across the channel."

"You won't be any use on your own if Stephen is marching with an army. I'll lose you and that's not really an option." Arthur began to pace. His expression grave. "How soon will Stephen reach Avalon?"

Merlin looked at the ceiling for a moment. "He's not making it easy for me to track him but if we leave now we might reach the town before he does. The weather will hold him back because he's journeying from further north."

Arthur nodded. "We take the Wolf Pack and fifty of my best regular soldiers. The rest will stay here to defend Camelot if something happens. Moran will be left in charge of the standing army," Arthur instructed me.

"Yes, Sire," I said automatically.

"Arthur," Guinevere's voice cut through his planning. "If I promise not to be a nuisance can I come with you both? I don't want to be left in Camelot, alone. Not again." Her eyes were large and the fear leaked from every pore in her body.

Arthur knelt beside his wife. "Sweetheart, the journey will be impossibly hard on you."

"I promise, I won't complain, please, don't leave me. I won't survive if I lose you and Lancelot." She blushed and looked down at her hands. "Whatever is happening between you."

Arthur and I stared at each other, we needed to tell her the truth and he needed to explain that taking her to Avalon was a monumentally stupid idea. As I stared at him I realised he'd see to the former but his heart would not hear the arguments against the latter. By the time the night grew to the darkest hour we were waking the castle and preparing for war.

I was going to Avalon.

CHAPTER THIRTEEN

LEAVING CAMELOT MEANT THAT sooner or later, I had to face Geraint and Else. I hadn't seen either of them yet, Geraint choosing to stay in rooms away from mine, until I headed for the stables.

I rounded a corner on the narrow dark back stair, which spiralled downward in a lazy curve. Not paying any attention to my steps, I collided with a body.

"Bloody hell," I snapped, catching myself before I fell and catching the person with whom I'd collided.

"It's good to see you too," came a muffled voice.

"Shit." I dropped the small body in my arms and stumbled back. My heel caught on a stair and I promptly sat. Else now stood a little taller than me. I looked up into her brown eyes. There were dark circles staining them but I don't suppose I looked too good either. I opened my mouth and snapped it shut, she smiled and a wash of self pity brought tears to my eyes. I blinked and pulled myself upright.

"I am sorry, my Lady Fitzwilliam." The honorific hurt more than I thought possible. I shifted to the narrow part of the staircase to move past her.

"Lancelot, wait, please, can we take a moment to talk?" She reached out to stop me moving. I kept going, her fingers slipped from my arm and I was gone. The stairs blurred. I almost tumbled down the rest of the flight and in moments I found myself in the royal stable. The cold night air hit me hard and I breathed in deep breaths of bitter cold air. Nausea swept through me and I stopped my flight to stand with hands on my knees, fighting for control.

A light touch made me jump. "Guinevere," I said, and I pulled the Queen into a tight embrace.

"What's happened?" she asked mystified.

"Else," I said into her hair.

"It's alright," she said understanding me and stroking my back.

I let Guinevere go and she smiled up at me, the moonlight washed out her golden hair and turned it silver. "Arthur's Wolf, how you suffer," she said, her fingers tracing my jaw. "I'll do what I can to keep them away from you on the road. Just stay close to me or ride with the men."

I nodded consent. I heard Arthur calling and all thoughts vanished from my mind in the chaos which followed. By dawn we were on the road leaving Camelot far behind. A long ribbon of steel glinted in the pale winter light and puffs of warm air flowed from the breath of the horses. We were all riding draining the stables of war bred mounts. If anyone attacked Camelot, it would be a siege, so the horses didn't need to stay.

I watched, along with Captain Moran, as the men filed past. The Wolf Pack and fifty regular soldiers is all we took to face Stephen's army. It wouldn't be enough but it did mean we could move fast and Arthur did not want to call on his right of knight's service from any of the lords in Camelot. He did not trust enough people and those he did trust did not have the necessary soldiers to call to arms in time.

I heard some bickering and squinted into the bright light of dawn. Gawain and Yvain were arguing once more over their horses. Gawain, his bright blonde handsomeness a contrast to Yvain's smaller, darker good looks, their heads were close together as thy bickered. They'd been friends since boyhood and were an inseparable team. Yvain stood a good hand and a half shorter than me, swarthy and dark, his family heritage made for interesting reading. Uther made his father a knight and gave him lands when the man killed the king's enemies in an efficient assassination. The new knight then brought his herd of spectacular horses to England from southern Europe. Yvain inherited his father's looks and gift with the animals. They weren't strong enough to hold a knight in full armour but they ran almost as far and fast as wolves. Both men adored Arthur and I was glad they were coming, I and the Wolf Pack enjoyed their effervescent company.

"You'll have trouble containing those two," Moran pointed out watching them ride past, they bickering turned out to be about some woman they both liked as well as the horses.

I chuckled. "If that's the worst of my trouble I'll be grateful."

"Time for you to go, my Lord," said the older man.

I nodded but continued to stand still. "I wanted to say thank you."

"Stop being afraid, Lancelot, but be careful. People can be tolerant if you give them a chance, they can also be cruel," Moran said.

"I hope you're right about the former and fear the latter. Merlin doesn't believe it's right."

Moran made an unpleasant noise. "That's bollocks. He just wants to keep Arthur under control and you too. Follow your heart, boy, and you'll be alright."

I mounted Ash and looked down into the scarred face. "Look after Camelot for us."

He saluted, as did I, then Ash turned and we cantered up after the last of the soldiers. I rode in the vanguard. We all carried our own equipment, no carts or camp followers. Unless you counted the Queen. She rode with Arthur at the head of the army. I saw Else and Geraint next to them. It gave me an incentive to stay and listen to Gawain and Yvain arguing over what mare to place on which stallion. I tuned them out and watched the dawn spread fingers of molten rose across the sky. The wind blew fresh into my face and I closed my eyes while Ash lopped along the road. The smile spread from the warmth inside my heart. I'd surrendered to Arthur and it felt good. Gossip be damned, he needed me and I'd consent to anything to see him happy.

The journey itself was cold. Snow fell with regular monotony. The Wolf Pack and the additional soldiers soon became a single fighting unit under Arthur's coaxing. All thoughts of rivalry between them were soon squashed. With Moran remaining in Camelot, Tancred found himself promoted. He wore his responsibilities well, efficient, calm and unafraid to ask for help when he needed it from me. We worked well together and I found his company a comfort. Arthur and Guinevere shared their lives like never before, which didn't stop him stealing the occasional moment with me but little happened. Just words but those words held me strong and happy, forcing dark thoughts about Geraint and Else away. They also helped the dreams. They were frantic, full of anguish and fear. Arthur eventually asked Merlin to help me after yet another night of broken sleep. The draft he prepared eased but didn't cure the nightmares. A man with my eyes laughed through the chaos inside my head. I refused to acknowledge his presence.

Guinevere surprised us all. Arthur and I raised a small tent for her every night, giving them privacy, but she ate with the men and spent her time in riding leathers. She walked painfully for the first few mornings and found sleeping difficult, but after five days she became one of us and I watched her bloom with great pride. We all loved her and she became our talisman against the torment of the weather and cold nights around inadequate fires. We would fight for Guinevere's honour. Whenever I thought about de Clare's hands on her flesh, my loathing made me sick and rage overtook me, burning through my blood. It slowly dawned on me that I loved her still, despite everything we'd done to each other. Not a terribly happy thought.

Eventually and without incident, we reached the small town we'd destroyed on our last visit. The wind came from the north, as did we, but it didn't prevent the stink of burnt buildings and rotting flesh making some of the newer recruits curse. We rode slowly down the treacherous hillside, the horses slipping on ice under the snow. The afternoon became evening and I realised we'd have to camp in the burnt shell of the town unless we rode through the night.

I pushed Ash up the ranks of men and joined Arthur. Geraint rode on his other side. He tried to smile at me, but I spoke briefly and only to the King, "I don't want us spending the night in the town, we either stop now and make camp before we reach the place or we ride on into the night. The men will not want to sleep among the ruins." I pointed to the stark fire blackened hovels just appearing in the gloom.

"It won't be safe to ride over the Levels during the night," Geraint said.

"It is never safe to ride over the Levels," Arthur said. We all remembered how horrific our last venture became at this point in the journey to Avalon.

"Then we stop here?" I asked.

"Here might well be safer than down there," Arthur said nodding to the flat, snow covered land below us. The wind whipped at the tousled heads of the willow trees making them wave and dance.

I pulled Ash's head around and rode back up the hill, he argued with me. He hated the snow even more than he hated me for making him be in the snow. His powerful legs high-stepped through yet another drift and I reached Tancred. Echo, Tancred's bay, sidestepped Ash's lunge.

"That beast is a menace," he grumbled.

"We need to make camp here," I said.

"Here? Are you sure?" he asked, pulling his scarf away from his mouth.

"Trust me, we don't want to go any further today," I said.

Tancred gave orders and we moved off the road into some woodland. Nature remained still and quiet. No birds sang the sun below the horizon and no game ran from our noise. Merlin came over to where I helped Arthur raise a tent for Guinevere.

"I don't like it here," he groused. "I can feel the death you wrought in the autumn."

"I'll be sure not to kill the bad people threatening Arthur next time and ask them to leave nicely," I said, lifting the damp leather canvas over the small wooden frame.

Merlin said something foul and wandered toward a fire starting nearby.

"He's right," Arthur said, keeping his voice down. "It's not good here."

"Well, there is nothing we can do to make this easier so we just post extra guards to reassure everyone and not let the wind scare us. I'm certain all the golem died." I tried to be practical but my skin crawled as darkness crept on silent paws through the trees.

I sat with Arthur and Guinevere, all of us eating a poor ration of barely warm food cooked on smoky, spitting fires. We were quiet and I gazed upward. The stars mocked us with their beauty, the moon hid from the sight, riding her dark aspect.

Guinevere stirred. "One of you share your cloak, I'm freezing," she complained. Arthur didn't move, lost in his own thoughts. I wriggled and opened my arm up for her to snuggle under. She pressed her small body tight into mine. "Thank you, noble knight," she giggled.

We were alone. The men tight to their own fires and unwilling to trespass on the King's unusually sober mood. "Lancelot, tell me we will win against Stephen and won't lose Camelot."

Guinevere gasped, her husband's distress upsetting her. I'd listened to Arthur's fears many times before battle. The burden of a leader weighed heavily on his shoulders.

"Arthur, we will win. De Clare will not take Avalon and with a little luck I'll kill the bastard before we are through," I told him.

"Can you hear that?" Guinevere asked. She sat straighter under my arm and turned her large blue eyes onto the woods.

We stilled and listened. Not for the first time I wished for the skills of the Wolf in my real life. Something made my back twitch. "I'll go and take a look," I said untangling myself from the Queen.

"Not alone," Arthur rose.

"If there is something out there, it wants you, not me," I said. I pointed to the log we'd shared. "Stay there." Tancred, two fires away saw me moving and rose. We came together and walked to the edge of the light from the fires.

CHAPTER FOURTEEN

"DO YOU THINK THEY are still out there?" he asked. I'd told him of the golem we'd encountered in the town during the autumn.

"I don't see how, but at this point anything is possible," I said.

"It's giving me the fucking creeps," he said. "I can feel something out there."

I glanced at him and frowned. "What do you mean?"

"We aren't all quite as thick headed as you, my Lord." He grinned.

"Come on," I said. "I am Camelot's greatest knight. I'm not supposed to be afraid of the dark."

"Modest too," Tancred said, mocking me. I couldn't help but chuckle. We moved together into the darkness, both feeling foolish but nervous. The wind didn't stir the fresh snow and none fell from the boughs of the trees. I felt the cold through my boots but the fine quality leather kept the damp out.

Well attuned to the night we moved on silent feet despite the snow, senses aware of everything. In the same moment, Tancred and I drew our swords, the steam from our breath mingling.

"Something is coming," he hissed and putting his back to mine.

"Why can't we see it?" I asked. The same feeling of dread the Wolf felt so often in the woods crept over my body like a swarm of ants, eating into my bones. "We should head back to the men."

"It might be too late," Tancred said, his voice growing louder on each syllable. I moved to his left, the unprotected shield side of his body and watched a wave of blackness, darker than any night I'd known, roll toward us.

"We can't fight that," I cried.

"Close your eyes," Tancred yelled. "Close your eyes and see your enemy."

"What?"

"Trust me," he ordered.

I snapped my eyes closed and the wood became alive with the bodies of the dead. I also saw Tancred, a glowing light beside me and the battle began in earnest. These were the townsfolk once more, hideous in aspect. When we'd faced them in the autumn they were people without minds, burning in fires conjured to kill Arthur. Now, they were craven beings of burnt flesh and open wounds where we'd hacked our way free of their clawing hands. I battled into the ranks of the dead, my shoulder tight to that of my comrade. The skill created through endless training made our weapons a flowing river of death, which wove around us protecting our bodies from the touch of the dead.

"We can't hold them off forever," I gasped.

"We don't have to," Tancred said. "Arthur is coming with Merlin."

With my eyes still shut I gazed over the heads of our enemies and watched three bright lights, one golden, another huge and bronze, the last of silver racing towards us. I knew Arthur for the golden light. He fought with the heart of a true monarch. The others must have been Merlin and Geraint. Behind them were the Wolf Pack, smaller glowing lights spreading out and fighting the enemy we faced. Some gold, some bronze.

"Lancelot," Arthur called to me.

"What are we fighting?"

"We need to protect Merlin and let him finish this or they will keep coming," Arthur yelled.

Tancred and I moved as one toward the others. We all formed a circle around the wizard, Arthur to my left, Tancred to my right.

The silver light of Merlin started to grow and pulse. "When I give the order, you must all open your eyes," he said. His confidence in us kept his voice calm and quiet, we all heard and knew to obey.

We continued to fight but I felt the heat behind me coming off Merlin and his voice speaking in a language which made my ears pound. Arthur moved smoothly and blended with little effort into my fighting style. The three us became one and my heart swelled with the pride such company and talent gave me, but it didn't stop the exhaustion slipping through the cracks.

The heat behind me grew sharp and painful. I cursed, wanting to tell Merlin we couldn't bear any more when he bellowed, "Now!"

I snapped my eyes open and saw nothing but darkness. A great heat washed over me and I found myself flung forward into the blackness. A cold so intense it should have stopped my heart attacked me before vanishing under the heat of

Merlin's spell. I recovered, panic gripping heart and looked for Arthur. He picked himself out of slush and mud. Merlin's heat had melted all the snow in a large circle around our fight, bodies lay among the slush.

"Instant thaw, marvellous," he griped.

"Are you alright?" I asked holding him by the shoulders.

"I'm fine," he smiled. "Don't worry, Wolf. You've done your job."

"Arthur?" Guinevere's voice cut through the wood. I watched Else throw herself at Geraint.

"I'm here," Arthur announced. His hand slid down to mine. "I could drag you into these woods for the rest of the night," he growled for my ears only.

I chuckled. "I could let you."

Arthur moved away and stood firm as Guinevere rushed into his arms. I strode over to Tancred and helped him up. "What happened?" I asked.

"Don't know, not my job, ask Merlin." He brushed mud off his leather hose.

"Are you alright?" I turned him toward me.

"Lancelot," Merlin's voice now snapped my attention away from Tancred who slipped from my grasp. "Here, now." I sighed wanting to follow my friend, something seemed very wrong but Merlin was an impatient man.

I walked to the wizard, his green eyes still shone with his inner fire, but he appeared tired and his shoulders were hunched. "I never thought to face something that powerful out here," he muttered and grabbed my arm for support. Together we made our slow way back to the camp. I found Arthur, his arm still circling Guinevere and sat Merlin beside her.

"So, what the hell just happened?" I asked.

Merlin wiped a tired hand over his face, "A mighty spell."

"I guessed," I said. "How did Tancred know what to do? About seeing it only with my eyes closed."

Merlin shrugged. "Right now I don't know anything. We just need to sleep."

"We need answers," I said.

"The darkness you saw should have covered the golem attack, how your boy knew to close his eyes you will have to find out, Wolf. If he hadn't known you would be dead and so would the rest of us. The sound of your fighting alerted us and when Arthur couldn't see you, but he could feel you, I knew you were caught, trapped in the dark. It was a fey spell, I know that, but on a scale I've never seen before. And now, Wolf, I am going to sleep." Merlin curled up inside his black cloak and just seemed to pass out.

"I'll organise the men into short watches," I said to Arthur. The look in Arthur's eyes held me still and my loins tightened. He stepped toward me, his lust thick in the air.

"Arthur," Guinevere's soft voice made us both jump. He opened his mouth to speak but I leapt in first.

"She needs you," I said.

"I need you," he replied.

"Family, she is your family," I told him.

I watched him struggle with his love for his wife and his desire. I smiled, attempting to reassure him, and walked toward the bulk of my Wolf Pack. They spoke about the events of the night but they were calm, practical men who knew we faced something out of our control, yet did not shrink from their duty. My pride in them grew. I wanted to speak with Tancred but he evaded me and I eventually gave up meaning to corner him later.

The following day we found ourselves riding into a blizzard, the wind vicious over the flat lands, coming straight in off the sea. The horses were fractious and we couldn't cover enough miles. I did not want us out in the winter for another night and we were all on rations, which wouldn't help us fight if we met Stephen on the road or we arrived too late. Arthur agreed. So, we pushed on that day and into the night, her cruelty making us bone cold and weary.

I finally broke ranks, forcing a miserable Ash up the hill, his knees buried in snow. I approached the large gates, pulled down my scarf and banged on the wood. The sound boomed outward. Shattering the peace cloaking the town. Nothing happened as I shivered. The men began climbing the hill.

I drew my sword and used the hilt to bang harder. A sharper, harder sound wove through the community. "Open in the name of the King," I bellowed.

"What the bloody hell is going on?" came a surly female voice.

"Open up, the King is here and needs council with your leader," I said.

"What king?"

"What King do you think?" I said to the hole in the door. "Just open the fucking gate."

"What is it, Maria?" came another voice. This one more delicate and educated.

I heard voices exchange explanations and the gate began to move against the snow. It stuck. The others caught me up, many of us dismounted and began clearing snow. In no time, we were walking into the Abbey precincts. The walls were tall, eighteen feet or more in places but they were decorative more than functional for defence. The grounds were open and vast, the Abbey slowly being rebuilt in stone, replacing the wooden sanctuary. The housing for the priestess and novices were stone, with thatched roofs and the guesthouse looked warm compared to the ground outside. This place could not house fifty men and horses easily, never mind the townsfolk. Arthur joined me and a small, neat woman approached us.

She curtsied and said, "Sire, we had no word of your arrival, though you are always welcome." It didn't sound as though we were welcome.

"Mother Superior." Arthur bowed low and kissed her hand. "Forgive us for arriving so late and landing on your doorstep in such an unhappy way."

She smiled, Arthur's presence already weaving its magic. She asked, "What has caused your arrival in such numbers and in such inclement weather?"

I tuned out Arthur's words. They would be platitudes and pleas for aid. I found myself watching Else being lifted off Mercury by Geraint. He wrapped her in his cloak, tight against his body. I'd spent the entire journey avoiding them, they camped away from Arthur and during the day when Geraint rode at his side, I rode with the men. They must have felt my eyes on them because Geraint turned and Else raised her eyes to my face. Geraint spoke to her and I watched her nod. He took his cloak off and gave it to his wife, swamping her in the fabric. He walked toward me.

I wanted to move but my feet wouldn't obey. Geraint approached and yet he stayed out of sword's reach. "Lancelot." His hazel green eyes were so tired. The journeys they had undertaken took their toll. "Can we talk?" He held his hand out in peace.

I briefly considered cutting it off. We'd not spoken since they announced their engagement when we were last in Avalon. Else moved to stand at his shoulder, her soft brown eyes stared at me and I saw the fear.

"Lancelot, I need some help," Guinevere's clear voice cut through my growing anguish. Why did it hurt when I had Arthur to love? I asked myself. I already knew the answer. I thought of her as my last chance at a family of my own and I thought she loved me despite my many flaws.

I turned to my Queen, she smiled but her lips were tinged blue. "Bloody hell, Guinevere, you look sick."

"Thank you, my noble Wolf," she managed through frozen lips. Her arms moved stiffly but she reached out to me and I lifted her from the gelding, Boxer, she'd been riding. His woolly chestnut coat lay thick with snow but he also steamed in the frigid air. More snow covered Guinevere, her lashes thick with it and her shoulders.

"Arthur, we need to get the Queen somewhere warm and the horses need shelter," I called out. I walked toward the doors to the Abbey's living quarters, carrying Guinevere who nestled against my chest. Tancred gave orders for the men to dismount and unpack in the Abbey precincts. I brushed past Geraint and Else, my eyes only on my charge.

CHAPTER FIFTEEN

I CARRIED THE QUEEN into the largest of the living quarters, the stonework new. White walls were marked with the beginnings of the frescos the nuns planned but the bright paintwork remained unfinished. Familiar with the territory, I strode through a flock of small women and into the refectory. I found the hearth blazing. I knelt and placed Guinevere on the floor. She shivered and her eyes fluttered, disconcerting me.

"Why didn't you tell me you suffered so much?" I asked, stripping her damp fur gloves off her hands. They were white with cold.

"I promised not to complain," came the stuttering reply.

"I need warm, dry blankets," I announced to no one in particular, assuming my orders would be carried out. More quietly I said, "We need to strip you out of these clothes."

Guinevere tried to smile. "You offering?"

I smiled in fondness at her. "If my King orders it," I shot back.

"Forever his, huh," she said.

"Forever," I agreed wrapping my arms around her slim shoulders. It didn't take long before warm blankets and warmer wine were being given to Guinevere. I sat at her feet. She now sat curled up in a large chair, swaddled in wool.

Arthur walked in, his armour chiming on the stone floor. I'd stripped off most of mine, leaving it in an untidy heap. He kissed the crown of her head and lay a hand on mine, it felt so good.

I began to move. "I need to assess the defences of this place."

Arthur unbuckled his breastplate. "No point, not tonight. It's snowing again and it's bad. You can't see a damned thing out there. Merlin says we are safe enough."

"Where is the old buzzard?" I asked.

"Talking to the Abbess about all things mystical," Arthur said. I rose from the floor and lifted his mail off his shoulders. "That feels like a miracle."

With our short rations, we relied on Avalon's kitchens to feed us. It took time to organise all the people and the horses but around midnight everything began to calm. Most of the nuns now shared their cells with at least one other woman while the men bunked three to a small cell. Where we'd put the townsfolk I couldn't imagine. Still, I doubted the siege would be a long one. I walked around the precincts, trying to see through the snow and realised we were officially buggered.

The place was indefensible. The high wall was only a single thickness of stone and surrounded a huge green space, which sloped up the side of the Tor. I could just make out its brooding presence in the darkness, a thicker black against the swirling snowflakes. I shivered and for the first time I wrestled with my fear about losing to Stephen de Clare.

"I can't lose," I muttered. If I lost, Guinevere, Else and all the women in Avalon would be victims to his army and Arthur would be dead.

"Lancelot," her soft voice broke my reverie.

I didn't turn, but I said, "You should be with Geraint."

"He's with Arthur," her voice came closer. "And we need to talk, please." A firm instruction, not a request.

I turned to look at her. "Alright, what do you want to say?" A part of me realised how distant our relationship seemed with the chaos of the last few weeks.

She stood in the snow, wrapped in a blanket over her cloak. I wondered if Geraint knew she was out here in the middle of the night. Her eyes were dark, her voice didn't waver. "You need to forgive Geraint."

I raised my eyebrows. "I need to forgive Geraint. Is that an order, my Lady?" My chest tightened and my back locked rigid.

Else fought her temper. I didn't understand what she had to be angry about. "He fell in love and offered me a life I wanted. I am sorry you were caught in the crossfire, but he needs you. Your friendship is important to him. You forgave Arthur."

A rough bark of a laugh spat from my constricted chest, "Forgave Arthur? My Lady, you have no idea what you are talking about. Geraint chose to take you from my side and frankly, madame, I am pleased." Anger ripped through me, real anger with her for not standing beside me and allowing Geraint to seduce her while I lay in my sick bed. "I am free of the duplicitous –"

"Lancelot," another woman's voice snapped. My Queen's words chimed through the snow, "I need you with me, now." The order clear.

I fought my instinct to follow her instruction. I wanted this, I wanted to rant at Else and tear her new perfect world to shreds. I wanted to give her an ounce of the pain she'd forced into me. I wanted to explain that her surrender of me made my love for Arthur bloom into something physical and beautiful but also caused a form of agony I didn't know if I could survive.

"Lancelot," Guinevere's voice became imperious. I bowed to Else and brushed past her to walk to my Queen.

"Your Majesty," I said arriving at her side. She stood in a plain white shift, on the steps of the main building. Her exhaustion hidden behind a mask of command. I found myself trapped by the fragile beauty she possessed.

"Wolf," her voice softened and I heard her love for me. "Don't torture yourself. Come to Arthur, he needs to talk to you." She held out her hand. I slid my rough leather glove into her small palm and mutely left the scene behind me. I left Eleanor Fitzwilliam alone in the snow.

Guinevere led me through the Abbey and I found Arthur in his old room on the second floor of the stone building. A rush of memories made my knees weaken in a way Else's presence didn't.

Arthur half turned as we walked in. "You found him." His relief swamped me in comfort and love.

I stood and thought about the conversation I'd just had with Else, "She thinks Geraint did the same thing to me as you did and she thinks I have to forgive him. Just like that." I snapped my fingers.

Guinevere made a soft sound of pain at the mention of our shared past, something we tried to avoid. Arthur's mouth turned grim. "Yes, she wants you to forgive him."

I grew more detached from the previous conversation. "But it isn't the same. She isn't Guinevere and he isn't you. We were so young."

"Yes, Wolf, we were," Arthur said slowly. I realised he feared where I wanted to take this confusion.

"It has taken us years to overcome that one act," I stated.

"Yes," Arthur said. Guinevere sat on the large mattress, which lay on the floor for their use. The fire blazed in the hearth, its heat almost suffocating me.

I stepped toward my King. "I love you but seeing her with him still hurts, Arthur. I can't help that. I feel like I have been robbed of something but at the same time I know I would have broken her heart. I don't know what to do and I don't know how to make it right with Geraint."

Guinevere, now in the periphery of my vision covered her mouth and tears stood on her long lashes. Arthur placed his hand at the back of my head and pulled me toward him. "I know it hurts, Lancelot. I need Geraint, don't let the pain overwhelm you, give it to me." His lips were just a finger's width away.

I became very aware of Guinevere in the room. "Arthur," I sighed his name.

His breath came hot and fast on my mouth. I wanted this, him but I didn't want to be swept into the confusion of sharing a bed with both of them. Guinevere rose from the floor, approached and lay a soft hand on both our faces. Arthur moved first and claimed my mouth. I groaned and folded into his arms, needing to cling to his physical strength. Wanting to forget my fears about Stephen taking the Abbey, about losing my last chance to have a wife and family, about the chaos my love for Arthur could bring.

We kissed and I pushed against him forcing him to the wall. He grunted as he hit it and his hand pulled my hips tight against his erection. We'd still not finished the dance we'd begun in Camelot so many days before. Our kisses were not graceful or compassionate. A greedy need filled our loins and bellies. I wanted to fuck this man hard and dirty, make him cry out my name in longing.

"I'll leave," Guinevere said.

Arthur broke from my mouth. "No," he said too loudly making us both flinch. I buried my face in his shoulder, unable to look at the Queen. "No, Guinevere, I need you to be a part of this, we are a family."

"I don't think your Wolf will cope, Arthur," she said. I turned to look at her through a mass of tangled dark hair, she smiled at me. "He is a simple emotional creature, who needs to be loved, not tormented. I've done him enough damage for many lifetimes. I will not hurt him again by confusing the issue."

"Guinevere," I said and wrenched myself from Arthur's arms. "You deserve more than either of us can give you." I ran my fingers against her head, a great handful of her hair sliding against my palm.

She turned her head and kissed the inside of my wrist. "I will always love you, Lancelot, but this…" She glanced at her husband. "This is too much for us both. I can give you tonight, the eve of battle but I warn you, Arthur, I want you in my bed by dawn and you'll make love to me after your Wolf."

Blindsided by her statement and demand I watched in awe as she kissed

Arthur on his cheek. He grabbed her hand before she could leave. "He can handle it, Guinevere. I know he can and I know he still wants you."

Did I? Maybe but I wanted Arthur so much more.

Guinevere frowned at him and pulled free of his grip. "No, Arthur. I know you think that if I give myself to your Wolf you'll be able to have him in our bed more often but I'm not prepared to stamp over old ground. Lancelot only ever wanted me because he needed to escape his feelings for you and you only married me so he couldn't have me. This stops at this point. There is a line and you're crossing it with this demand. You can share your love, even display it in my company, but I'll not share your bed, my King. Any baby we make is going to be yours and I'll have no one doubt that. Not again. I'll not go through any of that again and I'll never make Lancelot a victim of my lust. I've learned even if you haven't."

I watched Arthur during this impassioned speech. His expression shifted from amused, to mutinous, to desperately sad. He pulled my head back to his shoulder, sheltering me in his embrace but I could watch Guinevere as they stared at each other. Arthur nodded, a slow and deliberate movement, sealing my fate. I would have Arthur but only at Guinevere's behest and although I knew a different woman to the one she'd been before de Clare's violation, it scared me. I didn't want to be their pawn.

"Good, we understand each other, husband."

"We understand each other, wife," he said.

She rose on her toes and kissed my mouth for a brief moment then kissed Arthur's in the same way. "I'll return to you, I think. And you can make sure Lancelot isn't the only one to enjoy your body, Arthur." She turned away from us and left the room.

I looked at Arthur. "She's serious."

He nodded. "The baby making is serious that's for certain." The rueful tone made me relax a little. Arthur poured us some wine from a jug by the fire.

CHAPTER SIXTEEN

"DO WE NEED TO talk?" I asked, dreading the thought of an emotional quagmire.

Arthur shrugged and drank some wine. "She'll tolerate what we share but she's going to limit it. I don't know how to change it or even if we should. She'll help keep our secrets and for that we both owe her a debt."

I took the wine from his hand and took a gulp before filling the cup again and handing it back. "I will be your servant in all things, Arthur, you know that."

"But?" he asked, raising an eyebrow.

"I'm lonely," I confessed.

He sighed and leaned into me so I could hold him close. "I know, I can see it, feel it inside you. I want you to be happy, Wolf, but I don't know how to make it happen. I am a king and so we have some protection but we cannot vanish into the world and be together. I wish we could."

He shifted in my arms and I felt him nose at my neck, licking over my Adam's apple. It made me growl, soft and low. He stepped away from me for a moment, drinking more wine and replenishing the fire.

I watched the play of flames through his golden curls and the shadows that shifted over the strong plains of his face. I wanted him. I didn't want the soft skin and curves of a woman. I wanted the rough strength of a man to conqueror. I approached him and removed the wine cup from his grasp. He made a sound of protest until he looked at my face.

"Oh, bloody hell," he murmured. "Now I know what a sheep feels like, Wolf."

I had no words of soft seduction for my King. I placed a hand around his neck, tangled my fingers into his hair and pulled him towards me. Our lips met and I groaned into his mouth, our tongues sliding together, duelling for control.

He tugged me tight to his body and I felt his cock through my leather and wool hose.

Our hands began pulling at laces and buckles, tearing at the fabric that dared to separate us. Soft curses filled the room until we managed to be naked in the firelight. We sank together, locked in our embrace, to the furs and blankets. The muscles in my arms and back bunched as I lay Arthur under me and stroked down his flank.

"It's been too long, my King," I whispered, sliding a thigh between his legs and feeling him arch into it and push hard enough to hurt. "I will never stop wanting you, needing you."

He brushed my dark hair back, holding my face in both his hands as he stared up at me. "I love you. I don't know what the future holds or how much I can give, but I do love you."

He hadn't told me that in a long time and I didn't realise how badly I needed to hear the soft confession.

"And when the throne or Guinevere needs you more than that love?" I asked, threatening to ruin the moment but unable to stop the words.

He traced my lips with his thumb and I licked it. "I don't know, Lancelot." Tears stood proud in his eyes. "You've given me so much and I always want more."

"What if I took a lover, Arthur?" I asked for the first time. "One that we could trust." I held his hip in my hand and I felt the fine tremor in his body that my words caused.

"It would hurt, Wolf. It would hurt. Would you choose a woman of the court?" The tears slid down the side of his face. "Would you find your wife?"

I swallowed hard and let the truth of my words fill me. "No, I would choose a man."

Arthur's eyes widened in surprise.

"Making love to you has taught me that I need something I can only find in a man's arms. I can enjoy a woman but this…" I trailed a finger down his neck and chest, tugged at the blonde hair. "This is a hunger like no other and gives me so much more."

Arthur sighed. "But I cannot give you forever, and you need forever from someone, if it is a man I will learn to endure it."

"But not now, Arthur, not now, my love. When you are ready, and you let me go. I will never betray our love, I will never seek another while you want me and I will only take a lover with your understanding and consent. For now,

~ 86 ~

I will take this moment and hold it close for all my days," I whispered, wishing I hadn't said anything.

I bent to his lips and we kissed, a deep and tender moment as our bodies blended. Making love to Arthur was always a bitter sweet experience and I wanted tonight to be something we could both hold dear.

I kissed over his jaw, the rough prickle of his blonde stubble feeling more solid and right for me than the soft skin of a woman, so I licked him.

Arthur chuckled. "Enjoying yourself, Wolf?"

I hummed in contentment as I licked more of the rough skin and nosed at the scent under his jaw, drawing it into my body so I'd never forget how he tasted and smelt. Arthur pushed up against me and I felt the slick liquid we both formed as we rocked together, his light to my darkness.

"Lancelot…" he breathed, while I bit at the pulse in his throat, it pounded as I sucked hard. His thigh came up my flank, opening his body for me. "I want you, inside me, now."

"Is that an order, my King?" I growled against his ear as I licked.

"Just fuck me," he groaned.

I chuckled and rose off him for a moment. I rifled through his saddlebags and found the small, dark blue bottle of oil he carried to match the one I had. I drew out the cork and inhaled the soft scent of roses and lavender. I bought it from an apothecary in Camelot who didn't ask too many questions.

I dropped to my knees between Arthur's thighs and watched as he tugged at his cock, he was so beautiful, with the firelight turning his golden hair red that I couldn't breathe. He opened his legs wider as he smiled knowingly at my dumbstruck silence and let his fingers explore his balls, covered in a dark golden fur and then he went lower.

"Put the oil on my fingers, Wolf," he ordered.

Well, this was a new game.

I poured a little onto two fingers of his right hand and watched as he circled his tight entrance. I licked my lips, desperate to take his cock in my mouth but I didn't want to stop watching him enjoy his pleasure. He lifted his hips off the furs and I watched his finger slide into his body.

"All for you, Wolf, all for you," he moaned on soft outward breaths. He moaned, his eyes closed, head thrown back, mouth open, back arched off the bed as he fucked himself.

I played with my cock but most of my attention focused on Arthur, my lust forgotten in the wonton vision he presented. In and out the finger moved.

"Add another, Arthur," I told him. He whimpered but did as ordered. I watched, greedy for more. "Faster, harder." He did as instructed. "Don't you dare come." He groaned and moved to touch his cock. "No, Arthur." I slapped his hand away. "Open your fingers and use another." I poured more oil into his plunging hand and licked up his cock, swirling my tongue over his leaking head.

"Please, I want you, need you," he begged.

"Not yet," I told him, loving the power I had over such grace and strength. "I want you open for me so I can fuck you without pause."

He whimpered. "Can I change position?"

"Yes," I said.

He barely left his arse but flipped over into his stomach and dragged his knees under him. The view took my breath away. He now used both hands and four fingers to open his body for me. I reached for his balls and rolled them as I watched. The hunger in me for this man knew no end.

"Please, Wolf, please," Arthur begged for me. His back glistened with sweat as he fucked his fingers but couldn't bring himself to orgasm.

I bit his tight arse hard enough to mark, drawing a thin wail from my lover. I rose behind him and moved his hands. I traced the widened entrance with my finger and he moved to capture the feeling, needing to draw it inside his quivering body. I played with him for a while as he cursed and begged, the glistening oil making it easy to slide into and out of his straining body. From one moment to the next I'd had all I could tolerate of play. I needed more.

"Brace," I ordered.

His breathing came hot and heavy. I lined up my weeping cock, added a little more oil to make this easier and thrust deep in one movement. Arthur bit off a heavy grunt as he stretched around me and I held still, balls deep in one movement, trying to remember my reason for existing. I leaned over his back and we were as tight together as we could be.

"I love you," I whispered into his ear. His hand came up and caressed my head as we tried to kiss at the impossible angle.

"I love you," he murmured, his eyes shut and small tears leaking through his thick lashes. He pushed back against me and I knew I could ride us to completion. I straightened, gripped his hips and withdrew before punching my hips forward with a brutality I'd never used on him before. Arthur gasped, his body going soft and pliant as I pulled back and did it again.

"Yes, please, yes, more, faster. I want you deep inside me," he moaned.

I rode him, sweat trailing down my chest and back as I owned my lover, my King, the beginning and ending of my existence. I trusted Arthur with my heart, even as I felt the fear of that love, but watching him, feeling him wrapped around my cock, I knew a depth of feeling for this man that could make or break me.

When my balls grew tight and Arthur whimpered in need, his hands flexing into the furs of his bed, I grabbed his shoulders and pulled him upright. The major shift in position as I settled on my heels for him to be sitting in my lap made him cry out for me. We managed to kiss and the movement had brought that sweet spot inside him to me. As I remained deep, I found enough movement to keep the pressure on that magic place and within moments Arthur shivered, his body going tense. I reached for his cock and tugged hard. He came and pushed down on my cock as it filled him.

The tight, hot, pulsing of his body dragged me upwards and the pain in my balls surged through every nerve in my body as I came hard and deep inside my lover.

I pushed my face into his neck and held him tight to my body as we both trembled and shook with aftershocks. I never wanted him to move, to move would be to admit we were separate beings and give voice to the fear I might lose him to war or politics, or even his wife.

He raised the hand I'd wrapped around his softening cock and I licked his seed off my fingers, the taste making me push up into him again, he flexed against me but neither of us could recover that fast. I helped him off my lap and lay him on the bed, brushing back the sweat soaked golden curls.

"You are so beautiful," I murmured. "Being inside you is the most perfect moment I've ever known. I love you, Arthur."

He caressed my cheek. "My dark Wolf. My heart. No other makes me feel the way you do, no other draws such passion from me. You will always be my deepest desire."

I blinked back the sudden rush of tears. Was he saying something close to goodbye? I swallowed and refused to chase the thought. "Let me wash you, my love." The words were close to a growl and I rose to hide the sudden turmoil. I cleaned myself quickly before kneeling and washing Arthur.

When I finished I lay beside him and he tucked me under his arm so my head lay on his chest. "I promised Guinevere I'd go to her," he murmured.

I traced lines down his chest and belly, just wanting to sleep in his arms, just for one night. A soft knock at the door startled us both.

"Who is it?" Arthur asked.

"It's me," Guinevere said opening the door. I drew a blanket over my hips and covered Arthur, a sense of possessiveness overcoming me that made her eyes narrow. She still wore the long white shift over her small frame and she approached in silence to lay on Arthur's other side, words gone in the strange moment of her arrival.

Her small fingers laced with mine over Arthur's belly and she kissed his cheek. "Sleep, both of you but, Lancelot, I want you gone when I wake."

"My Queen," I murmured. Arthur's arm pulled me tight to his side and I couldn't resist the call of sleep.

CHAPTER SEVENTEEN

I SLEPT LONG AND deep, dreamless for once and woke to dawn's pale light nosing through the narrow window. The fire burned low but the embers still fought the cold. I found both Guinevere and Arthur pinning me to the bed. I must have shifted because Arthur roused and lifted his sleepy head off my chest. My heart swelled when I looked at his smiling eyes. He rose up the bed and landed a quick kiss on my mouth. My courage began to waver and so many of my fears from the night before rushed back in a foul chaotic mess.

"I need to start work," I said to him.

He frowned. "Good morning to you too."

I grunted and tried to peel Guinevere off my chest. She smelt of sex, of Arthur and her own warm scent mixed with the blankets and furs we were buried under.

"What's wrong, Lancelot?" Arthur asked laying a hand on my chest to stop me escaping.

"Nothing's wrong, I need to defend the indefensible. I need to protect Avalon from Stephen de Clare. That's going to take time," I said pushing against him.

Arthur knew the truth on the surface of those words so he released me. "Alright, I'll let you go." Arthur also knew me well enough to know the signs. I couldn't cope with this new twist to our relationship. I gazed at Guinevere and I wondered if I would ever survive the chaos.

I dressed and Arthur watched me, remaining silent. When I buckled on my sword he said, "I need you, Wolf."

I glanced at him and raised a smile from the tumult. "I know." I left the small room, pushing everything complicated to the back of my mind. War, I know war and I'm good at it.

The men were gathering as I walked into the Abbey's yard. They stared at the walls, as disbelieving as me. Tancred joined me. "This is going to be impossible, my Lord. Those walls are useless."

"No wall is useless, Sergeant. The King needs this place defending and we shall defend it." I clapped him on the shoulder and called the men to attention. They were all tired, I could see that, but we needed to work and fast. Stephen would be on us at some point soon.

I began to give orders. We worked in efficient small groups of men, along with the townsfolk who vanished into the snow to find wood for us to create the towers we needed. I discovered any number of the locals could use a bow, so began organising them to help us defend their walls. The priestesses and other women were organised by their Mother Superior and Guinevere. I saw her just once across the yard. She smiled as she carried a small child away from the men. I smiled in return. I tried hard not the think about the previous night. I didn't want life to become more complicated. I spoke briefly with Geraint and for the first time felt sad about the distance between us, I missed my friend.

By the middle of the afternoon, we had a number of towers around the walls, the gates were reinforced and Arthur stood beside me on a tower overlooking the main road. "I have a splinter," he moaned as he picked at his left hand. He'd worked just as hard as the rest of us.

I grabbed his hand and looked. "That's not a splinter, that's minuscule," I said just as one of the soldiers shouted.

"My Lords, they are here," Yvain added his voice to others.

Arthur and I glanced upward. I dropped his hand. There, coming from the north a dark smudge. I focused on them, individual men and horses came into view.

"Fuck," I cursed. "That is more than two hundred men."

Arthur hissed, "We are badly outnumbered. There must be four hundred at least."

"All for one woman," I said, thinking of Stephen wanting Guinevere.

"All for Avalon," Arthur said, not hiding his dark hatred. "They are here to destroy the soul of England."

I glanced at him. "Is there something more I should know?"

Arthur shook his head as he moved away from the wall. "No, Wolf, just make bloody certain we don't lose." He bellowed Merlin's name and vanished from my side.

I had a bad feeling about this one. Something terrible walked toward us and we were weak. I began organising the men into standard formations. We were in groups of four, two archers, two soldiers. The archers would fire down and out into the enemy, then if they managed to breach the walls, which they would, the swordsmen had to force them off the ladders or fight to defend the archers.

We spent the day dragging in supplies and I had a bitter argument with the women guarding the some sacred well in the Abbey grounds. Apparently, that water wasn't for general consumption. I disagreed. I won because I held the sword. The children helped by collecting stones, even pulling down low walls to supply us with improvised weapons. The makeshift towers carried small amounts of these and water to warn off scaling ladders and fire, we also relied on increasingly desperate prayers when the enormity of our task marched into view. Some of us followed the old ways and were blessed by the priestesses, some of us the new. I believed in me and Arthur.

Tancred joined me to view the enemy. They camped just outside the edge of the town. "We should have laid traps in the town. Fire pits and things."

"Arthur didn't want the town destroyed in the winter," I said. "The people would soon die in this weather."

Tancred grunted. "They are going to die anyway without a miracle."

I sighed, I needed my men to at least believe we could win but even I didn't believe we would win. The army outside the town squatted in the snow.

"Lancelot," Arthur yelled. I turned and looked down, he stood dressed in full armour, "Fancy baiting the bear?"

The grin which spread over my face made Tancred step back. "My Lord, I don't think…"

I didn't hear the rest. I leapt off the tower and ran to Arthur. We raced toward the horses' pen shouting orders on the way. Men scurried to saddle Ash and Willow.

"What's brought all this on?" I thought to ask.

"You never know, he might accept a formal fight and we can save a few lives," Arthur said.

"Bollocks, it doesn't have anything to do with that," I told him.

Arthur laughed. "No it doesn't, I just want to fight the son of a bitch."

We mounted the horses. Guinevere, Geraint and Else all came tumbling from the Abbey halls.

"Where the hell are you going?" Guinevere snapped. I hadn't seen her really angry since our return to Camelot. It made an entertaining change.

I grinned. "To wind Stephen up," I said trying to help.

Geraint placed his hand on Arthur's bridle, Else approached Ash. I looked at her and she dropped her hand, but she said, "This is madness, please don't do it."

"We don't intend to engage," Arthur said. "I just want to make him angry enough to force some mistakes."

"And what if something happens to you?" Geraint insisted. "If you are set on this Arthur, allow me to ride with Lancelot in your place. I'll even take Willow so they think it's you."

"No," Arthur said. "I am his King and he defies me. I will lay my challenge before him."

Geraint's hand dropped. Arthur pushed Willow forward and Ash bounced with excitement beside him.

"Lancelot," I heard Guinevere's voice but had to concentrate on the damn horse. "Bring him home," she implored.

The men opened the gates and we rode into the town. The snow in the streets lay in shallow drifts, the low stone houses and their thatched roofs protected them from the worst. It lay pristine except where we'd been dragging logs to make our towers. I felt the silence of the small town wrap around us. Ash danced and made life difficult while Willow stepped high to stay out of the snow. The excitement running through me relieved me of the bizarre events of the day before. My King did not speak. He just focused on our enemies. I imagined he prepared a speech to deliver to Stephen.

After a quarter of a mile, we reached the edge of the main street through Avalon. The last houses in the town were humble affairs, as we left them behind we both closed our visors and the wind rose. Not enough to be a problem but it made my armour a colder shell.

We stopped just out of bow range. I watched a man in fine armour mount a great dark bay and ride toward us, I recognised the Boar on his shield. De Clare. I heard Arthur exclaim, "Why are we worried about these men?"

"What?" I asked, confused.

"There aren't four hundred. We were right, there are only two hundred," Arthur said. He laughed. "This is going to be easy."

De Clare, in the last of the daylight sat on his horse at the edge of his camp. He waved a hand and I watched as two hundred men advanced. It was not even half the army.

"Oh, my God," I breathed. "They aren't men at all."

What I now bore witness to I knew would haunt my nightmares for years. A horde of golem moved toward us, with more standing behind them. There were men amongst the monsters but the core of the army contained the burnt dead remains of people. I watched de Clare raise his visor and even at a bow's length, I saw his smile. We would be fighting the silent, foul ranks of the dead. They marched in perfect time. A deadly enemy we could only stop by destroying their heads. No other shot would prevent them from moving toward their goal.

Arthur turned in the saddle, "What are you talking about?"

I pointed and raised my visor. "Those, Arthur, those fucking monsters."

"What monsters?" Arthur asked. "Have you been drinking?"

"Lancelot," Tancred's voice forced me to look over my shoulder. He raced toward us on Gawain's fine, fast stallion. "Get him out of there."

I knew I had to move to save Arthur but the shock of seeing the monsters under Stephen's control made me slow to react. I grasped Willow's reins, just as a hail of arrows came toward us like a small black cloud. I raised my shield to cover Arthur and try to protect the horses. The arrows hit us like giant deadly raindrops. A sharp pain in my side let me know I'd leaned too far out of my saddle and my armour no longer protected all of me. All down my right side, I felt the darts hit me. Ash remained still, trusting me to make this right. Willow however panicked as the smell hit us of the burnt dead bodies. He threw his legs in the air and screamed at the now clear sky. I lost my grip on his reins and Arthur lost his balance. I had a great deal of practice with unpredictable horses, so didn't fall even as Ash reared to fight Willow. Something infected the horses and I watched Arthur roll away from Willow's lashing hooves. I jumped from Ash and landed almost beside him. The warhorses turned and raced back toward the Abbey.

I stood in front of Arthur, he rose from the snow and said, "I don't understand, men can't shoot that far and there aren't enough of them." I just watched the reload. Men might not be able to shoot this far but golem could.

I had no idea why Arthur didn't see the monsters I watched but I knew I had to move him. I grabbed his arm and yelled, "Run!" pulling him with me. I heard de Clare laugh and almost turned back to fight him before another cloud blotted out the pale low sun. I pushed Arthur to the ground and covered us both with my shield as I landed over him. The arrows made a deafening sound when they hit my armour. The ones bouncing around us whispered their potential for death while they buried themselves in the snow.

"Sire, quickly." Tancred reached us.

I rose, hauled a surprised Arthur to his feet and lifted him bodily behind my Sergeant. Yvain raced to a skidding stop and held out his hand to me. Neither man wore armour so they were light and would die if we didn't run fast enough. Despite the growing pain in my side, I grabbed my friend's arm and jumped onto the fast horse. Yvain turned us and we galloped after Tancred and Arthur.

We made the Abbey grounds in record time. Ash stood there, shaking, as Else tried to calm him. Willow backed himself into a corner, against a tower, making it rock. Gawain began to deal with him.

Arthur ripped his helmet off. "What the fuck do you think you were doing?" he bellowed at me.

I slid off the horse Yvain rode, the pain in my side made me slow. Well, that and the fact Arthur looked angry enough to smack me in the face. His mailed fist caught my jaw. I stumbled and raised my hands. I'd torn my helmet off on the mad gallop back to the Abbey, so the fist caught me hard. Blood filled my mouth, my teeth catching my cheek.

"Arthur!" Guinevere screamed. She raced across the square, no one else moved. All of them too shocked to think. Arthur prepared to hit me again. I dropped to my knees. I would not stand against my King. He brought his fist down just as Guinevere threw herself between us.

"What the hell are you doing?" she gasped, fighting his arm.

"He turned coward, he dragged me from facing Stephen. I wanted to kill de Clare, he raped you," Arthur shouted. I rose to move Guinevere out of his line of sight. I had never seen him lose his self control like this.

"Didn't you see those things?" Guinevere asked refusing to move.

My face ached but I'd known worse. Arthur frowned, "See what you mad woman?" He stepped backward and swayed.

"Arthur." I grabbed him, he moved in fitful jerks, trying to brush me off, then he collapsed against my body. "Arthur," I cried out.

Everyone moved, the spell of our own creation dissolved. Merlin rushed forward, Else and Geraint joined him. Yvain shouted orders to the soldiers, forcing them to man the towers and gates.

"Else, they are the golem. I don't understand. Why couldn't he see them?" I asked her.

Else looked at Merlin. He said, "There is a mighty spell over the army. I didn't sense it until you raced out there like a couple of foolish children." He looked tired. "Arthur, wake up you bloody idiot." Merlin slapped the King's face a few times and Arthur's eyes fluttered open.

"What happened?" Arthur asked, breathless and confused. "Lancelot, you're bleeding." He twisted out of my lap and touched the growing bruise on my face. Blood trickled out of my mouth.

"You hit me," I told him.

Arthur paled. Merlin said, "The spell or I should say series of enchantments, hides the dead from those of us who are almost or completely human."

"So, everyone who has fey blood in their veins can see what we face?" I asked.

Merlin nodded, "They are trying to spilt us, using our own strengths against us."

I handed Arthur to Guinevere and stood. "Men," I yelled, loud enough for the whole Abbey to hear me. Everything stopped. "All those that can see the dead men walking out there, pair with a man or woman who can't. Help your comrade fight what they might not be able to see until too late. Aim for the head. They only stay down when you destroy their heads. Do not allow the fear to dull your minds. We face a mighty enemy but we will prevail. For Camelot, for the King, for our Queen's honour, we will win."

I am not Arthur and I don't make pretty speeches but everyone cheered and began to reorganise themselves. I heard many of those who couldn't see the golem ask confused questions.

Geraint said, "They are the same as the ones we faced before?"

I glanced at Else and she looked surprised. Geraint didn't have a drop of fey blood in his veins.

I said, my heart twisting at the words, "Else, stay with Geraint. If he can't see he can't fight and I need him on those towers. You are a fine archer so I need you too."

She looked at me, her heart in her eyes. "Yes, my Lord." She rose and dragged Geraint with her. I watched as she vanished from sight.

"Right," I said shaking myself. Guinevere held Arthur, he struggled upright. "Merlin, why can't Arthur see the dead?" I asked

"They are attacking him," Merlin said. "The death and rage in the golem is all focused on Arthur. His fey blood is making him weak. That's why he attacked you."

"Get him inside," I said.

"Lancelot, they are coming through the town," Yvain yelled.

"Go," Guinevere said. She rose. "Just be careful, I cannot lose you, Lancelot." She lay a soft hand on my face and I felt her love wash through me, it made my heart race anew.

"My Queen," I kissed her hand, turned and raced to the tower on the left of the main gate.

CHAPTER EIGHTEEN

I STOOD ON THE makeshift battlement and watched the hidden army move toward us. Gawain and Yvain were involved in a detailed question and answer game. I discovered the reason Tancred and Yvain came to rescue us lay in their blood. Gawain remained fully human. I saw Tancred on the other tower playing much the same game with William.

I did not have a partner, under other circumstances I would fight with Geraint but right now, I had no idea how to speak to him. The best thing for me, as Commander in Chief until Arthur arrived, would be to stand and fight in the most vulnerable positions.

The late afternoon light made me nervous. They were going to attack at night, we were all exhausted from the day but I knew golem don't tire. This would be a fight for survival.

"I want torches, lots of light, when dusk comes we will need more light," I said.

A young small woman said, "Yes, Sir." She jumped off the ladder to race from tower to tower giving my orders. A lad replaced her. Someone had organised runners for me.

The horde advanced through the town, marching up the hill at a measured pace. They carried scaling ladders and ramps with them, they also had battering rams, but no trebuchet. I guessed the complex war machines were too heavy for the boggy ground on The Levels. But they were prepared. De Clare knew we were here.

The worst part of what we faced came not from the vision of burnt carrion that moved like men, but the silence. In the snow, they moved silently. When men march on a castle for a siege there is a mighty sound. The defenders yell defiance and the attackers yell abuse. There are orders being given and screams as people start to die. There is the sound of armour, of swords on shields, of arrows hissing and fire crackling. This time I heard nothing but the wind. Even our torches sounded mute.

The golem came within firing range of our bowmen and women. "Draw," I bellowed into the stillness. Fifty bows were pulled back. The creak of the ash wood audible. "Remember to aim for the heads," I said. "Fire first volley." The rush of air as the arrows sped over the walls of the Abbey made me smile grimly. I watched that rain of death hit the front ranks of our enemies. Only a few of the golem were hit accurately enough, they dropped, arrows sticking out of their heads. The rest continued to move forward. The mortals among them took cover behind a shield wall. We needed to wait until they were closer, a dangerous game.

"I fucking hate the waiting part," Gawain said as he hopped from foot to foot.

I lay a hand on his shoulder. "You'll have your share fast enough."

In the last of the light at the dying end of the day, I ordered another volley of arrows. More golem fell but not enough to matter. Their archers, having to shoot upward and over the walls, attacked. There were no orders, but a third of the golem stopped, lifted their bows and fired as one. Death descended but we were prepared. I heard the occasional yelp but no screaming and no grieving. I did however hear the enemy rush toward the wall as we sheltered from the arrows. They rattled down among us and children were soon scurrying about retrieving them for reuse. I rose as soon as it stopped and peered into the gloom. They moved and were within twenty feet of the wall, too fast for us to react.

"Archers," I yelled. "Fire at will." I should not be giving this order so soon.

A hand clamped down on my shoulder making me jump. "Arthur," I sighed in relief. "Can you see them? Should you be here?" He looked pale but his eyes were hard and determined.

"I can see them. Merlin's almost killing himself to break the enchantments. He says the lacing of power is something he's never known. He's punching holes in the spells but I don't know how long it will last." He peered over the walls. "This is not good."

"No, you can take over if you like," I said.

"I don't think so, there is no guarantee I won't succumb once more. You keep command and tell me where I need to go if I become confused."

"You're trusting me with Camelot?"

"So what else is new, my Wolf?" He smiled. "Now I suggest we do something about those scaling ladders."

I grinned back. Having Arthur at my back gave me great comfort. The archers were picking golem off one at a time, but we didn't have enough people to make a huge dent in the enemy's ranks.

"I thought only two hundred were standing against us?" I heard one of the local men saying.

I thought the same thing but Arthur said quietly, "They are creating them as we wait behind these walls. Merlin is trying to stop them."

"You don't want the men to know?" I asked.

"Not yet, despair isn't an emotion to court under the circumstances."

I didn't argue with him, I just watched the golem advance. "Ready poles," I ordered. "And the oil." A dangerous gamble this one considering our towers were wooden, but if we greased the ladders, they would be harder to climb and we could light them when desperate. Besides, fire had spent the day heating the oil, and waking corpses or not, the golem wouldn't like their faces and hands melting. The worst of this remained the silence. Even as they fell under our onslaught, the golem remained silent. We too were quiet. I'd never known anything like it.

Then we were there, in the thick of it. We could only defend the front wall, it ran such a long way. I had gambled and left the sides and back unprotected so the hills sheltered us, it proved the correct decision. Stephen could throw his monsters at us all night and never run out. He wanted us to die before breaching our walls, making hand to hand fighting unnecessary, by far the best option. The ladders were shoved toward the walls, we pushed them back. When we began to lose control of pushing ladders off the long wall, we tipped heated oil and grease over the rungs. It worked, the golem couldn't hold the rails and many slipped down, but they just kept coming, melt faces included. I heard orders and realised men controlled the dead. The golem washed back away from the walls for a moment and we watched, waiting, the night now on us. Men made certain they pushed the remaining ladders away.

I descended into the Abbey grounds and began checking the supplies of arrows, water, anything to take my mind off what we faced. We dare not fail but to succeed we needed a miracle. I walked around a large pile of hay for the horses and found Else. With her back to me, she didn't realise I'd arrived in the stables. Ash shared a small stall with Mercury and she held his head. I heard her weeping.

I almost turned and moved away. Whatever grief she felt, now was not the time to deal with it, but I didn't leave. "Eleanor?" I asked.

She turned as though stung by a hornet. "Lancelot." She rubbed her face. "I wanted to make certain the horses were secure."

"Of course," I said feeling distant and confused. She looked up at me, her eyes red but her face composed.

"I want to tell you why I said yes to Geraint," she said. "I know what our odds are of surviving this and you need to know."

"I don't need to know, you need to tell me," I said roughly.

She shrugged. "Perhaps, but if we do survive this, you will be faced with us at Court and we need a united front. It has to be said."

I remained mute and just stared at her. She made a small sound of protest at my stubbornness.

"It is important we know where we stand," she hesitated, "I owe you an explanation."

"You are being cruel and we don't have time."

"I am being honest. It is one of the things you value about me."

"Why are you doing this?"

Else paused. We had not moved but the world span away from me. The centre of that world looked sad. "You never loved me, were careful to never say it. I needed to be loved, Lancelot. You wanted to possess me. You love Arthur. But you want to possess me, you still do."

"Don't flatter yourself," I shot back. Possess her? Of course I wanted to possess her, to watch her flower under my protection, care and love.

"Ask Guinevere, she will understand. You are not just a man, Lancelot, you are the Wolf and you own what you profess to love. Arthur is the exception. He is the one you follow, the one who can tell you his dreams and you will help him achieve them. He is the one you allow to flower and grow. The rest of us, you want to wrap in silks and furs but never permit us to reach for our sunlight."

I didn't know what to say. How could she say she loved me and know me so little? I did not behave like this, I did not crush those I loved. I stood and watched her stroke Ash's nose.

"And I suppose Geraint offers you an uncomplicated love? I told you I'd surrender Arthur," I said confused.

She shook her head. "You will never surrender Arthur. You can't. The more I watch the two of you together, the more obvious it becomes. I don't know how Guinevere can stand it, having such terrifying passion surrounding her all the time."

"Lancelot," Arthur's booming voice captured my fraying control. "They're back."

I wanted to reach for Else and pull her to my chest and make her understand how I wanted her. I wanted time to convince her I didn't want to possess her. I wanted to watch her bloom. To convince her to leave Geraint. It wasn't too late.

"Else," I stepped toward her.

"Don't," Else stepped back. "When I am with you I cannot think clearly. I care for you too much for that. Go to Arthur, he will keep you safe. He loves you more than I could."

None of this made sense, but, "Lancelot!" Arthur's panic touched me at last.

I turned and ran back to the tower by the huge nine foot gates. I raced up the steps and took in the enemy. All the golem had cloth wrapped around their hands. They picked up their ladders and placed them in firm hands against our walls. Now they would climb with ease, unless we lit the ladders.

"You alright?" Arthur asked.

"Else," I said, the dull ache inside me translating to my voice.

Arthur turned away. "I am sorry, my friend."

There were no more words and no time for confusion. Maybe Else picked the perfect moment to tell me I was useless at the kind of love a woman wanted, because all I thought about was death. The smell of the golem reached us first. Those with delicate stomachs retched and vomited until they grew used to the stench of burnt death. The golem tried to breach the walls and we tried to push them back. When so many of them scaled the walls we no longer had the time to push the ladders back for sheer weight of numbers, we began to fight.

Arthur and I fought back and forth over the tower and narrow runways we'd constructed behind the Abbey walls. We fought on the wooden scaffold into the darkest part of the night. At one point, we were alone surrounded by death, our tower overwhelmed.

A sword slashed through the darkness and tried to rip Arthur's head from his body. I forced him down with my hand, he ducked and turned around me, pushing his blade into my enemy as I deflected and sliced into his. We danced around each other over and over, deflecting and slicing into the golem surrounding us. They were thickest here, they knew Arthur stood on this tower and they attacked without mercy.

Just as we began to falter from exhaustion, I heard a great cry. Tancred led a group of my Wolves from his tower, along a ladder he'd stolen from the enemy and hauled over the wall, to lay between us over the gate.

He screamed defiance at the golem and rushed headlong to the cry of, "Save the King." Others from all over the Abbey rushed to our tower and soon they climbed the sides to pull the golem off us, only to smash them when they reached the ground. The townsfolk became rabid in their desire for vengeance.

"Impeccable timing," I said as Tancred and others pushed the largest of the ladders away from our part of the wall.

"I do what I can, my Lord," Tancred said, grinning through a mask of blood.

"They are attacking the gate," William informed us. We peered over the edge, then retreated. A short volley of arrows came over.

"There are so many of them," Gawain said as he appeared. He looked hurt, his sword in his left hand hung at his side.

I glanced at the moon. We were barely half way through the night. "We can't keep this up."

"We won't have to." Merlin appeared at the foot of the ladder. "I need a word."

Arthur and I glanced at each other and as one we half climbed half jumped down the tower. I caught a glimpse of Else and Geraint. She carried him toward the Abbey hospital. I focused on Merlin.

"I've almost shredded the main part of the enchantment." He seemed to have aged a hundred years in the process. "The Abbess and I can force them to retreat but it will only be a matter of time before they come again. Their spells are renewing even as I speak. Whoever is in control is very powerful. More and more golem are growing from the earth, they don't even need the bodies of the dead. I have never seen such magic."

Arthur lay a hand on Merlin's shoulder as though to steady his torrent of words. "What will you have us do, old friend?"

Merlin took a deep breath. "Just hold out a little longer, there is a fog coming off The Levels, from the sea. Once night has fled, the golem won't attack. This many cannot be controlled during the day. Necromancy of this level is too difficult for the hours of the sun. A few, like those who attacked you, are one thing, but an army is something else."

Arthur nodded as though it all made perfect sense. "Right," he said to me, "tell the men we fight until dawn. Then it will end. If they know they have a specific time then they will find the courage and strength necessary."

The orders were given. We poured oil and stones down on those attacking the gate, shot arrows into them and then, an hour before dawn, just as the gates began to splinter I gave the order for fire. We could do no more but watch in horror as the monsters below us burnt. They made no sound and continued until their arms burnt off and their heads exploded or melted or whatever the hell the dead did to finally know peace. When they relented on the doors, I ordered water to douse the flames but the damage to the old tarred wood had been done. They wouldn't sustain another attack for long, no amount of reinforcing helped under these circumstances.

Dawn broke, the fog rushed in and the golem retreated. Arthur and I stood, watching them vanish into the mists, as silent as when they had arrived.

"We cannot have another night like that," I said.

"No," Arthur said, his blue eyes dark. "But we have little choice."

CHAPTER NINETEEN

WE CLIMBED DOWN, LEAVING some of the women as sentries. Exhaustion was a huge cloud and followed us into the Abbey. We found Merlin sat by a great fire eating a potage.

"What news wizard?" Arthur asked.

"The fog has come?" Merlin's eyes were haunted. The green, dull and lifeless like old dug up bronze brooches.

"It has," Arthur said trying to undo some of the straps on his armour. I moved to help. My hands were numb my right particularly stiff and it ached. We struggled until he freed himself from his breastplate. Merlin remained silent but nodded.

I looked about me. The stone floor appeared to be littered with blood and bodies. Some groaning, some talking quietly, some asleep. Women and children were trying to feed those who could eat, while others tried to staunch wounds. We couldn't deal with another night like the one we'd lived through. Guinevere appeared from the kitchens, a goddess in leather with golden hair. She smiled as she saw me and I realised I needed to stop this battle a long way short of defeat. I would not survive the afterlife knowing that woman had become a victim of de Clare's.

"Why so grim, Lancelot? We have survived," she said as she looked up at me.

"Merlin," I said turning back to the crumbled figure. "If we kill the person responsible for creating the golem will they fade? Cease to exist?"

He frowned. "What are you really asking, Wolf?"

"If I kill the enchanter making those things, we win, right?" I asked.

"Yes, but you can't kill the one responsible, I don't think."

"Can you?" the seeds of the idea gave me a flush of energy. I crouched at his feet. "Can you kill this person if I get you in there?"

"In where?" Guinevere asked.

"Inside Stephen's camp," I said looking at Arthur. "If we can stop these things then the match of men is equal, more or less and a siege won't work. You need more attackers than defenders for a siege. And I know a hell of a lot of the blood on me is from mortal men I've killed."

"Slice the hydra's head off," Merlin muttered. "It might grow back but if we cauterise the wound it will send a message. Perhaps now is the time."

I recognised the metaphor but still didn't understand it. "Are you willing?"

He grinned. "Wolf, you are all you should be and more."

"This is madness," Guinevere said. "It's suicide to try to go in there."

"It is genius," Arthur said.

Guinevere opened her mouth. Her fear lay in her eyes, bright and clear, she didn't want me to die by going into Stephen's camp. The fear lost the fight against her instincts as Queen. She knew we were lost without extreme measures. I watched her nod as though confirming her internal dialogue.

"When will you leave?" she asked.

"Now." I rose and promptly swayed as my head spun. Arthur grabbed me.

"Lancelot, that's your blood," he pointed to my right leg.

I looked down. Blood did flow. "It's just a scratch from when we first went out there." *So long ago*, I thought.

Guinevere hissed, "Then you aren't going anywhere until I've cleaned you up." She knew better than to talk me out of anything. "You will also need to eat and you need water."

"See to it," Arthur said. "I will organise a small group to go with you."

"I want Tancred and only him," I said. "He's steady, he can follow orders and he's capable of thinking on his feet if something happens to me. I'll have Gawain and Yvain placed in the town to act as cover if we find ourselves racing out of the camp. Or as a second attempt if we fail."

Guinevere grabbed my shoulders, turned me and forced me out of the large room. She pushed me down a corridor grumbling about the mess I made as I walked. I found myself in a small room, a nun's cell. She stripped me of armour, still chiding me and made me pull off my chainmail. It took far too much effort. A bowl of water sat on a tripod in the fireplace. The room reeked of herbs used to clean wounds. Lavender and wild garlic overriding everything else, they did not make comfortable companions.

She pulled at my shirt, found the wound sitting over my hipbone and tutted, poking at me.

"Ouch, Guinevere, go steady," I complained.

"And you a big brave knight of Camelot," she poked again. I caught her fingers up and brought them to my lips.

"Gently, my Queen, or I shall be forced to retaliate," I whispered over her knuckles. She blushed.

"Lancelot, stop, I think our courting days are long gone," she mumbled.

I touched her jaw and realised she entrapped me as much now as she did when we were barely more than children. "I have done nothing but use you since Arthur and I returned. You have been good to me, Guinevere."

She blushed deeper. "You saved me from so much," she spoke of my punishment. We were both still and silent, our fingers interlaced, her body close to mine.

I grabbed her and pulled her into me. I needed to hold her to keep me in my world. I felt the white doe race away into a sunlight deprived me. The call of a falcon made the Wolf raise his muzzle. A fine peregrine circled over the Wolf and the Hart, who stood at his side. The vision began to fade. I found my head slumped on Guinevere's shoulder, her fingers brushing my hair.

"I love you," she said. Then she drew away to repair the damage to my side. Her fingers were soft, her words softer. She cleaned me up, washed my hands, my face and bound the slice over my hip the arrow made.

I dressed once more, the pain of abused muscles and the numerous lacerations taking their toll. Guinevere took my hand. "Food now big man."

She led me to the kitchen and I found Merlin sat at a table still trying to eat. He looked a little better. I sat and Guinevere served me herself. "Eat, I need to find Arthur." She kissed my head and vanished.

I stared at the food, barley, oats, meat and vegetables, sat in the thick juice. The weariness of the night devoured me and my hand shook as I tried to raise my wooden spoon. I felt Merlin's green eyes on me.

"Are you well enough for this, Wolf?" he asked.

My expression twisted in grim acknowledgement of my weakness. "I will be. It's been a difficult few days."

Merlin snorted. "You've slept, what, half a night in the last two days?"

"I've managed half that, but I'll be fine. I won't let you down, old man," I said.

Merlin broke some bread and handed it to me. "It will line your stomach."

I grunted and we ate in silence for a while. The bread worked, I began to feel human.

My companion suddenly said, "Geraint is the right man you know."

I looked up, eyes hardening. "Tell me what the plan is and who we think we are killing."

Merlin sighed. "There is no plan, we go, we find the person responsible, we stop them."

"No clever insights?" I asked.

"Not unless you talk to me about my daughter and how you feel."

I stared hard at the tabletop. "Fine," and I told him of the vision I'd had in Guinevere's embrace. "So, I know it's over," I finished.

Merlin nodded. "Powerful symbols, my friend, and sad. But I feel a new beginning for your family, Wolf. The falcon is a good sign. She will see things you cannot." He pushed his food away. "I can't eat another thing. This strike of ours is a dangerous game. From what I've been able to discern the creature who is helping Stephen is not human."

"I guessed that much," I said.

He looked at me sharply. "Hmm, well, I think we are going to be facing some of or just one of the fey king's court. I've never heard of any of them being powerful enough to raise an army of the dead but we might be looking at a coalition."

"So, more than one to kill?" I asked looking for useable intelligence.

"You will have your share of death, Wolf."

"I'm not all about killing you know," I protested. "Is that why your dear daughter chose Geraint because you think I am unsuitable?"

"She chose Geraint because he doesn't drown her and Else has decided she does not want this world." He raised his arms to indicate the Abbey. "She is far from human, just as you are, but Geraint is not. She needs his weight in this world to help her survive."

"I'm as human as the next man," I snapped, the anger souring the food in my guts.

Merlin raised his eyebrow. "That depends on who the next man is."

I wanted to retort but Arthur walked into the kitchen and sat beside me. "Guinevere said you are exhausted but she thinks you are able enough with some refuelling. I need an honest answer, Lancelot, can you manage this?"

"Do you want someone else doing it?" I asked grumpy with everyone.

Arthur raised an eyebrow at my tone but said, "No, you are the best man for the job. I just need to know you can do it."

"I can do it."

"Good, then the others are ready," Arthur said, declaring my breakfast over by rising and pulling on my shoulder.

I followed, concentrating on the near future and what I already knew of Stephen's camp. The set up would be similar to many war camps I'd been in, so it would have the commander's tent in the centre. We would have patrols to avoid and men to kill. I needed to take more than one knife.

In the large central hall, I found myself being dressed in a new gambeson. Arthur said, "I've had the women strip it, then place the mail inside. You need to be protected but you need to be able to move silently." His fingers flickered over me and his words tripped over themselves. The gambeson felt heavy and uncomfortable. I tried moving around, the padding and chain tangled with each other making it impossible to move.

"A good idea, Arthur but I'll be better off with my leather armour," I said.

He glanced around him, no one watched us, they were all wrapped up in their own siege dramas. His right hand flexed on my left bicep, his blue eyes filled with deep emotion. "You have to come home, you know that right? Regardless of what's happening with us and how you feel, you come home."

I smiled, my hand at the back of his neck, holding him tight. We bumped foreheads together. "You are my reason for living, Arthur. I'm going out there to stop Stephen taking Guinevere and killing you. I'm not going out there because I've had my heart broken and I plan on dying."

"I know."

I laughed, "No you don't."

We walked out as close as we could be without holding hands. Tancred, Merlin, Gawain and Yvain were all in the courtyard. Merlin handed me a white cloak. I shrugged it on. It would cover my dark clothing and my hair in the fog.

A small group of us walked up through the Abbey grounds to the low wall at the back, hard against the hill. I glanced up, half expecting to see the entrance to the hidden cavern beneath the Tor. The fog hid even the closest of trees. Guinevere and Arthur walked with us in silence. When we reached the wall we all stopped.

Arthur spoke, "You know your duties and you know the lives of those of us left in the Abbey depend on your actions this day. I am humbled by your sacrifice in order to protect us." He hugged Guinevere.

"We could do without the speeches, Arthur," Merlin grouched. He'd forgone his black robe for practical clothing much like my own. "It's cold and I want to go to sleep before dark."

The others giggled. Arthur sighed, "And I had such a wonderful speech too, very rousing."

Merlin grabbed Gawain and Yvain by their necks and pulled them through the gate, Tancred followed. That left me with Arthur and Guinevere in the fog.

She kissed my cheek and vanished without a word. Arthur sighed, "She relies on you being with me. It helps keep her stable."

"Arthur," I said with deliberation, "I have a request of you as my King."

"Name it," he said.

"If something happens to me and we fail." I gazed after Guinevere for a long time. "If we fail and Stephen wins Avalon..."

"I know," Arthur said, matching my grim words. "You have my word as your Lord and King, Lancelot. Guinevere will not be a victim to Stephen. My life on it."

I nodded. It worried me that Arthur knew my request without me having to voice it aloud. "And Else, Arthur."

"I think Geraint –" Arthur began.

"I don't give a fuck about Geraint. Do not allow Stephen possession of his sister. Your word on it, Arthur."

He nodded. "My word, Wolf."

We embraced. I kissed his mouth and left my King in the fog.

CHAPTER TWENTY

I CAUGHT UP WITH the others and we made our careful way around the Abbey grounds and back into the town. Despite the fog hiding us, we moved quietly, we didn't talk and we kept to the darkest parts of the narrow streets. We moved in single file, the snow helped cover what little noise we made but we left terrible tracks. We wove to the edge of the town so we could circle around the camp and come up from behind. We left Gawain and Yvain to hunker down covering the last houses on the main street. They would wait in the cold and snow, bows warming next to their skins for the fast draw if necessary. We all knew if we succeeded we'd be coming out of Stephen's camp like weasels from a rat hole. If we were coming out at all.

I grasped their arms as we parted. They both nodded and left, vanishing into the fog. The three of us continued around the camp. We approached at an oblique angle. All the orchards surrounding the town now lay shattered, branches stripped from the apple trees and left so their trunks could be used against us as ladders and rams. It would be a hard few years for the locals.

We had little cover so we moved through the thick layers of fog as they drifted around the battle camp. I stopped us at one point, while the fog cleared for a moment. The golem did not guard the camp. Instead, men stood, every thirty feet, too far for them to see each other in the thick soupy air. Stephen had not adapted to the new weather conditions. I grinned. I would have men every five feet or so, I would not keep a standard formation, as Stephen had done. He'd made a mistake.

I glanced at Tancred and he nodded, understanding without me needing to explain. He pointed while hardly moving. The ground at the back of the camp dipped, a man stood there, but he would not be seen by his comrades. I felt the glee of an easy victory and moved us on toward the guard as the fog closed over the land.

I pushed Merlin close to the ground. Tancred asked a question with his eyes and I lowered him to the snow. I'd go alone. They would be less likely to spot one man. The fog swirled in thick and I raced to keep pace. I no longer saw my opponent but I allowed instinct to carry me forward. I felt the ground slope and I knew I'd reached the dip. A dark shape loomed out of the smothering fog and I reacted before he saw me.

The knife I held in my right hand found his throat. I stabbed down, between the base of the neck and his shoulder. I sliced into the unprotected flesh. The blade, long and narrow found its target. My hand covered his mouth. The body struggled for a moment. I held tight and a sigh carved the fog. The body dropped, freeing my blade. The dead man hardly bled, the wound closing. I'd found it a good way to kill in the past, it left little mess.

My blood pounded through my head as his blood sang to me through the death rattle. It is one thing to kill a man in battle, it is quite another to murder, even if they are your enemy. The rush made me tremble like never before. I breathed deeply trying to force away the desire to race through the camp like a mad bear tearing everyone to shreds. Or perhaps the Wolf wanted its freedom.

I dragged the body deeper into the hollow and stood to take his place. Tancred and Merlin dashed toward me, white blobs racing against the drift of the fog.

When they arrived, they both looked at the dark corpse. Merlin said, "You kill well, Wolf."

I grunted, "Just remember that, old man."

He chuckled. We moved into the camp. There were fires for warmth everywhere but the men stayed huddled in silent groups, leaving us to move unseen between the small tents. No one spoke loudly and many snores rattled tent poles. The night fighting would be as hard on them as it was on us.

We hunkered down behind a large tent where the snoring seemed loudest. Merlin brought our heads close to his face. He smelt of herbs, a bitter yet alluring scent; one which invited danger but gave the illusion of safety. It made my hackles rise and I had to force down a growl.

"We are near the centre of the camp and I can feel the power," he whispered.

"Where are the golem?" Tancred asked.

"A long way from the horses I should imagine," I said. "They will also make the men nervous." While we'd crept through the camp I'd heard many men mutter curses about being in Avalon. They did not like this war they fought. Always nice to know.

"So, what next?" Tancred asked. Merlin pointed, we looked, the mist parted and a large pavilion crouched like a toad twenty yards from our position.

"I can feel the source of our plague is in there and the source of Arthur's pain," Merlin's eyes glazed.

"De Clare," Tancred said.

We moved off to approach the grand tent, caution being our watchword. There were guards at the front. Tancred and I shared a single glance before he vanished behind the pavilion. I slid up one side, ensuring I didn't crawl into the light from the torches. Counting slowly I tried to leak to the front of the tent, rising from the snow. A slight movement, I only noticed because I looked for it, and I realised Tancred was in place. I stepped behind the guard. Tancred matched my movement. The blades slid across the throats of the men as though I pulled both knives myself. The men gasped but did not fight. They sank in silence and their blood stained the snow. We grasped the bodies and pulled them back into the shadows. Tancred stripped one of the guards and threw the tabard over his head. He then stepped out as though he owned the place, kicking at bloody snow on the way.

"He's a fine man," Merlin said.

I nodded. "What next?"

Merlin held his ear. I listened and realised I'd been so focused on the guard I'd missed the conversation in the pavilion. I heard Stephen and some woman, they were having a bitter argument.

"I want the golem back out there before dark," Stephen yelled.

"I can't do it. I'm not even certain it will work at dark. I didn't anticipate Merlin's interference. I thought I'd be able to sweep through the Abbey's defences and just destroy Arthur and Lancelot. I cannot fight the wizard, fuel the golem and keep the spells in place for confusing the humans." I could hear the exhaustion in her voice.

"Then what fucking use are you?" Stephen snapped. "I thought you were the most powerful the king has."

A long pause. "I am," she ground out. "You expect too much, sir." I wouldn't want that voice angry with me.

"I want to speak with your king," Stephen said.

Merlin touched my sleeve bringing me back. "We need to stop her doing that. It will give her more power."

"Do you know who she is?" I asked.

"Morgana," Merlin said. "I don't think you should go in there."

I frowned. "What are you talking about?"

Merlin looked at me, pulling a strange face. "The trouble is I'm going to need you." He sighed heavily. "This isn't going to go well."

"Why don't we just get on with it, Merlin, and stop buggering about." I don't appreciate forbidding doom being prophesied. He sighed once more and decided to move. He rolled his sleeves up and cracked his knuckles.

We walked straight past Tancred who would be responsible for keeping enemy soldiers out as long as possible.

Merlin swept back the tent flap and stepped into the boar's den. There were guards. I drew my sword as Stephen yelled an order. One died without knowing what happened, the other drew his sword and might have been good, but he tripped over a low table. My blade found his heart. The scrap ended. I turned to Stephen, my side ached but my breath remained even.

"Du Lac," his hissed, drawing his own blade.

I smiled. "De Clare." I tilted my head in welcome. "I think it's time we ended this, don't you?"

"Wait," the woman's voice cut through our tension. Stephen's hand flexed on his sword hilt. She walked into our line of sight. "Put your blades up gentlemen while we talk for a moment."

"Morgana, we have no wish to talk," Merlin said. His power washed over me, I attacked Stephen without conscious thought. We were well matched and I found it hard to break his defences.

"Killing each other isn't going to be constructive, Merlin, dear," Morgana said. My sword became too heavy to lift and my legs buckled. I crashed to my knees. Stephen grinned and raised his sword. I couldn't move.

"Too easy, Morgana," Merlin said and Stephen collapsed just before his sword fell over my head.

I found myself able to move around on my knees. I shifted, movements heavy and looked at the fey witch.

Morgana – her beauty almost felled me.

Luscious thick black curls cascaded over her shoulders, dark blue eyes that radiated power, with long black lashes. She towered over me as she walked toward me. A tall, statuesque woman, her dress glided over the rugs on the floor, the velvet a deep blue bordered with gold. Her hand reached out. I didn't want her to touch me. Her red lips, a smile like a cat's, perfect, full, pouting, rising to cheekbones so fine they mesmerised me. I tried to pull my head away, I really did.

"My cousin, you are as beautiful as I always wished you to be," she murmured. She bent and laid a kiss, none to chaste, on my frozen lips.

"Enough, Morgana, leave him alone," Merlin snapped, striding to my side and pulling her back. I thought I saw sparks come from the contact but neither mage flinched.

She released me physically but I still could not move. "Ah, Merlin, he doesn't know does he? Despite Nimue's declarations last autumn. You have never told him." Her laugh shivered over me like a wolf's soft fur.

I didn't like this, I did not like being this vulnerable and confused. This did not make me a happy soldier. I focused on Morgana and I pushed. Inside my head, I pushed. I pushed against the weight in my mind. When in doubt, fight and I fought Morgana with blind instinct. I forced the fey witch away.

Her eyes widened and her smile expanded. I rose to my feet, the weight on my shoulders impossibly brutal. "I know all I need to, my Lady," I growled. My hands flexed and I found my sword remained in my grasp. Stephen did not rise against Merlin's suffocating magic.

"So the wizard has given you an idea of your heritage, cousin. The bastard born half bred whelp," she sneered. "Your dear father has marked you for death. He doesn't want you as Nimue does." Well we now knew the fey queen lived at least. Morgana continued, "Aeddan wants you dead, wants Arthur subjugated or dead and we want Guinevere finally siring the children we've stopped her having."

Merlin's breath hissed and Stephen twitched, the wizard losing control. "So, her barrenness is caused by you. I bloody knew it," he cursed. "I just couldn't find the trigger."

Morgana laughed. "That's because you are not all you wish to be, just another half bred mongrel."

The grief Guinevere suffered because she believed she was barren raced through my blood. "Enough," I said. "By my King's command, I order you off his land and away from this place. If you don't leave you will die."

Morgana laughed with genuine amusement. "You intend to take on the whole army?"

"If I must," I stated, the power growing inside my guts, readying me for action.

"If only you would betray Arthur for us, we could give you so much,"

Morgana said. "Guinevere is a lucky woman and so is that little pixie bitch, Eleanor, but she and the Queen will once more belong to our Boar before we have finished." Morgana almost sounded sad at the prospect. "He is such an oaf but he is useful." She glanced at Stephen and I saw him flex against Merlin's control.

I glanced at Stephen. "He will never be king," I growled.

Morgana sighed. "I fear he will. It's a little unfortunate. He's ungovernable when it comes to women and we needed the Queen. I suspect we will never be able to tear her willingly from Arthur now."

Merlin stepped between me and the witch. "Leave, Morgana. You have lost this one. If I am here I can stop you, don't make me prove it." We wanted to avoid a confrontation as the assassination had failed and I wanted to take the news home that Arthur could be a father given a chance.

She laughed again. "Try, old man."

Stephen rose. Merlin's focus changed and I felt my body flood with power when Morgana shifted her own magic. De Clare roared and we came together in a rush of steel and determination. I flexed and dropped back, rolling away to give myself space. The leather armour meant I moved with far greater speed. My feet propelled Stephen over my body. I heard men shouting outside. Tancred would soon be overwhelmed by his enemies. I needed to finish this. Stephen rolled, using the power I'd supplied to force him over me to roll and return to his feet in one smooth movement. I caught sight of Merlin, down on one knee. A shimmering in the air between him and the witch the only evidence of their battle. Stephen rushed toward me, we parried, both too canny to waste time exchanging jibes.

I didn't have the room I needed in the confines of the tent. With the long knife I carried I slashed at the pavilion walls and stepped into the fog and snow. Stephen must have thought he had me on the run but the space gave greater scope to my fighting style. Men began to rush toward us. Tancred yelled a warning.

"Are you afraid to face me as an equal, Stephen?" I asked. The first words we'd spoken. I planned on him ordering his men back.

"You are not my equal, you are nothing," de Clare said, his hate dripping like acid from each word.

"I am the son of a king," I said and laughed at how ludicrous that sounded. An arm snaked around my neck.

"I have him, my Lord," someone shouted in my ear. I smashed my right fist into his face. He grunted. I back fisted him with my left hand in the groin, grabbed his arm and twisted. He rolled over my left hip and as he landed, I thrust my knife into his chest. I rose and moved in a circle to keep everyone at bay.

Tancred struggled in the arms of three men. Blood fell from his nose and a cut in his head. A rag filled his mouth. Thirty men surrounded me. Stephen held up his weapon.

He laughed. "It seems your mission has failed, scum. Assassination is a desperate move on Arthur's part. Especially as he is sending his bed warmer to do his job. After all the Queen is a lousy fuck."

Men laughed. The blood inside me filled my ears, the fog became the red mist of my nightmares and something inside me snapped, never to be fixed. The Wolf raced through my body. The weapons in my hands became an extension of tooth and claw. I attacked.

I was hopelessly outnumbered but refused to admit I should lie down and die. Men screamed and I moved. I became a living breathing instrument of death. Tancred found himself freed in moments and took the fight to the enemy but he dare not come close. I sensed his fear. I tasted all their fears and guilt over this fight. I knew their minds and their sins. I realised Stephen began to throw men at me, forcing them to fight, forcing them to their death so he would remain protected from the Wolf.

I ploughed through these poor wretches and reached de Clare once more. His fear tasted sweeter than any other I'd ever known. We were no longer evenly matched. I overwhelmed him in moments. The ground below us became slick with dead men's blood and the moans of the injured. De Clare knew he faced his death.

I delivered a sword smashing blow toward his head and his blade snapped in two. The movement carried my weapon around and down, ready to deliver a strike to his guts when I stumbled. I stumbled and my arms disobeyed me. My hands lost all feeling. My legs folded under me.

CHAPTER TWENTY-ONE

"NO!" SCREAMED TANCRED.

My knees hit the bloodied snow. I realised something in my back hurt. I reached around and found the hilt of a knife sticking out of my back. "Fuck," I managed.

Stephen rose before me, our roles in this evil drama reversed. He wheezed as he laughed. I still held my knife and my left hand managed a brief conversation with my brain. De Clare drew back his sword. The broken blade glinted with the fog's beaded moisture. The sword descended. I smiled and drove upward for the last time.

"You will not be the one to kill me, de Clare," I said, driving my knife toward his throat. I missed. My knife caught his cheek, entered, his teeth broke, the blade hit the other side of his mouth. Blood rushed to cover my hand and hit my face. He screamed and jerked backward. The knife twisted in my grasp, pulling through his face, to stick out of his mouth, like a tongue made of steal and oak. I lost possession of my blade. I also lost my balance and I hit the floor. A woman's scream filled my head. Merlin's deep voice cursed my name. Hands, I felt hands on my body. I moved.

I heard a conversation drift in and out while I floated on a soft bed. "I don't know what happened, Merlin. He became a thing possessed, then that woman," Tancred sounded like he wept. "That woman ran from the tent and a knife... A knife rose from the ground, just as he... And then it was in his back. He dropped."

"Alright, son," Merlin's voice sounded soft. "It's alright. He's alive. Though for how long I don't know." His voice dropped, "So much death, Wolf. You have caused so much death. I hope you are not claimed as well, my friend."

A hand stroked my cold face. A sharp pain in my back made me moan. Oh,

I could talk. "Arthur," I whispered. I tasted blood but it might not have been mine.

"We'll make certain you see your King, Lancelot," Merlin said. I focused and they'd turned me onto my side. He smiled, not a comforting gesture. "Tancred's gone to steal a horse. The camp is in uproar, we should escape well enough."

The ground vibrated under me. "Here he is. Now, Wolf, I'm going to put you to sleep so you don't feel this and I'm hoping it will slow down your bleeding."

"No." I tried to clutch at him.

"Yes, Wolf. Arthur won't forgive me if I don't take you home." Merlin touched my forehead and I began fighting but lost. Darkness swallowed me. I remembered snatches of the journey home. The pain of hanging over the back of a horse. Tancred and Merlin trying to run through the snow, pulling the beast with them. The frantic conversation with Gawain and Yvain. The shouts as arrows were exchanged, to keep the enemy at bay while we made our slow way back to the Abbey.

The gates opened. I heard them. I heard the shouts. I heard Guinevere cry my name. My hands and legs were cold. "Lancelot," Arthur's voice broke the last of Merlin's weak spell.

"Arthur." I moved on the horse. Hands took hold and pulled me back. I heard instructions about not allowing me to lie on the knife hilt, to make certain I didn't move it, or twist it in my back. It felt good to be looking at the dull grey sky. More orders came to man the walls and gates.

My King's face came into view. Tears stood in his eyes. "Lancelot, you came home."

"I promised I would," I think I said but my ears made the sound in my head twist. "I've hurt Stephen but I failed you, he is not dead. He needs crushing, Arthur."

"Shush, you have done all you can, Merlin and Tancred say the golem are gone back to dust and you killed almost half their mortal army on your own." Arthur smiled but it wavered and the tears spilled over his cheeks. "You are hurt, my Wolf, but we will do everything we can, you just have to hang on. You have to survive. You cannot leave me. Without you there is no Camelot for me, do you understand? Do you understand, Wolf?" he spoke with a desperation I found painful to hear.

"Arthur," I said before darkness stole me from him.

I woke laying face down on a soft mattress, the air cold. Voices surrounded me.

"Get out, Arthur, you are not helping us," Merlin snapped. "I cannot concentrate with you jabbering."

"Come, Arthur. We are no use here, come," Guinevere's voice coaxed him.

"Else," Merlin said. "I need you to be ready to cover the wound the moment I take the knife from his back. He can ill afford to lose anymore blood but there will be more."

"I am ready," Else said. Her voice made my heart ache. I twitched and groaned. I wanted to tell her I was sorry. I just missed her. I realised so many things as life swirled around me.

She knelt. "Quiet, Lancelot, you need to stay still." Her dark eyes were hollow, she looked so tired. Her small hand stroked my hair. She smiled. "We are going to pull the knife out but it is very close to your spine, Merlin's worried. You need to be still. The Mother Superior is here and we are going to spend time making certain you are healed." She kissed my temple. "Just rest now."

She did not use endearments. She loved another. I didn't want her to move. I didn't want her to release my hand and leave me. I felt the knife in my back twitch as someone touched it.

A voice I didn't recognise said, "We should give him something to force him to sleep and to take the pain. He might go into shock."

"He's lost too much blood and I have no more magic left," Merlin said. "He'll stay still."

I moved my arm, my right and grabbed the leg of the bed or table or whatever I lay on. I heard soft words, the knife wriggled inside me and then a wash of pain made me gasp. My body locked rigid and I wanted to scream but no breath came.

Something replaced the knife and pressure, heavy pressure on the centre of my back below my ribs pinned me to the mattress. I gave up fighting. I didn't want to know. The frantic voices. The yelling of instructions as blood flooded from the tap in my back. Sleep. Escape the chaos, I told myself firmly.

The dreams came, as I knew they would. The Wolf lay broken and dying, whining in pain. The stag pushed with his nose at the wet fur, trying to force the Wolf to rise. The falcon screamed overhead. The grief, the terrible grief of the stag made the Wolf fight but I couldn't stand. I fell deeper into the wolf's mind. I found myself remembering the woods, the hunts, the smell of the forest, of the wind, of the blood. I wanted to run from the pain and I felt so alone. I realised it was not just me that needed a wife, the Wolf needed a mate and a doe cannot be the mate of a wolf. But neither can a bird. In my fevered dreams, I knew the stag and the Wolf to be equals but we were not the same.

The dreams flew through me, the images, the meanings a blur of dark conjuring. Until the picture of a woman, a woman with red hair, tangled in the wind. Her eyes greener than beech leaves in the spring, walked to the wolf. I lay in the grass, the stag nearby but unable to help any longer. She walked straight to me, sat in the long grass, lifted the great head and placed me in her lap. Her lips moved and I realised she sang in a language I didn't know, but it made me warm and safe. I wanted to stay there, with her. Long fingers buried into my coat and I smelt summer hay on her skin and clothes. When she bent over me to kiss the fur near my ears, her hair left the fragrance of roses.

"Do not die, Lancelot, we have yet to meet and I want to know the greatest Knight of Camelot," she whispered. She breathed sweet breath into my face and with it came power, strength, light, and a reason to fight.

Leaving the body of my Wolf and returning to the dark cold Abbey didn't feel remotely fair. Air rushed in and out. I groaned as I tried to rise off my belly and fire shot through me.

"Don't move," a woman ordered. "Tancred, fetch the King. He has woken."

I didn't recognise her voice. I heard a door close and running feet. I began to panic. My legs didn't want to obey my mind.

"Hush, hush, Lancelot. You are safe. You need to move but only a little and you cannot move far. Please be patient and I will help you roll over." Strong fingers took hold of my shoulder and lifted me, while also supporting my hips. I lay naked under a pile of blankets and rugs. The pain made me whimper, my eyes tight shut, but I only moved onto my left side, while my back lay against something soft. It hurt so much and so deep inside.

"Fuck," I conceded to the pain.

"Easy, now, I hear the King." The hands vanished before I could bring myself to open my eyes.

"You're alive," Arthur's voice made me respond. His love for me poured over me as he sank to his knees beside my bed. He kissed my hand and stroked my face, words tumbled from him but I didn't understand any of them.

"Your Majesty, I think you need to slow down. He has travelled a long way from us here and his soul is still trying to catch up. He doesn't understand," the soft voice focused me further. The words so warm. I sighed in contentment.

"Arthur..." I managed. I smiled. I think.

"You have been sick for so long," he said, his voice breaking. "We thought you were going to die. It has been over a week." He looked tired, fragile and thin.

"I'm fine," I sighed and my eyes fluttered closed.

When they opened again, I found myself staring at Guinevere while she sewed something on her lap. Light hit her hair and it shone gold.

"At least Arthur will sleep and eat now he knows his Wolf will live," she chattered to someone.

"The King is in need of rest. His love for his friend serves him well. They are a fine team," I recognised the voice but not the face. I blinked in an effort to focus and shifted position, my arm numb under me.

"Hello, hero," Guinevere said and her smile lit the room like cherry blossom.

I frowned and swallowed. "Drink," I managed.

A woman came to my side, holding a wooden cup, her eyes were old but kind and her hair lay in a thick silver coil over her shoulder. She smiled at me making the world warm. Her handsome face kept her years from encroaching, but her hands were old and rough. Her figure remained slim and she moved with more grace than most. As I studied her face, her smile widened, it curled at the ends like a cat.

"Here, young man, drink this it will help make you strong." She offered the cup and I held it in trembling fingers. It tasted of herbs and honey. It tasted of life.

"Thank you," I managed as she retrieved the cup.

Guinevere appeared and began feeding me soup. "You've been in a terrible fever for days, Lancelot. Merlin and the Mother Superior called Rose in to help. Merlin's been very weak since you returned."

I focused on Guinevere, her chatter filled my head and her soup filled my aching belly. She smiled a great deal and told me all the news in a great rush of information.

Stephen's camp broke up and moved off after making one more failed and weak attempt on our walls. With the golem gone and half the mortal army dead, thanks to me apparently, they decided to run. My Wolf Pack chased them but not too hard. De Clare lay wounded. We did catch a deserter who informed

Arthur, quite promptly, that I might not have killed Stephen but I'd wounded him badly. He lay in as bad a state as a man could without dying.

I'd been sick for over a week. Sinking into terrible nightmares. Arthur remained at my side until his own exhaustion made him ill, when he'd consented to others watching my every breath. Rose, the woman summoned from the town, brought with her a vast store of herbs and healing ways, which dragged me from my sickness. I didn't think she came from the town for one moment, but I didn't want to argue or interrupt Guinevere. Something about the woman, Rose, made my mind itch.

The Queen ran out of steam by the time I finished my bowl of soup. "I'll go and wake Arthur," she said, kissing my brow and vanishing.

Rose chuckled. "I don't know which of them worried more. You are well loved, Knight of Camelot."

"I owe you my life," I said, wanting to steer clear of emotional references to Guinevere or Arthur.

Rose moved around and I tracked her with my eyes. "The whole town owes you a great debt, my Lord. You saved us all. The little I do by my healing is all we have to pay our debt to you."

"Call me, Lancelot. I'm not a great one for ceremony," I muttered. I tried to move but waves of agony shot through my back and belly. The soup began to rebel.

"Oh, no, bad man, you cannot move yet." Rose rushed to my side and strong fingers took the pressure off screaming muscles.

Arthur appeared and I found his arms around me, lifting me gently so Rose could prop me up. He lay me back down but grasped my hands in his own. "How do you feel?"

I smiled for him. "I feel better than you look." His blue eyes were pained and weary, his face drawn.

"It's been a rough few days. Someone I care about has been messing me around making life hard," he said.

I nodded. "Have you spoken with them about it, encouraged them to be more reasonable?" I asked straight faced.

"I'm hoping it won't be necessary. If they make the effort, I should be fine," he said, his fingers tightened on my own.

"I'm sure they will make the best effort they can," I said as a promise to my King.

We sat and talked until it became clear I needed help for personal duties.

Evidently, Rose had taught Arthur how to handle me in sickness. Between them they helped me stand, and to my credit, I only cried out once. I relieved myself, then they set about washing me and changing my small bed. Every service Arthur performed for me spoke of his love. Once the simple tasks were finished, my exhaustion overwhelmed my ability to listen.

He kissed my hands. "I'll be here first thing, Lancelot. There will be someone here to help you at all times, so don't panic about being left alone."

I nodded and began to drift, not really caring. His lips brushed my brow and I slept. The Wolf whined in his sleep and opened an eye, a small white nose poked his ear and warm sweet breath filled his lungs. He raised his great shaggy head and looked into the soft brown eyes of the white doe.

Firelight lit the room and Else sat in a large wooden chair, her eyes were closed and fabric draped over her lap. I lay on my side once more, so I could watch her with ease. I sighed, she stirred and her eyes fluttered open, turning to me.

She smiled. "You're awake." She placed the tunic down and rose, coming to my side.

"What are you making?" I asked.

Her cheeks coloured and she looked away, my lips twitched. "Something for your husband," I stated.

She reached for the wooden cup once more. "You need to drink this. I was left with strict instructions."

"Does Geraint know you are caring for me?" I asked, perversely determined to hurt myself even more.

She placed the cup down and sat still on the stool by my bed. "Yes, Lancelot, he knows. Arthur asked me to help care for you and I agreed without hesitation."

"That was good of you," the petulance made me sound childish.

"Lancelot, you need to come to peace with this, for all our sakes."

"I really don't, Else." But I did want peace. I just wanted to find it in my own way and I wanted her to stop pushing.

"Our whole relationship was built on lies. I lied to you from the start," she said sadly. "I want peace and Geraint offers me something you cannot."

"Which is?"

"No Arthur or Guinevere."

"So you are settling for safe? Does he know that?" I asked my own tears making it hard to see.

"I think so," she said. I heard her misery. "But he doesn't care. He loves just me."

"Will the potion in the cup help me sleep?" I asked.

She nodded and handed it to me, her small hands held me while I drank. It knocked me out in no time. The mercy of sickness.

CHAPTER TWENTY-TWO

I WOKE TO THE softest of light, dawn light, whispering over me to dance my eyelids open.

"I am glad you are awake," an unfamiliar male voice startled me. I raised my head, my muscles protested. A man sat in the chair by the fire, his form elegant, long black hair trailed down his back as he leaned toward the fire to place a new log on the hearth. His eyes were as dark as my own but his skin almost glowed in the pale light.

"Who are you?" Fear spiked through me. I wanted to scream for Arthur. I tried to rise, to fight, nothing happened.

He chuckled, his teeth were slightly pointed. "You are strong, Wolf, and my family would make you stronger, but you are not strong enough to face me."

He held no knife, carried no sword, made no obvious threat but I had never been so scared. "Who are you?" I repeated, relying on my stubbornness.

He rose, his fluid grace unnerving as he sat next to me. He smelt of summer. I cringed away. His hand reached out and touched my brow, brushing away stray hair from my face. His finger traced a line over my stubbled jaw. His own would always be as smooth as a woman's.

"My son," he said in soft wonder. The sun caught his perfect face, highlighting his flawless bone structure. I froze. The dreams rushed back with terrifying clarity. I suddenly wished Arthur a thousand leagues from me if it would keep him from this man.

Aeddan smiled, now sad. "Watching you, my son, I often think you are my finest creation, but you will defy me. I don't want to hurt you but you stand with Arthur."

My mind screamed in anguish. Arthur lay asleep and vulnerable. My father's smile grew feral. "I know, son. It's exciting isn't it? Will I rise up and cut his throat myself?" His dark eyes sparkled in merriment. I sweated.

"Why are you here?" I asked, while I prayed Arthur still breathed.

"I came to give you fair warning, my boy." His skin felt cool as he held my hand. His fingers were smoother, longer, slimmer than my own. "I will have your King at my feet and you will help me before we are done."

I heard voices, shouts outside the door. Merlin yelled and someone beat the library door with a sword hilt. Arthur bellowed his right to entry. I did not want him near me. The Fey King rose, a gentle smile on his lips once more. "We will talk again, son."

The door burst open. Merlin raised his hands and yelled something. Arthur and Geraint moved past him into the room, swords drawn. The Fey King pressed a kiss to my brow, his lips burned. Arthur yelled a challenge I couldn't hear. My father straightened, turned his back and walked into the sunlight. I blinked and the room darkened for a moment. The Fey King vanished.

"Lancelot," Arthur cried out, dropping his sword and rushing to my side. He lifted me into his arms and hugged me close. I shivered and trembled, grateful and fearful all at once.

"What the hell just happened?" Geraint asked.

Arthur lay me back on the bed. I glanced at Merlin. The older man, still looking weak and tired, sat by the fire. He sighed. "This is bad."

"He called you son," Geraint said, pointing his sword at me. Arthur pushed the blade away irritated.

"You haven't told them?" I asked Merlin.

"I didn't think it wise and convinced Tancred not to speak." Merlin spoke to his hands.

"You scared him into not speaking," I said. Merlin shrugged.

I gripped Arthur's hands, "You know I am Aeddan's son but he wants me dead because he believes I will never betray you and if I am dead he can force you to submit to his power."

Arthur went white, his lips paled and his eyes dilated.

Geraint exploded, "You are what?"

I ignored him and continued to concentrate on Arthur. "He told me I am to betray you, Sire, or die saving you," I said quietly. The worms in my belly writhed.

"You will never betray me," Arthur said.

Geraint continued, "That's the missing piece of the damned puzzle, that bloody maze in the hill." He gestured madly toward the Tor. "That's what those final marks meant. He has more of a right to your throne than Stephen.

He is the one you should be scared of Arthur. He has the most powerful fey blood imaginable."

"Get out," Arthur said quietly to Geraint.

"What?" he asked. "Arthur, please, don't let your emotional attachments –" He never finished.

Arthur rose, no longer my friend, but my King. "Get out, Fitzwilliam. If you had not stolen Else from under his nose, I would not be responsible for Lancelot's happiness. Don't challenge me on his position in my family."

Geraint opened his mouth, glanced at me, bowed stiffly and left the room. Merlin rose as well. "No, wizard, you sit. I will have my answers," Arthur ordered.

He made me recount everything I remembered of the fight with Stephen and the conversation with Morgana. No one had told him about her words to me, or her relationship as my cousin. No one told him the fey were the reason Guinevere remained barren. He did not know how I'd lost myself in the battle madness, killing so many of Stephen's men the rest fled. Arthur grew angry but he turned it inward until it manifested as weary sadness.

"Why did you lie to me, Merlin? If I cannot trust you, then who can I trust?" he asked, still sat on my bed.

"You were grief ridden. Lancelot was dying until Rose arrived. I could not tell you, Arthur, it would have broken you." Merlin sighed even more than usual. "I have choices to make. I've always know what, who, Lancelot is, that is why I've allowed your bond to grow tight. The only times I've asked you to be careful is when he can be used against your crown, even if I've known he needs to be close to you as a man."

The door opened once more and Rose, my nurse, appeared. She stopped, sniffed the air and said, "I see you've met your father."

"What?" Arthur asked, as I said, "Who?" and Merlin muttered, "Fuck."

She smiled, her faded green eyes became brighter by the moment. "You've grown careless, Merlin. Aren't you supposed to be protecting your King from our kind?" Her skin fleshed out and tightened over her strong bone structure. Her hair gained colour. It shone like fox's fur at the height of the summer. Her figure slimmed in some places and thickened in others.

"You are the woman from my dream," I said.

Arthur rose and drew his sword once more, the woman laughed. "Oh, do put that away, didn't your mother teach you not to play with toys indoors?"

"Merlin, what is happening?" Arthur growled.

The woman spoke, "Please, Sire, put up your sword. If I wanted you dead, I could have achieved it when you slept beside your lover. Instead I saved his life and through that Camelot." She stepped up to Arthur. "I rather think you owe me, Arthur Pendragon."

"Put the sword down, she won't hurt you if she hasn't already," Merlin said. He looked defeated and exhausted.

"What do you want?" Arthur asked.

"One thing at a time," the woman said. She'd grown strong and beautiful, her lips were full and curved into a slightly mocking smile. Her green eyes shone. She pushed to my bedside and knelt. "He didn't hurt you?" she asked.

"No, but he did touch me," I said.

"How?"

I told her how and when I mentioned the kiss, she lay her hand on the spot, closed her eyes, then frowned. "He's a bastard," she muttered before a searing pain through my head made me yelp. It lasted just a moment. When my eyes refocused I looked into her, literally, just for a heartbeat. Her soul glowed with power and beauty, just as nature did, but nature's harshest winds can be beautiful when you are locked in the safety of a stone keep. If you are faced with them in the open, they are cruel and hard. Winter can be cosy when you have food to eat and wood to burn, but if not, starvation is a vicious way to die. This woman represented the most powerful of nature's elements in mortal clothing.

"Who are you?" Arthur asked again.

She turned away from me, breaking our connection. "I am here to help you. I saved this man's life so he would be free to save yours. I do not believe in what my king or queen are doing and I want them stopped. So, I am going to help you defeat them."

"You still have not given me a name," Arthur said.

"Merla will do," she said, her smile bright.

Merlin snorted. "If that's what you chose, little blackbird."

"Don't push it, wizard," she said.

"You know this woman?" Arthur asked him.

"Aye, I do." Merlin scowled. "She is brethren to the Fey Queen Nimue."

"Why are you standing against your own kind?" Arthur asked.

Merla sat on the floor, her hair brushed my fingers, it felt like fox fur, soft and strong all at once. "The fey have grown fat on the power men have given us through their adoration. They crave that power and do not want men to move away from their attachment to the fey and our ways. I, however, having once been a goddess among your kind, know of the power of corruption and we are being corrupted. I want my kind to remember their own, so called, old ways. The gifts and the world we were given before mankind, when we were pure and light. Humanity must find its own path, we've manipulated you for too long. We were never meant to become so dependent on mortal worship."

"You want to stop your fey king from taking Camelot so we maintain our sovereignty and our right to worship whom we chose?" Arthur asked.

"Basically," Merla said. Then she grinned, her teeth were not pointed. "I also want to stick one in the eye of the old bastard and teach him some humility. Helping his bastard half bred son to defeat him will be amusing to watch. Aeddan has become a problem but we of the fey cannot stop him."

Arthur sat, the weight of the world bowing his back. "How did you save Lancelot's life?"

Merla smiled. "Worried that I've corrupted your boy?"

His eyes spoke of his fear. Merla rose and knelt before the King. She looked up into his face and said simply, "I broke a spell Morgana lay on the knife to plant inside the wound. I healed the brewing poison through traditional means. I called him back because you could not, he wanted to come home to you, Arthur, but he grew too weak."

A tear rolled down the King's cheek. "I thought I'd lost him for good."

I glanced at Merlin, the pain in the old man's face for Arthur's fear scared me. How could I be that important?

Merla said, "We need to speak of how to save your crown, Pendragon."

Arthur offered his hand to help Merla stand before him as an equal, he nodded. "We won this round but only just."

"Aeddan wants to intimidate you, that is why he showed up here. It would have cost him power but he hopes to turn Lancelot against you. He will manifest in your dreams and in the world."

"Why doesn't he just appear as a friend and kill us both? That's what he threatened," I said.

"Because Aeddan believes in nonsense, in prophecy and portents. He believes that if he kills Arthur by cheating he will make your King a martyr. He thinks more fey will want to return to the old ways and they will abandon their king. He thinks he must usher in his new dawn of fey power through your death or surrender. His mortal bred son must become either his weapon or be destroyed. But as he's half mad on the power he's already stolen he might believe anything by now." Merla's green eyes shone with her anger and bitterness.

"So what do I do?" Arthur asked.

"You face him directly," Merla said. "If you fight him through Stephen he will just find another mortal who wants your throne and throw them against you. You cannot win every war and if you fight, you cannot grow your crops and farm your land. Your people will starve."

"I had hoped that by coming here I might have prevented a war," Arthur said.

"You may well have delayed it somewhat and you have bloodied him but this is far from over, Arthur. Your enemy is a driven man, he wants your throne and believes he has a right to it," Merla said.

CHAPTER TWENTY-THREE

MERLA DECIDED I NEEDED to sit up and we all needed to eat. She bustled about, bullying Arthur into helping me stand, dress and move, it hurt. I hurt and I already felt exhausted. We heard the Abbey beginning to wake. Arthur and I sat beside the fire, Merlin now occupied my bed and Merla sat beside him. Merlin didn't appear to be happy at the prospect.

I tried to think past the pain in my back, which spiralled up my spine. "What do we do about defeating this fey king?"

"There is only one thing to do," Merla said. "You and Arthur must face him." She said it with some glee.

We glanced at each other. "No," I said.

Arthur said, "Alright."

I glared, "No, Arthur. You need to return to Camelot and you need to lead your people, this is my job."

"You have done enough, Wolf," Arthur said.

"You both need to go," Merla cut across our argument. "And we need to pick something up first."

Merlin shifted on the bed. "Don't do this," he muttered.

"There is only one weapon that can achieve such a task and only a true King of England can wield it, a sword. One that only I can give you," Merla ignored him and spoke only to Arthur.

"Please, Merla, don't do this," Merlin whispered.

"What's wrong?" I asked him.

"This sword is a fey weapon. It is old and blessed in the fires of the fey smiths. It has enchantments in the blade and it bonds to the soul of the man expected to use it," Merlin said sadly. "Arthur is destined to carry this sword."

"And you have delayed this gift long enough, which is why I am here,"

Merla snapped. "The sword will not harm Arthur, it will save him. The sheath will stop your wounds from bleeding and the sword will never break, helping you to win every battle you fight. It is the only sword which can be used against Aeddan. But a fey cannot wield it. The blade was made for a man of England. I had it made for you, Pendragon."

I looked at Merlin. "What do you mean, it bonds with his soul?"

"The more he uses it, the more it will pull him from us and into the mists of their world." He glanced at Merla.

"But what if I use it just for this?" Arthur said. I glanced at him, his blue eyes shone like a summer evening sky.

"You won't, Arthur," Merlin said. I'd never seen him look so defeated.

"Then we don't use this sword and we find another way," I said.

"If you can find another way, I wish you luck," Merla said.

"Where is this sword?" Arthur asked. I sat back in my chair. I knew that tone. We were going for the sword and I couldn't stop him using it. Merlin and I shared a long silent exchange. He wanted me to protect the King. I nodded briefly. Keeping Arthur safe from this thing would be my goal.

"The sword is kept safe from Aeddan in a place only I can reach. A lake near the place we will summon him so we can face him. We will be going to the oldest of temples that link the fey with mankind."

"The stone henge," I said dully. A place even more full of magic and tricks than Avalon. Only one other site in England held more power. We all avoided such places.

"I will gather my men," Arthur said rising. His decision already made.

"No, Pendragon, you and the Wolf go alone," Merla said.

That jolted me. "I can hardly walk."

"You'll heal," she said.

"No," Arthur stated. "Lancelot has done enough. He will not face his father. I will not allow it."

Merla watched us both for a moment. "Your destinies are welded together, Arthur. You have stated Lancelot is the heart of Camelot. You share your dreams, you share your love."

We also shared his wife but I declined to comment on that score.

"You cannot do this alone. You may be the only one to wield Excalibur, but your Wolf will be the one to lead the way. I can only summon Aeddan by using his son," Merla said. Her green eyes challenged Arthur's blue. I felt myself being drawn more tightly than ever into Arthur's orbit. If I were a fire, able to burn those who strayed too close, Arthur was the very sun in the heavens. I could not resist the warmth even if I knew it would destroy me.

A wave of exhaustion threw itself against the shore of my mind, devouring my strength. I did not want to do this, I wanted to talk about light and love. I wanted a home and I wanted the killing to stop. How many had I killed in Stephen's camp? How many mothers and wives wept because of my actions? I did not have the strength or the will for this fight. Not yet. Perhaps not ever. I felt shattered and terribly alone. I lay my head back on my chair and my eyes fell on Arthur. My heart swelled, I would suffer anything for him, I always had and I realised I always would. I had no life. I was Arthur's Wolf. Else was right not to marry me. No woman should be asked to cope with my dedication to my King.

Loneliness rushed over me once the exhaustion drew back from the shore. It rushed into my mouth, down my throat and burned inside my chest. Tears welled in my eyes and I screwed them shut. I gripped the arms of the chair.

"Get out," I managed.

"Lancelot?" Arthur broke off from his argument with Merlin.

"Please, leave, all of you," I said trying to hold back the agony of my burning gasping lungs as they attempted to breathe in the suffocating loneliness.

Merlin rose. "Out." He pulled Merla to her feet and reached for Arthur. The King tried to argue. He wanted to stay at my side but Merlin snapped, "Arthur, for the sake of all that is holy, leave Lancelot alone."

They closed the door just as my lungs exploded and a huge racking sob escaped me. The wave rushed over me and swept back, washing the grief and death of my life into me, through me, drowning me. The anguish so much worse than the pain in my back.

I slid off the chair and knelt on the floor, my face buried in my hands, my body rocking. I felt lost, adrift, alone. So alone. I could see in my head the terrible darkness surrounding me, engulfing me.

Arms, strong arms were suddenly there and a soft female voice began a soothing litany. The Wolf howled inside me, desperate for someone to join him. The words became an anchor and the Wolf turned as he heard the gentle bark of a friend. A smaller, russet Wolf walked from the darkness with her head down and eyes rolled up. As she drew nearer she dropped closer to the ground, seeking acceptance before reaching me. Telling me she'd never threaten me, that I could trust her. I walked toward her, lowered my muzzle to her dark nose and licked her mouth. She rose, rubbed her face against mine and my Wolf was not alone.

My mind grasped who held me as I wept for the grief. Merla rocked me, her long legs either side as she tried to hold as much of me as possible close to her chest. She murmured and stroked.

"It's alright, Lancelot. You are safe, you are not alone, you will never be alone. I promise. You are loved for who you are, for what you are," she said.

I began to calm and allowed her to help me relax in her arms. I forced my hands to let her go and I pulled away.

"Fine Commander I turned out to be," I managed after a long period of quite.

"You are a fine Commander but you are a finer man," Merla said.

I glanced at her face for the first time. Her own tears stained her cheeks. Her green eyes were soft, more gentle than I'd ever seen them. She smiled at me. Where my skin retained a swarthy warmth regardless of season, Merla's remained pale. Her deep red hair lay in thick rivers, not a fine mesh like Guinevere's. I realised for the first time it held small leather ties, pieces of metal and jewels.

"I thought Merlin forced you to leave me alone," I said. Having a huge emotional meltdown in front of a powerful fey, didn't seem like the most sensible thing I'd ever achieved.

"I heard your pain," she said carefully. "And the old man is easy to avoid. You need help, Wolf," her words were soft, her eyes wide and wary, begging for acceptance and understanding.

I touched her jaw and she closed her eyes, peace sweeping over her face. "Who are you?" I asked confused.

She smiled. "I am not what you think and I have no wish to make your life more complicated. But you need a friend and I can be your friend."

"You have not answered the question," I said.

Her eyes were very wide and she blinked. "I can run with you, Wolf, at least for a little while. Please just accept my gift and hold it to your heart as a healing balm."

"You just want me to accept who you are and pretend there is no agenda?"

She smiled and kissed the corner of my mouth. "Yes, that is exactly what I want you to do. I've listened to Arthur over these last few days during your illness and the burdens he places on your shoulders are mighty indeed. You need help, Knight of Camelot. You need to share your burden, or the madness you suffered when fighting Stephen will sweep you away for good."

I stiffened and tried to stand. The pain brought me back to the floor so I said, "How do you know about that?" Only Tancred and Merlin would know how I killed that day. I'd given Arthur the edited highlights.

"Your Wolf called to me in your madness. How do you think I came at a time you needed me? I arrived as Rose because I knew Arthur and Merlin would never accept a full fey as your carer under the circumstances. Your fey blood called for help in its agony. The fey protect themselves when they are forced to kill, you are powerful but alone and unprotected. Your heart is breaking and you feel death sitting on your shoulder waiting for the next prize you deliver," her words were gentle but felt like hammer blows. Tears coursed down my cheeks once more. She wrapped her body around me and held me as another, gentler wave of grief washed over my soul.

I calmed and Merla helped me stand. I felt lighter, calmer and happier than I'd managed since I'd heard of Stephen marching on Avalon. Her words though haunted me, death sitting on my shoulder waiting for me to feed him. It was disturbingly accurate. Every moment my mind found itself unoccupied I relived those moments in Stephen's camp, trying to see the faces of the men I killed. Trying to remember them, so they were not yet more faceless dead waiting to torment me when my own time came.

I forced myself to listen to Merla and we slid into effortless mundane conversation. The day began to pass without pain. I relaxed and dozed as my recovery dictated. A soft knock at the door roused me and I realised Merla had lain a blanket over my knees. She went to the door, opened it and bowed low.

I couldn't twist far enough to see who stood the other side. "Can I come in?" Guinevere asked.

I smiled, she had changed so much over the last few months. "Of course you can, your Majesty," I called.

She walked to my side, took my face in her hands and kissed my cheek. "You look tired but better," she said.

"I feel better, it is good to see you," I said and meant it. What hope did I have when I loved both Pendragons?

"My Lord?" Merla drew my attention from Guinevere. "I should see to your lunch." She bowed as though to leave.

"No," the panic induced within me at the thought of her leaving me alone shocked us both. She'd rescued me from drowning and I could not let her go in case I sank again into the mire. "Please." I held out a hand, Guinevere moved away as she heard the fear in my voice. Merla came back to me and took my hand. "Don't go. Not yet. Someone else can deal with the food."

She smiled and nodded. My heartbeat began to calm as she walked toward the window. Guinevere frowned, confused, but stayed quiet. Clearly someone had explained I'd become a little fragile.

"Arthur told me about your father, I am so sorry," she said. Servants are easy to ignore when you are used to them. She'd already forgotten about Merla.

I smiled tightly. "It's not me that I'm worried about but Arthur."

She knelt before me so she could lean into my knees and lay her hands in my lap. "You always worry about Arthur. He's not the one with the hole in his back. I am worried about you."

"You don't mean that, Guinevere."

She sighed. "No, I suppose not, or at least not completely. Arthur's told me I cannot go with you. I have to return to Camelot and become a Queen who can go to war if he doesn't make it home in time." I heard her fear and I understood it, she did not want to be alone.

"You'll be a great Queen if you follow your instincts," I said, as I stroked her hair. She'd taken to wearing it in a long braid, wisps escaped.

"I'm pregnant," she announced from nowhere.

My hand froze, a hundred different emotions swept through me. She looked up with her huge blue eyes the colour of an early clear winter dawn. "Oh, Guinevere," the smile spread over my face, settling my initial response. "I am so glad. You have told Arthur right?"

She bit her lip and her face clouded. "I was going to but he is trying to understand and prepare for this sword. I didn't want to burden him."

I laughed. "Go, Guinevere, if you are here asking for advice. Go and tell him."

"What if I lose it? It would kill him," she wailed in fear.

"Go and tell him," I ordered, lifting her to her feet. "Go, you will not lose the child. You will give him the boy you both need. Go!" I slapped her backside.

CHAPTER TWENTY-FOUR

I LEANED BACK, EXHAUSTED. Things were changing. Else had married Geraint and our friendship would mend with time. Arthur would become a father and I? I would go on. I would endure. Merla didn't speak. I heard Arthur yell from somewhere else in the Abbey and soon pounding footsteps were rushing to the library. Arthur burst into the room. "Lancelot," he yelled.

I managed to rise and fix the perfect welcoming smile on my face. "Arthur." He rushed into my arms and we embraced.

I saw Merla bow and leave the room. I hoped she wouldn't go far. I'd need her back the way this day was turning out. I found I held a six foot excited puppy in my arms. Arthur babbled and I smiled and I laughed. All the time knowing things would change forever between us because of this one declaration. I felt proud and happy for my friend, my King, but the hovering sadness within me knew yet more loss. He bounced and then rushed off to find Guinevere, whom, I pointed out, probably needed him more than I did.

I stood alone, wishing I didn't have to think any longer. Then I was no longer standing alone. Merla lay a soft hand on my shoulder. I turned into her. It felt so good to be held and gently nursed through such a day. Although smaller than Arthur, her strength gave me an anchor.

As I listened to the frantic happiness outside my sick room, I grew numb. Merla remained quiet after he left, allowing me my thoughts before beginning our evening ritual. She produced food, she cleaned my wounds and helped me wash. I lay on the bed and found her sitting on the edge in her chemise.

She stroked my face. "You need to heal fast, Wolf. It is time you let me in."

"What are you talking about?" I asked.

"Lancelot, you need to heal because Arthur needs your help. I know you don't believe me right now, but there is hope for your future. I promise you." She planted a kiss on my scarred knuckles.

I blinked, exhausted and grim. "There is hope?"

She smiled. "You are loved, Lancelot. Where there is love there is always hope. I know you feel alone but you aren't, not really." Her green eyes shone in the firelight, her hair cascaded around her like the living flame. Merla lifted my blankets, lay down with her nose close to my chest and her arms around me. "Heal, Wolf," she murmured as my arms encircled her back and I slept.

Fey magic laced my fevered dreams, but the Wolf did not join me, he lay quiet allowing Merla to wrap herself around my body. The scent of summer hay and roses filled my head and when I woke, dawn graced the windows and I found my stiff cock trying to bury itself through Merla's chemise. I didn't really think, I just began kissing the back of her neck and my right hand found the swell of her breast.

A hand clamped down on my questing fingers. Merla's body locked rigid as she rushed from her own dreams. Awareness rushed back and I realised I did not share my bed with a woman who'd given her consent. I pushed my hips back, away from her and relaxed my hand.

"Sorry," I muttered embarrassed.

Merla rolled and we lay facing each other, she smiled. "You feel more alive than you have since I've met you, Knight of Camelot. I have done well, don't be sorry."

"You are a beautiful woman," I told the captivating green eyes.

"I know that but I am not your woman. I have no wish to be crushed by a man as powerful as you are capable of being, you burn too brightly, Wolf." Her words, so similar to Else's, sliced through me.

"A Wolf always runs alone," I muttered morosely. I rolled onto my back and released Merla from my arms. She slipped out of the bed and dressed. I closed my eyes trying to pull back the hurt, trying not care that Arthur lay with his pregnant wife and not me.

Merla's hands pulled mine down from covering my eyes. "You cannot be jealous of an unborn child you know he needs. Perhaps Arthur is not the one you need, just the one to show you the path you need to take to find the happiness and companionship you crave."

"I cannot begrudge Arthur his son but I don't believe I will ever find my heart's desire without him and I know I will lose him," I said, now desperate.

Merla chuckled, I looked at her. "You are a bloody romantic aren't you?"

I frowned, she kissed my nose. "You will be happy, Lancelot. It may not be exactly what you were expecting but you will be happy." She pulled on my hands as she rose, "Come, up, I want to see how well I did. I haven't tried healing someone with fey power in decades."

I stood. I stood with ease. I wriggled my hips and my balls bounced. I grinned, no pain. No weakness, no vulnerability. Merla laughed. I grabbed her and lifted her off her feet. Energy filled my muscle and bone. The door opened and Tancred stood there, he looked at me as I placed Merla back on the ground and stretched. "Look, I'm whole," I said grinning.

He raised one eyebrow and blushed. "So I see, my Lord."

I laughed, naked as a babe. I walked up to him, grabbed his face and kissed his brow. "I feel alive at last," I told him. "And I don't want to be cooped up any more. Fancy a ride?"

He blinked and frowned. "Arthur told me I was not to move from your side."

"Good, then we shall go for a ride. There must be somewhere out there we can hunt." I walked away from him.

"I'll go to the horses," he said as he fled my company.

"What's wrong with him?" I jerked my thumb over my shoulder.

Merla shook her head. "Not all men are as confident as you are, Wolf."

I frowned. "What do you mean?"

"I mean he's wrestling with his desire for someone, don't you pay any attention to your companions?" she asked, while rousing the fire.

I helped her with the logs and thought about Tancred being attracted to someone. It made me feel odd, imagining him with a woman in his arms. I didn't like the image at all. "Who is she?" I asked.

Merla laughed, deep and throaty. "Oh, you men are always so anxious to place people in tidy boxes. It's not a woman he wants, Lancelot."

"Tancred's interested in men?" Despite my own lifestyle I felt shocked. Idiot that I am.

She laughed again, turned and kissed my mouth, it felt good. "You daft sod. Yes, he loves men or rather a man, so go gentle and take care if you don't want to love him in return."

"Me?" I asked in shocked awe. "Why would he love me?"

Merla raised an elegant eyebrow. "I can't imagine. After all, you don't represent the pinnacle of knightly prowess or virtue."

"I'm a fine warrior," I agreed with all seriousness, "but I wouldn't say I was virtuous."

"Really, you do surprise me," Merla said with a straight face.

"Besides, I only love Arthur," I said, my perpetual litany.

Her eyes calmed and darkened. "I know that and you always will, even if it means your soul's destruction." She slapped my naked chest. "Dress, Wolf and leave me alone to deal with a pregnant queen."

When I finished dressing, I walked from the library feeling whole. I made it outside without being spotted and found Tancred. He held his bright bay gelding, Echo, while trying to stop Ash from taking chunks out of the gelding's neck.

"I've informed the King of our trip, he says we need to be home by dark," Tancred said as he danced away from Ash's hooves. "Why are you so much better, my Lord?" he asked.

I heard the concern. "I have no idea but I'm grateful for it. I do not make a good patient."

He grinned. "I had noticed. But aren't you concerned?"

I shrugged. "Merla curled up with me all night and by morning I'm whole. I don't need to worry about the details. Merlin and Arthur trust her with my life, that's sufficient for me." I put my foot in the stirrup and mounted before Ash could whip around and bite me. He danced and bounced as soon as my backside settled in the saddle. I cursed him.

"You are bedding the fey woman?" Tancred asked just as I realised I'd delivered the first of what would be many mistakes now I knew how he felt. The thought of another man, a man I worked with, seeing me as something other than a normal companion felt odd. A strange swirling wriggled inside my belly. Had I crossed a line never to return? Or perhaps a new world stood before me? I certainly enjoyed sex with both men and women, but somehow my relationships with women never really worked. Perhaps I'd find another way. I decided I didn't want to burn bridges so I thought before I spoke.

"Erm, no, not really, nothing happened. She just seemed to think it was the only way I'd heal quickly enough," I said as we began to leave the yard.

Tancred didn't say anything for a moment then managed in a neutral tone, "If she makes you happy that's all that matters. I just worry that you don't understand what she is and what she is capable of, none of you do."

I turned Ash's head and pushed him hard in the ribs. He whipped around and we cantered from the Abbey. We rode around the side of the town and I decided I wanted a good view. I forced Ash up the side of the Tor through the snow. I remembered my time with Arthur up here during the autumn. I forced the memory into the wind. It rushed past my face viciously, the cold fierce but enlivening. Nothing stood on the hill but us and the sunshine. The flat, watery world of the Levels opened up before us, covered in a white blanket, the few ridges in the land supported villages and sheep. Willow and ash, with a few scrubby oak and hazel littered the bog.

We enjoyed the view in silence. The horses calm after the steep ride up the hill. I pointed to a ridge about a league off. "We'll see if there's anything to hunt over there. Should keep me out of trouble for the day."

We slithered the horses down the hill and rode toward the ridge. Tancred had provided us with short hunting bows so we spent the rest of the morning hunting fat wood pigeons and rabbit. At midday we built a fire and dressed the meat. We talked of childhood adventures and I learned I'd underestimated Tancred. The information Merla gave me forced me to reassess our relationship and I discovered I valued his friendship a great deal, he was not just a sergeant for my Wolf Pack.

After we'd finished our lunch I knew we'd have to return to the Abbey. I did not want to return, I wanted to stay on the road. A simple road, a simple journey, with no Else, no Arthur, no Aeddan. Fat chance.

We rode toward the Abbey and my mood darkened as did the weather. Before we reached the town, I pulled Ash up, the wind whipping at my cloak. "I thought my future lay in this place," I said. The weight of rejection lay heavy with me.

Tancred leaned against his saddlebow. "Perhaps it does, just not where you think."

I looked at him. His dark eyes were open and frank. An invitation perhaps? Surprisingly tempting if it would take the confusion away for a few minutes, but that's all it would be, a diversion. He deserved more if his feelings were real. I couldn't love him, Arthur filled my thoughts.

I sighed, unable to meet his gaze for a moment. "Arthur will be expecting me."

Tancred flinched. "Yes, my Lord, he will."

I watched as he rode away from me before I nudged Ash forward. I liked Tancred. I cared about him as a brother in arms but I could not desire him. Could I?

Sounds of the celebrations in the Abbey echoed toward us long before we reached it and my mood began to twist. They would be thanking whatever God or gods they believed in for deliverance from Stephen de Clare, the pregnancy and the marriage of my best friend to my woman. I needed to do something to release the pressure building in my heart. I didn't want to see Else in Geraint's arms and I sure as hell didn't want to think about their sex life.

"I need to get drunk," I announced before we rode through the Abbey gates.

Tancred turned in his saddle, the falling gloom of the day hiding his face in shadow. "There's a tavern in the town," he said. "We could go there. It's rough but nothing unusual."

"There you are," Arthur's voice bounced off the stone walls. "I've been waiting for you for hours. What have you been doing?" He walked across the yard, his footsteps a little unsteady. "I've been wanting to share a toast with my friend for the safe delivery of my son," he announced.

Tancred's shoulders slumped. I wouldn't have noticed if I'd not tuned into his behaviour. I rode Ash into the yard and as I passed him, I briefly lay my hand on his leg. He looked at me with shocked surprise, I held his gaze longer than I should have done but something in me yearned for the peace we'd found in each other's company that day. He bowed his head a little in acknowledgment of something changing between us. I joined Arthur.

I slid off Ash and handed the reins to someone, Arthur grinned at me and I realised he'd drunk a great deal of wine. Definitely more than he should have done. We walked to the library and I found the fire awake, cold meats on a plate and warm mulled wine in the hearth. Merla's work no doubt. Between her and Tancred I realised I'd found two people who seemed to care about me, it felt good.

My peaceful thoughts were scattered when Arthur roughly pulled me into his arms and kissed my mouth. He over balanced and his teeth caught my lip. It split and blood caught my tongue.

"Bloody hell, Arthur, be careful," I snapped, stepping back from him and dabbing at my mouth. "What the hell's wrong with you? You should be with Guinevere, your pregnant wife, remember?" My anger surprised me, but it flared real and hot. He should not be here and he should not be drunk.

"I miss you, and you are well, strong, back," he said as he grabbed my coat to pull it from my shoulders.

"Stop, Arthur, this is insane," I insisted. I began to battle with his fingers and hands, he giggled. The King giggled. I realised this wasn't just the wine.

His lips brushed my neck. "I saw you in bed with the witch. Trying to replace me already?" he hissed.

"No, Arthur, I'm not." I stepped back and fell into the bed. "Nothing happened with Merla, we are friends. I needed to be healed so I could help you and that's all she did. Something fey but it worked. We are friends. Nothing could replace you." Though at that moment as he tried to climb over me I decided I'd like to replace him given an opportunity.

A soft knock and Guinevere's voice.

I panicked. "Not now. Fuck," I snapped as Arthur bit me hard.

He laughed.

Guinevere opened the door. "I knew it," she said. Her eyes filled with tears. "You bastard, you promised we would talk first. I'm carrying your child and all you can think about is him." Her agony hit me hard and it hurt.

"No, Guinevere, please it's not…" I began.

Arthur's head whipped around as though someone had pulled his tail and he wanted blood for the insult. "Of course I'm here, at least I can have a decent fuck, you bitch."

Guinevere went white. She swayed and grasped the back of a chair. I stared in horror at Arthur. His eyes were blood shot and his mouth set in a mean snarl. I'd never have recognised him. I pushed him off me and rose. I placed myself between the King and Queen, not the best of ideas perhaps.

"Arthur, apologise, you cannot speak to your wife like that," I said.

"She's a sow, a pig I must breed from, you are all I want." He lurched towards me. Guinevere gasped and backtracked. I caught Arthur's hands and held him.

"What are you talking about?" I asked as I searched his eyes. The irises were like piss holes in the snow.

"Now you've fucked her you don't want me, is that it?" he snarled as spittle ran down his face.

I turned my head. "Guinevere," I snapped. "Find Merlin and Merla while you're at it. Something is wrong."

She stared at her husband in horror. "This is what I lived with when you were gone," she whispered.

"Guinevere, if you don't help, he might be gone forever," I began to wrestle with Arthur, trying to maintain control.

Her eyes focused and she nodded. As she left the room, Arthur began to tear at my clothing. "I am going to fuck you whether you like it or not," he ordered. "On your knees, you are my vassal. You are at my command."

I dropped. He calmed instantly. "That's good," he cooed as he bent over me and stroked my face. I closed my eyes and prayed for forgiveness. I hit Arthur.

CHAPTER TWENTY-FIVE

MY FIST CONNECTED WITH his jaw in the prime target and he flew back. I rose with the punch and caught him before he slammed into the chair. His eyes rolled back in his head and he passed out.

I breathed easy for a moment before I unbuckled my belt and tied his hands. Merlin burst into the room, followed by Guinevere and Merla.

"He's sick," I cried out. "He's behaving like he did when he was poisoned."

Merlin rushed to us, Merla spoke softly to Guinevere and the Queen left the room. Arthur stirred. His eyes opened. "You bastard," he snarled. "I'll see you hang for this."

He strained against the belt, something gave and his hands came free. He pushed against Merlin as the wizard tried to stop him moving. I saw a flash of metal as he rose and rushed toward me. Merla stepped back. I raised my hands but Arthur batted them away, his strength out of control. He slammed me against the wall and the knife in his hand pricked my neck.

"Arthur, please, stop, think," I begged. I didn't have the courage to hurt him again.

"Would you rather fuck the witch than me?" he asked, his face a mask of hate. I realised blood tricked down my throat from the knife.

"No, Sire. I explained, Merla is just my friend," I said forcing my breathing to calm, my Adam's apple bobbed against the blade.

"Liar," he said as he pushed with the knife. I heard a command from Merla and Merlin. Arthur flinched before his eyes glazed, half a breath later I descended into darkness.

"Lancelot, wake up," Merla's voice and hands nagged at me. I obeyed.

"What happened?" I asked feeling like a dragon sat on my head.

Merlin lifted Arthur onto the small bed I'd been using. "He's been wrapped up in a spell."

I frowned. "How?"

I watched my companions share a long look. Merla broke their silence, "It's Aeddan, I can taste his magic."

"I thought you said he wouldn't be powerful enough to do anything else after yesterday," I said pushing myself upright. I touched the blood on my neck. I'd been out long enough for it to become crusty.

"He shouldn't be," Merla said. "I don't understand how he's done this but Arthur isn't safe until I reach somewhere I am stronger."

"So, Aeddan shouldn't have this kind of power?" I repeated in an attempt to understand.

"Yes, Wolf, you have the right idea," Merlin said. "And no, we don't know where he's taking it from."

"Is Arthur going to be alright?" I asked.

"He'll be fine, we both used the same spell in the same moment, it knocked him out and the backwash hit you." Merlin lay his hands on Arthur's head and closed his eyes.

Merla turned to me. "I need to get Arthur away from here. Avalon will act as a focus for Aeddan. It is Nimue's land and she is his wife. He can use that connection."

"It's night," I said. "And winter."

"We have to leave now. Someone you trust must pack Arthur's things and we need to leave for the sword. Only then will he be safe." She didn't hide the urgency and fear in her voice.

"I'll pack, I need to talk to Guinevere anyway," I said and left them fussing over Arthur.

Their room lay a short distance from mine. I realised they'd co-opted the Abbess's office into use, she'd be pleased. I opened the door without knocking. Guinevere lay on the bed in floods of tears. Moving toward her, I scooped her up and held her tight to my chest, she wailed.

"It's always you, he always chooses you over me," she said, as small fists hit my chest. "And you always choose him but I love you," she said between the tears.

I rocked her and stroked her head. After a while she calmed and looked up at me, her eyes were red and her nose ran, but she looked so perfectly delicate my heart jumped in my chest. I smiled at her.

"Don't do that," she said miserably, hitting me again. "I love you and I wish I'd married you instead and I wish this baby was yours."

The pain in my chest grew, expanded. I wished the same and had done for years. She'd done this before, thrown these words at me when she'd grown angry with Arthur. I don't know if she knew how much they hurt but I never reacted to them.

"You don't mean that, Guinevere," I said forcing myself to be kind. The pain in my chest burned and I realised how small and how warm she felt in my arms. Her scent began to fill my head and her words blurred as she spoke of the King's anger.

"Don't think about him," I told her. "You belong to me," the words came from my mouth but I didn't remember thinking them. Guinevere snapped her mouth shut. I took hold of her jaw and kissed her mouth. None too gently as it turned out because she twisted away.

"What the hell are you playing at?" she said as she wriggled off my lap and stood.

I rose to match her, the heat in my chest diving for my groin. I ached for this woman. I lunged for her and she stepped back. Guinevere slapped me hard across the face.

"Bitch," I snapped as a wave of pain made my knees weak. It didn't stop me catching hold of her and pulling her into my chest.

"Lancelot, stop!" she yelled.

Then I heard her scream, the sound was warm as it drove through me. She pulled back against my bite on her neck and her skin tore. I fought with the dress she wore and began to win. I sat her on the desk and forced her legs wide. She screamed and I wrapped a hand around her throat. A part of my mind grew frantic with the need to stop my body. The war between my instinct and my true love for this woman made me pause. I held her so effectively she didn't stand a chance.

The door crashed open behind me. I glanced over my shoulder. Tancred and Gawain stood there, a wall of muscle. I grinned, "Well, if I can't fuck I can fight."

They didn't speak, they simply rushed into the room. Merla stood behind them and I realised she was the real threat. I released Guinevere, who rolled away. Merla raised her hands, muttered under her breath and I charged at the men trying to stop me. I never reached them. I fell. Tancred caught me and the lights in my head died. So did the pain in my chest.

I came to feeling as sick as a dog and my head pounded, the world shifted horribly and something dug into my guts. I groaned.

"He's awake," said a voice I knew but couldn't place. I groaned again. The jolting stopped, small hands raised my head and I looked into Else's eyes. They were dark in the moonlight, her skin pale.

"What the hell is going on?" I asked. I felt more hands undoing things which controlled my movement. My eyes reported to my brain something useful. I hung over Ash's saddle.

"Bring him down gently," Merla's voice guided.

"Arthur's waking too," Geraint's voice came next.

"Are we having a party?" I managed as Tancred lowered me to the ground. Else knelt by my head.

"How are you feeling?" she asked.

I knew how I felt. I flipped over onto all fours and puked. Her small hands rubbed my back. When the urging relaxed, I sat back on my heels. Tancred handed me a flask of water. I drank. "Tell me what happened."

Arthur appeared beside me with Geraint's help and sat. We leaned against each other and looked up into the faces of our companions and the horses. Merla stood dressed in riding leathers, she looked great. Else stood beside her with arms crossed, the expression on her face caught between concern and anger. Geraint stood next to her, I didn't bother looking at him. Next came Tancred.

Merla crouched and peered at us. "You both feel as you should?" she asked.

Arthur and I looked at each other. "If you mean, do we feel like we've been drinking for a month, then yes, we feel great." The sarcasm didn't escape anyone.

"He's fine," Geraint sounded disgusted. Else reached for his hand.

"Sorry," I snapped, "did our brush with madness ruin your night? She's used to being –"

"Lancelot," Arthur barked, stopping me from saying anything more.

Geraint's face darkened. "Careful, du Lac, you don't need any more enemies."

"With friends like you, trust me I'm well aware of my vulnerability."

"Stop it," Else said stepping between us. I realised the ground I sat on made my arse wet. I struggled upright, pulling Arthur with me. "I know you are angry, Lancelot, and I'm sorry, but it's done. We don't want to be here any more than you want us here."

"Then why are you here?" Arthur asked.

Merla walked to my side, her arm crept around my back and she laid her head on my shoulder. I peered down at her in surprise. "I need help keeping Aeddan from hurting you both. He placed a spell in Lancelot that I didn't find.

I have underestimated him to our cost. I didn't know he'd grown so strong or so cunning. This isn't his style at all. The spell used the connection you share through your love." Her hand flexed on my chest. "It slithered through you both to attack the object of your desire."

"Is Guinevere alright?" I asked. I felt sick once more when I remembered her fear and my disgusting behaviour.

"She will be, she's safe, that's the main thing. She will return to Camelot. I believe, Gawain and Yvain are in charge. And they have Merlin with them," she said as Geraint nodded. "I need Else's gifts to enhance my own until we reach the lake where I am stronger. I have not fought another fey for a very long time and living among mortals has weakened me. Geraint is the grounding I need and Tancred can be used in an emergency, although he has no training. Neither you, nor Arthur, can stray from Eleanor or myself. We are all that holds Aeddan's magic at bay."

Else and I looked at each other. The last time we were the victims of a fey spell, we were lovers. That hurt. Geraint drew her to his side protectively. I glanced at Tancred. He looked tired but remained his usual unruffled self. He accepted his orders and he smiled as our eyes met.

"I want to return to check on Guinevere," Arthur said, his distress palpable.

"You can't," Merla told him. "It isn't safe, she might be hurt again. Merlin will protect her and the child she bears. Until we defeat Aeddan we need you to stay away from the Queen."

"Does she know I didn't mean it?" he asked. I heard his anguish and it mirrored my own all too closely.

"She will, Arthur," Else said taking his hand.

We remounted the horses and I rode with Merla and Tancred. Arthur stayed beside Else and Geraint. In the darkness, we couldn't ride fast and we wouldn't be going far, but to be honest I'd have rather ridden all night than stay in this company, cursed by magic once more.

We called a halt when the cloud thickened and the moon vanished. We were in a small wood, so didn't leave the road. I watched Geraint walk with Else to find wood for a fire under the snow, Arthur stood beside me.

"This isn't good," he said. "And you have a bastard of a right hook."

I half smiled toward him, hardly able to see his face in the darkness. "Sorry. But you make a terrible rapist."

He barked a harsh laugh at my pathetic joke. "I understand you aren't too clever either."

The comment sobered us both. "She's never going to forgive me," I said. I'd hurt Guinevere, even in madness I didn't think such a thing were possible.

"She'll forgive you, my friend. She loves you. Once Merlin makes her understand she'll forgive us both."

"I would suffer anything for the two of you," I said, my voice thickening.

"You already have suffered far more than you should, my friend."

I grunted and moved away to help make a camp for us, trying to remain busy. Geraint and Else returned. We'd set the fire going and I knew the look in her eyes under the firelight. They'd been busy with things other than collecting wood. She shivered and Geraint pulled her into his body.

"Fuck," I cursed. I rose in one fluid movement making everyone in the camp jump. I suppose they thought I'd draw my sword and kill the bastard who'd stolen my future. Tempting. I didn't. I walked away. Soft noises followed and Merla appeared beside me.

"You cannot leave my side, Wolf," she said. "No matter how much you need to be alone."

"I can't stand it," I said. "Watching them. It hurts."

Merla took hold of my shoulders and turned me to face her. I must have walked quickly. We were so far from camp I couldn't hear them or see the fire. She held my head and forced me to look down into her green eyes, just a few inches lower than my own. "You are meant to feel this pain and hurt. If you didn't you would be a callous monster. Don't lose your humanity and the love of a fey because this has wounded you. There is so much out there to love, Lancelot, if only you could see it. Don't close yourself off."

I placed my hands on her slim hips, my fingers splayed over the top of her backside. "And what am I to love next, fey witch?" I asked as my cock twitched. "Am I to love you?"

She laughed. "Oh, no, Wolf. There are times when I look in your eyes and I see your father. I'll not fall for that again. You'll not use me to forget your pain. But you can use me to keep you warm. It will help and you need to sleep."

I kissed her full, smiling lips for a moment, I couldn't help myself. She tasted like honey. Her hands pushed me away even as I stepped back.

"I will take first watch over our camp. I know we are still close to the Abbey but Stephen's men might be out there somewhere."

I found a place to wait out the night. I wrapped my cloak around me, pulled the hood over my head and leaned against the large bowl of a tree. The wind beat the bare branches of the trees, setting up a rattle which reminded me of skeleton bones jangling in the wind. I shivered and my mind strayed to the people in the camp.

Arthur, my King, the man I loved had spoken few words to me since our fight. He'd be uncomfortable with what happened, he'd be very unhappy about my behaviour toward Guinevere. We needed to talk, clear the air properly.

I also knew we needed to close the intimate side of our relationship. I did not want him to be tangled up with me when his child arrived in the world. Guinevere and Camelot needed him. The thought caused my stomach to cramp and my lungs to burn. I blanked my mind and controlled my breathing. I'd grown to live with this pain, this loss when he'd married Guinevere. I could do it again, I hoped.

Next, my thoughts strayed to Else, for further self-flagellation. Wrapped in Geraint's arms, doubtless soon to be swollen with his child. I crouched down, headless of the snow, with my back pressed into the tree, waiting for the pain to leave me. This felt sharp like a knife and it twisted, pulling hard at me, unravelling my fragile peace. I tried to push this away as I did with thoughts of Arthur, but I couldn't, I didn't have those tools. The old griefs were not strong enough to unman me but these new ones tore at me with claws sharper than any knife. I wanted to howl, to scream. Why couldn't I just let her go? Forget the promises of a future never to be real? I knew it was over, I kept releasing her but my heart kept pulling me back to an illusion which would never be real. I had loved Else and Guinevere but not as I loved Arthur. My fingers pulled at my hair as I buried my face in my knees. I wanted normal, safe, calm, I wanted peace and I wanted to love, I wanted a family.

"Calm, Wolf, calm." Merla crouched in the snow and mud beside me. "Your soul is screaming, Lancelot. Calm or you will damage yourself forever. The scars will be too large and you will usher in the darkness to take your mind, your heart. You have to learn to control your grief."

I closed my eyes, held her arms as though the wind around me tried to tear me from her presence. She pulled me toward her, roughly took hold of my face and her hot lips were tight on mine. Her tongue forced itself into my mouth and suddenly I could breathe. I breathed and I groaned as the kiss grew. Hot, passionate, frantic. Merla pulled and collapsed backward in the same movement. I found myself lying over her, my heavy body pressing her into the snow. I didn't want to think too much, I devoured her mouth, her lips, her jaw and neck. She gasped and squirmed under me, her hands trying to pull up the layers of clothing. Between my woollen coat, surcoat, mail, gambeson and shirt, she didn't stand much of a chance.

She whimpered in desperation. "This is not a good idea," she groaned as I tried to unlace her clothing in the darkness.

Certain parts of my body thought it a very good idea. I felt hard for this woman, something so normal, something I understood. My common sense though made me pause. I did not take women against their will. Guinevere's horror flashed through my mind and helped to cool my lust. I placed my elbows either side of her head and lay still between her thighs. I could just make out the colour of her eyes.

"Why is this a bad idea?" I asked as gently as I could manage.

"Because I fear you, Wolf," she said, her eyes dark and sad, even as her fingers finally brushed against my bare skin.

I reared back further and frowned. "Fear me? Merla, what happened with Guinevere was the spell, I would never hurt you."

She laughed. "I know you won't hurt my body, Wolf, you can't. What I give I give willingly. But my heart you will steal and I fear you will crush what remains. You are not meant to be mine."

I realised Merla might well be experienced but we were not meeting on equal ground. I wanted to bury myself inside her to forget. She wanted me so we could build something new. They were bad foundations. Merla was not a woman of the night to be paid fairly and forgotten. If she gave me even a part of her heart, I needed to treasure it, not abuse it.

I kissed her mouth, her jaw, releasing her reluctantly. "Can you bring yourself to sleep near me here?" I asked her. "I don't want to be alone."

"Oh, Lancelot, you are more a man than your father could ever be," she said. I heard the tears as I forced my aching body off her hips. I'd need to relieve myself soon or something would explode.

I built a nest from the leaves, not all of them dry, but they were soft. Merla rose and helped. I sat with my back to a tree and she placed her head on my thigh. My thoughts were quieter as I stroked her hair, I wanted her but I did not love her and just as I needed to be careful with Tancred, now I knew how he felt, I needed to be gentle with Merla. I didn't know why these two people cared for me so much but it was a privilege and one I did not want to squander.

Merla spoke the truth when she said I had hope and I horded it close to my heart against the darkness trying to swallow my soul.

CHAPTER TWENTY-SIX

I DOZED AGAINST THE tree and watched the sky lift from black to grey. The clouds remained thick overhead, but I could now watch Merla. She breathed deeply, lying on her back, her lips parted. I heard the others beginning to wake. My hand had spent most of the night on her chest, so I moved it to her face and stroked her soft cheek until her eyes opened. She smiled, the day brightened a little.

"You make a wonderful pillow," she said.

"Well, at least I can perform some small service for you, my Lady," I said.

She sat up and stretched. I stood and realised I wasn't as young as I thought. My back ached from sitting upright all night and I'd spend the day feeling very tired but as we walked back to the main camp I felt a great deal calmer.

I managed to shock the hell out of everyone by walking to Geraint, who stared at me as though I might swing a punch at his head, and held out my hand. "I owe you a congratulations and thanks for helping us with this latest disaster."

All eyes stared at me, he looked at my hand and he smiled with relief. His forearm hit my palm and I grasped his arm in return. "Thank you, my friend and you are welcome. I owe you an apology."

"Let's not go too far, Geraint, one step at a time," I said trying to hide the flash of anger despite my attempt at reconciliation.

Arthur rescued me, "Well, this is good news. Now, can we eat and find this sword before my wife decides she wants no more to do with me."

Else and Merla scattered the fire, we packed the camp and tacked the horses. We were off soon enough and pushed the pace. We rode through woodland most of the day, the land lay quiet around us, spring may be trying to push through, with the snow beginning to melt but winter did not want to make it easy. The few people we did see were wary of knights riding swiftly and made themselves scarce. Mud hampered us in places and driving rain in others. We covered well over ten leagues that day and by dusk were looking to make camp inside somewhere warm. We'd been travelling east all day and never saw the sun behind the miserable cloud. Despite this I felt good. I'd ridden with either Merla or Tancred all day, Arthur choosing Geraint and Else for company. So when we reached the small town of Maiden Bradley, I found myself looking forward to an evening of gentle companionship.

The town boasted only one inn, a surprise considering it existed on the main road between Avalon and Salisbury. I asked the innkeeper when we stabled our horses.

"We don't like to encourage your kind," he said. "Soldiers, knights, you're all trouble." He sloshed ale over my hand as he plonked down the tankard.

I shook the brew off my gloves and wanted to prove him correct. Instead I muttered, "What about king's you prick?"

Arthur joined me. "Cheerful isn't he."

"I don't know why we can't tell them who you are and have them all scurrying about like blue arsed flies."

He smiled but appeared distracted. "Can we talk?" he asked. My heart sank. I didn't want to talk. I wanted to drink too much, flirt with Merla and find a few minutes peace to ease the ache in my balls. I also needed to sleep. I'd nodded off in the saddle several times during the day.

"Do we really need to?" I asked.

He blinked and frowned. "You don't think we do?"

I sighed and lowered my voice, "Arthur, we are in a dangerous situation and you are going to be a father. I know what that means to you and I know you want to turn back to Guinevere." I grabbed his arm. "I also know you find what happened to us because of Aeddan disturbing. It's alright, we are still friends but I know it's over."

He opened his mouth and his eyes betrayed his sorrow. "I don't know what to do. I should let you go, tell you to run into Merla's arms, but I don't know what to do," he repeated. "I want to be with you but I owe Guinevere so much. When I have a son…"

"Nothing will ever change how I feel about you." I didn't say love, there wasn't much point and he rarely used the word himself these days. "But I need something you can't give me, I need something that belongs to me." Was I really doing this? Was I really cutting him out of my life?

Something in me reached out for him, my hand tightened on his arm and my breathing hitched. His blue eyes widened as he felt my terrible desire for him take control. I wanted to release him for his own sake, not for mine. If I held onto him, I would make him miserable, far better to cauterise the wound.

But plans are for fools who have nothing better to do.

Geraint walked past us, Arthur's free arm whipped out and he grabbed our friend. Geraint turned surprised as Arthur said, "We're upstairs, not to be disturbed. We'll be down for food later."

Neither of us waited for a reply, we both moved to the small staircase and vanished upstairs. There were two small rooms, we poured through one door and found a mattress on a low bed.

"Hardly adequate but it'll do," Arthur muttered as I pulled him tight into me and we kissed. I melted into the comfort of his body. He held me and surrendered to me all at once. Our familiarity made our movements confident and we knew where to go to find those sweet spots. We pulled our surcoats off, put needed time to unlace the mail, which slowed us down.

As Arthur pulled the mail shirt over my shoulders and it slid into a metallic puddle on the floor he said, "I am sorry."

I looked at him, the room had a small fire, but the flames were low and I couldn't see his face clearly. "Sorry for what?" I asked.

"Sorry for not being able to release you, so you can find happiness somewhere else." He stopped stripping me of clothing and I watched his shoulders slump.

I began undoing his gambeson. "You are all I've ever wanted, Arthur."

"That's not true. I ruined your relationship with Else. If it were not for me you would be married," he said. His misery sounded genuine.

I pulled his padded shirt off his body, his shirt underneath smelt heavily of him, it made my cock surge with desperation. "I don't think I'd have ever made her happy. Not really. Our relationship began on a bed of lies and grew from deceit. I don't think we would ever have been as happy as she will be with Geraint." I used her words to ease his conscience.

"Doesn't stop you wanting her," he said just as my hands reached under his shirt.

"I love you," I managed as my brain closed down to concentrate on physical completion. We finished undressing and lay on the small bed face to face. Arthur caressed my face, my chest, my hips, tracing the lines of muscle and bone. This moment of isolation a rare treat to be savoured.

"I thought you'd died," he whispered.

I kissed his lips. "If I'd died, I'd have had to leave you and I cannot do that, I promised, remember?"

His hips moved toward mine and our powerful erections touched for the first time in many days. We both groaned at the sensation and laughed. "How," I said, "are we ever going to be able to stop doing this?"

"I never want to stop, Wolf," he said. "Becoming a father or not."

I didn't believe him but I didn't want to argue either so I pulled him closer and we began to make love with determination. I kissed down his neck, licking the scent of him into me and I nipped hard enough to mark. His fingers laced through my tangled hair and held me tight to his flesh as I hurt him. My left hand traced down his thigh and pulled it up, so I could trace his backside, trail my fingers over his sensitive hole and roll his balls in my palm. Arthur put his arm in his mouth, watching me with desperate eyes and trying to keep quiet.

I licked and nosed the join between his body and leg, inhaling him so I would never forget his scent.

"Fucking hell, Lancelot, please, take mercy," he moaned.

I chuckled. "No mercy, Sire."

"Wolf," he growled.

I licked up his thick cock and he yelped before biting his arm again. I sucked him into my mouth and rolled my tongue over the velvet head. He leaked into my mouth and the earthy taste made my cock drive into the bed under my hips. I released him and attacked his balls, the fine golden hair tickling my lips.

"Touch yourself for me," Arthur whispered, straining to remain quiet.

I wrapped my fist around my cock and sucked him back down, taking more than I could handle but wanting all of him.

"You look so fucking beautiful," Arthur said, stroking my head.

"I want to be inside you," I said, licking his cock, my lips and breath making it bob.

Arthur pushed me off his body and grabbed his leather purse. He returned with a small glass bottle, dark blue in colour and thick.

"Yes and make it soon," he said, pushing it into my hand.

I took the bottle, opened it and poured some onto my thick fingers. Arthur knelt before me on hands and knees. I grinned, we both loved this position, because we could use all our strength against each other. I trailed it down his crack and swirled it around his hole. Arthur's head hit the pillow and he groaned, pushing back.

"Now, Wolf."

"Bossy."

"I'm your fucking King, do as you're told."

"Yes, Sire." I pushed my index finger into him and he whimpered, pushing back. "Fuck you feel so perfect," I muttered. Hot, tight, straining to take me but sucking me deeper.

"Just do it, Lancelot, I need you." He gripped his cock, trying hard not to come.

I made short work of breaching him with two fingers and worked to make him wider. He was fucking my fingers and looked magnificent, all that muscle and power at my mercy.

I kissed the firm globes of his backside and moved into position behind him.

"I want it all in one go," Arthur ordered over his shoulder. His blue eyes were dark and hard.

"I don't think –"

"You know what's at stake, Wolf, I need to remember this moment forever."

I knew exactly what was at stake. This could be the last time I ever got to worship his body so intimately.

I pushed my aching cock into his tight heat and folded over his strong back as I buried myself inside him.

"Fuck, yes," he groaned.

It must have hurt but he didn't care. He pulled off me and pushed back, hard. I grunted and gripped his hips, forcing him to stay still as I snapped my hips forward.

"Yes," he begged, dropping his head between his quivering arms.

I fucked him, hard and fast, driving into him. Driving through the terrible wave of grief and sadness I knew lurked behind our desperate actions this night. I forced myself to remain in the moment, despite knowing the future roared towards me to steal my love from me forever.

I fucked him because I knew Camelot would take him. Guinevere would take him. Our lives would tear us from each other.

Arthur tightened around me and I fucked hard over that sweet spot. A pained moan escaped him. "I love you," he cried out.

That tipped me over the edge. I came hard, deep inside the man I loved and I felt tears on my cheeks as I knew it might never happen again. I lay over him, wrapped my arms around him as he lowered us to the bed, keeping me inside his body.

"You needed that even more than me," Arthur said, trying to keep his voice light as he panted a little. He rubbed his head against my face.

I rolled onto my back, releasing him. He flinched as I pulled from his body but came after me so he could lie on my chest.

"I've been a little short of privacy and a cooperative partner."

"Merla?" he asked.

I reached out to caress his jaw. "It's nothing, Arthur and nothing has happened but a kiss."

The light caught his eyes. "It is your life and happiness that is important. If she makes you happy, you should go to her and convince her to let you in." Was he trying to say goodbye to me already?

I traced his cheekbone, the edge of his beard prickly. "My happiness is here," I told him, believing it but also dreading it in the same breath.

He drew my questing fingers into his mouth and I shuddered as my body remembered other sensations delivered by that warm wet spot. "You want a family and you deserve to be complete. I'm not certain Merla is the right woman considering she's full fey but you need someone."

"I don't want to think about it, Arthur," I said. "We have a king to kill, that's what's important." I realised sleep beckoned making me giddy. I yawned.

"Come on, you should eat before you pass out." Arthur rose and hauled me upright, we washed in a small basin. He helped me dress because my fingers stopped working and dragged me downstairs. Our small group of friends all watched as we reappeared.

Else and Geraint's expressions remained neutral. Tancred watched me with a hunger that caught me unaware. I blushed under his hot gaze and realised we were brewing something I didn't know how to handle. Merla smiled. As the one everyone thought I'd bedded, she had the ability to make this a good or bad evening.

She rose, walked to me and kissed my cheek. "Good evening and it's nice to see you so happy."

I was happy but I knew it was ephemeral. Even as he sat, Arthur spoke to Geraint about sending a letter to Guinevere, begging for her forgiveness.

Merla followed my gaze, "He loves you, never doubt that."

"I don't," I said roughly, feeling him slip from my grasp.

"You are his greatest weapon, Lancelot. Not some sword fashioned for him. I just hope he understands the difference between a living weapon and a piece of cold heartless steel." She sighed so heavily I wondered if she would deflate.

Too confused and far too tired to figure out all the words, I just sat beside Arthur and felt his hand sit on my thigh, possessing me. Food arrived, a stew with some indefinable meat and rough bread, but after another pint of ale, I didn't care very much. The voices of my companions washed over me as we ate and I felt the heat from Arthur's thigh become a calming sensation. My eyes began to close and I drifted on the murmuring and laughter.

"Hey, sleepyhead." Arthur's hand rubbed my leg and I jerked awake. "Time for you to sleep." His blue eyes shone with tenderness as I focused on his face. I smiled, deeply content for the moment.

"I need to organise the watch, Sire," I mumbled.

His smile widened. "I think Geraint and I can take care of that, Wolf." He peered over my shoulder, "Merla, can you take him to the room? Geraint and Else can have the other room, we can bunk in together."

I tried to protest but found myself being bullied into the bedroom. The fire lay dead, so Merla lit some small candles from our packs and ordered me to strip. She brushed against me and I grabbed her, pulling her toward me before soundly kissing her cheek. "Thank you," I said.

She didn't pull away, but cocked her head to one side. "What for?"

"For being a beautiful woman," I told her my head full of sleep.

She smiled, her expression indulgent.

I tried to speak but no word formed, I descended into my hard won and peaceful sleep.

I woke sometime later. Tancred shook Arthur awake for his turn at the watch. I tried to protest but Arthur, sleeping in his clothes, pushed me back under several blankets and rose. I plunged back into sleep. I next woke when he returned, cold and shivering. He stripped off his outside clothing and I pulled him against my body. I curled around him, his rough shirt and hose annoying. I soon vanished back into darkness.

CHAPTER TWENTY-SEVEN

THE SOFT VOICES WOKE me. I'd ended up on my back with Arthur half laying over my chest. I wouldn't be able to move unless I woke him. He often slept as though trying to pin me to the mattress.

Merla's voice sounded full of concern, so I concentrated. "Brother, you really should tell him."

"How can I, look at them," Tancred's voice hit a nerve with his misery.

"He needs you, brother," she said coaxingly.

"He needs the King. He will never see me."

I heard Merla sigh. "He won't if you don't tell him."

This was not a conversation I should be hearing. What the hell did Merla mean, brother? The rest, well, I managed to join the dots.

"Gods, Merla, I don't know. Look at them, they are at peace in each other arms. He deserves this peace," Tancred said.

"How long do you think that peace will last now the Queen is with child? And what about you? You've been pining after him for years," Merla said, not hiding her irritation. "You went to Camelot to help them and now..." her voice trailed off.

"Now, he looks at you with lust and the King with love. He doesn't even know I exist," Tancred said. "You've flashed your big green eyes and stolen him."

Merla chuckled, "Jealous, brother?"

"You know I am," Tancred said. "I just don't understand how he can give so much to Arthur. I know he needs to be the King and I believe in our mission, but Arthur's been responsible for so much of Lancelot's pain. I held him when he was dying, I watched when they flogged the skin off his back and I could, I can, do nothing. Do you know what it was like to watch him suffer under the whip?" His anguish touched my heart.

"Yes, brother, I know," she said, all compassion now. "I remember your nightmares."

I couldn't listen to any more of this but I needed to wake without disturbing them, or frightening Tancred. I rubbed Arthur's back and he moved, waking, snuggling into my neck. The part of the conversation which disturbed me most was not Tancred's obvious emotional pain but the fact we had never known his full heritage.

Arthur woke and Merla rose as though he'd disturbed her, he kissed me briefly before leaving the bed. I rolled onto my side and watched Tancred untangle himself from his blankets, his face a mask of control. I didn't know what to say, how to feel about his deceit. We all met in the taproom for bread and cheese. When Tancred left to see to the horses, I followed. He first went to Willow, who stood next to Ash in the barn. I picked up a brush to rub off the mud, which had dried overnight on everything.

"Did you sleep well?" I asked.

Tancred's eyes were shadowed. "Yes, well enough considering. We have a long way to travel today."

I nodded. "Can I ask you something?"

I moved around Ash. Tancred knelt at Willow's front hooves trying to untangle his fetlocks.

"Of course, my Lord," he said without turning. I looked at his back and anger fuelled my movements. He'd lied to me, to Arthur, another fey full of tricks and deception. I'd trusted him with my life, with Arthur's life and Guinevere's, but I'd never known to whom I'd given that trust. He'd been following someone else's agenda for years.

"Stand up," I snapped. I'd planned on grabbing him before he knew what hit him but I wanted to see his eyes. I wanted him to not have lied.

Tancred heard the tone in my voice and looked over his shoulder at me, his brown eyes far richer than Else's. He rose slowly and realised he'd trapped himself against Willow's shoulder.

"My Lord?" he asked.

"Why have you lied to me?" I asked, my voice hard. He glanced at my fists, they were bunched tight.

His winter pale skin grew paler. "I would never willingly lie to you, my Lord."

"So the lies are unwilling?" I snapped.

He opened his mouth and his anguish washed off him in waves just as my anger beat at him in torrents. "I have never lied to you in a way which would hurt you, my Lord."

My control snapped. I grabbed his shirt in both fists, twisted him away from the horses who jumped at the violent movement and pushed him to the back of the barn. Ash stamped and pulled against his halter. I hauled Tancred up the wall.

"What are you?" I growled.

He did not resist or fight me. He did not cry out. He said, "I am your man in all things, my Lord."

"You fucking bastard," I bellowed. "You lying shit. You are just as bad as all the other fucking fey. Just as bad as Eleanor fucking de Clare or your fucking sister." I realised I'd lost control. All the disappointment and hurt of the last few weeks spilled out, like a lever had been pulled and I'd opened the entrance to a hole for the darkness to flow out. A festering wound I'd not understood until now.

Tancred grabbed my hands as I slammed him into the wall over and over. "I gave you my trust. I gave you my King and you are not the man I thought, you have fucking lied to me."

"I know, Lancelot, I'm sorry, please. I am your vassal, you are my Lord, I swear allegiance only to you," he choked out while I tried to throttle him.

"Tancred, no," Merla cried out.

"And you," I barked, still pinning Tancred with one hand while pointing at Merla. "You bitch, you scheming bitch. You had spies in Arthur's Court for years and you've done nothing to protect him from the poisoning and twisted politics. You didn't help Guinevere against de Clare and you didn't warn us about Avalon." The others poured into the barn and froze. Else stepped toward me but Geraint pulled her back. I laughed bitterly. "Do you know what you've bought there, my friend? You have yet another fairy bitch who will lie to you thinking they are doing it for your own good, or for a higher purpose. They all fucking lie." I pulled my fist back to finish Tancred. He merely closed his eyes.

"No, Lancelot," Arthur's voice boomed over mine. "Stop."

"They are manipulating us again, Sire," I cried as he began robbing me of my target.

"Let him go, du Lac," he snapped. The warrior warred with the soldier. The warrior fought on regardless, the soldier followed orders. The soldier won. I released Tancred. He dropped to one knee and held his hands out in supplication, as any squire would to his lord or a knight to his king.

"I beg you, my Lord, forgive me. I swear allegiance only to you. I always have and always will. Your path is my own," he said.

"Gods, Tancred." Merla approached but took one look at me and remained far out of reach. "Please, brother, I never meant you to do this. We don't need you to finish this, please. I can make them understand."

I frowned and looked down at Tancred. He raised his eyes, they were the deepest, richest most perfect brown I'd ever seen. "I will give my life in service to you, my Lord, Lancelot du Lac," he whispered. "I swear my allegiance only to you."

Those brown eyes hypnotised me with their intensity. They became the centre of my world. I gazed into them and saw everything. The Wolf inside me drove me into that deep warm brown and I witnessed Tancred's soul surrender. His own animal – another wolf – lay down, throat exposed. I witnessed a hard life and his need to be accepted by his alpha whom he'd chosen willingly. My Wolf, dark and black, bent his head and held the throat of the slightly smaller brown male. He whimpered as I bit hard, tasting blood.

"Lancelot, stop, please," I heard Arthur from a long way.

I saw in my head the White Hart bow his head before me and touch the Brown Wolf with his nose. His hot sweet breath calmed my desire to taste more blood. The surrender, the supplication of this wolf to mine, meant pack, meant family, meant an easier hunt.

I backed down. I released my pack mate and he rolled onto shaking legs before licking my muzzle.

Air rushed into my lungs. Tancred still knelt before me, his hands out. I took them in my own, as Arthur had done with me. "I will accept," I said simply.

Tancred smiled, his eyes closed and he collapsed.

I dropped to my knees beside him. "Tancred?" I tried to rouse him. Merla knelt beside me. Blood stained the straw. I lifted him, there were deep teeth marks in his neck, the blood flowing.

"What have you done?" Merla wailed.

Else appeared, a cloth in her hand. "Hold this to his neck." She thrust the cloth at Merla. "The rest of you leave us," she snapped.

"What?" I asked.

"You've made your point, Lancelot, now fuck off, all three of you. Leave us," Else said, as she pulled Tancred from my arms. I rose, with Arthur dragging my shoulder. We left the barn, just as Else said, "Why didn't you tell me you were using us both and what he is?"

"You are not full fey," Merla replied.

"I am Merlin's daughter," Else argued. We beat a retreat.

"What the hell just happened?" Geraint asked. He looked shaken – good, welcome to my world.

"Tancred is Merla's brother. He is full fey." I felt numb. I just wanted to wrap Arthur around me and stay in his arms forever.

"I guessed that," Geraint said, he surprised me with the softness of his tone. "I meant, what just happened to you?"

I looked at him. "I don't know, I didn't mean to do anything. I just wanted to stop the lies. I wanted to stop worrying about Arthur being hurt by his friends. I trusted Tancred with the things most precious to me and he lied."

"You mean Else lied," Geraint said. His hazel green eyes were sad.

"Yes," I said. "I am angry with her and I am hurt but Tancred is given a level of trust no other can claim."

"He has never threatened me," Arthur said. "He is fiercely loyal. He stood beside me even when I my world began to dissolve around me. He saved your life and he fights like you, he is a brave man."

"It's not as simple as that," I said and I explained the conversation I'd overheard. Arthur sat, Geraint cursed. "They planted him in your court, Arthur. We've been used."

"He loves you?" Arthur asked again.

"Focus, your Majesty," I said. "He is a plant from the fey."

Arthur waved his hand, "I have enemies around me all the time. Tancred is and never has been a threat. In fact, if he hadn't been there things may have been worse. I have no argument with him other than the fact that he chose to keep this a secret. He is a loyal man who is your friend. All friends need forgiving sometimes, Lancelot."

The reference was not lost on me. Geraint spoke into the silence, "What happened to his neck?"

Arthur and I shared a long look, I answered, "Tancred is wolf, or at least that is how I see him." I knocked my head with my finger to indicate where the Wolf lived. "He gave me his throat. I bit him and the marks are manifest. It happens sometimes."

"That's not all that happened," Arthur said. "His love for you has done something more." I frowned, not understanding, he continued, "It's something I can use, Merlin taught me. I chose not to because it can be dangerous, but you have come close to stepping over the line, my friend." He took my hand.

"Lancelot, he's given himself to you. It's a fey thing. His life is yours. Literally. The concept of vassal and lord is taken to the extreme. You can order him to die and he will. I don't mean by throwing himself on a sword. He will quite literally shatter his heart for you."

I sat dumbfounded. "He's done what?"

"You are his Lord, his reason to live, his existence depends on you. It's a form of union. It keeps men loyal, which is why Merlin wanted me to use it," Arthur said. "And he loves you, desires you. The poor bastard must be a wreck. Love is hard on fey, even half breeds." Meaning me, Else and to an extent himself and Guinevere.

"Eleanor says the stronger the bloodline of the fey the harder it is to deal with powerful emotions," Geraint said.

Arthur half smiled. "That explains a lot about you," he said looking at me.

I grunted. Merla called, "I need you, Wolf."

Arthur looked up at me, "You need to be kind to him. If you are angry it will hurt him."

"I can never be angry with him again?" I asked incredulous.

"The ties you share are new and he is vulnerable," Arthur told me as a final piece of advice.

I walked toward the barn, my mind racing with this new layer of insanity. The interior seemed dimmer than before and I found Tancred sat on a pile of hay in the darkest corner.

Else rose from his side when I appeared, as she passed me she said, "Go gentle."

He looked terrible. His eyes were red and he had a handprint on his cheek, also wraps around his neck. I sat next to him but didn't speak for a while.

Finally, I said, "Merla hit you?"

He nodded. "She thinks I've made a terrible mistake. She thinks I've allowed my lust to cloud my common sense."

"She might be right," I said. He'd confessed his desire for the first time. My heart raced but I didn't react. I dare not, I didn't want to scare him again.

"I don't think so," he said in a sulky tone.

"I take it this wasn't part of the plan? Her plan," I qualified.

"No, I've tied my fate to yours, a dangerous thing for a fey. But you are the one. I know it. You will bring down Aeddan. You will stop this madness among our kind and you will take your rightful place among us one day." Tancred's hands were knotted together.

I grabbed those hands. "Tancred, I am Arthur's man, you do know that right?"

He nodded, too fast, too often. "I know. You are the King's vassal. I am yours though and you could be a king among us."

"I don't want that. I am Arthur's, always will be." I felt the tension in his hands. The death grip he had on himself. I moved so I could look in his face. A flash of light drove through the dusty air and I saw for a moment, the face of the wolf in Tancred's eyes. My wolf. My pack mate. I touched his face, "But I would be honoured if you remained at my side."

His eyes, haunted and fearful a moment before, gushed with hope. "You won't send me away?"

"No, Tancred. You belong with me but I belong with Arthur. At least for now," I said trying to let him know what I needed from my life.

He lowered his eyelids, so I couldn't see his pain, but I heard it, "I understand."

His pain became my pain in the abstract sense. I pulled him toward me. I wrapped my arms around him and held him close. He trembled and I think he wept but he remained quiet. He pulled back and something new stirred within me as I looked into his now quiet eyes. I kissed those soft lips, just briefly.

"Don't let me hurt you," I told him softly as I spoke close to his mouth.

"I love you, my Lord, you will never hurt me unless you send me away." His breath warmed my lips. I realised I had exactly what I wanted, a partner for life, I just had to let it happen. The thought scared me and I backed off, hauling Tancred to his feet.

"We are behind schedule, Sergeant. Time to get us moving," I told him.

"As you wish, my Lord." He bowed and walked to the horses.

CHAPTER TWENTY-EIGHT

TANCRED SAT ON ECHO, pale but calm. I rode beside him. I glanced at him constantly, my need to protect him growing by the league. Arthur rode behind me, talking in low tones with Merla. Else and Geraint rode behind them in silence. I think Geraint now appreciated how complicated his life could become with Else as a wife. The fey are a difficult breed to love for a long time.

"Why didn't you tell me?" I asked my companion.

Tancred sighed. "I wanted to, as soon as I arrived in Camelot but you were in trouble and I couldn't reach you." Understatement of a lifetime. "Those of us who want to stop Aeddan and Nimue from using you and killing Arthur, made me promise to wait until they gave me the order to speak with you. Then you were sent away." He kept his eyes on the road ahead. "I thought I would die when I knew you'd been banished. It was bad enough watching..." he stopped and shrugged.

"Don't think about it," I told him. I'd had enough in the past of dealing with Arthur's grief and pity over my punishment. I didn't need it from Tancred as well.

"Hmm, as you say, that's done now. I just had to stay in Camelot and hope the King would relent. Alone, I couldn't help the King. I couldn't stop him or his enemies. Who'd believe the youngest of the city guard? If I'd confessed to being fey, I might have been killed and my task was to contact only you. Then you returned with Else to fight for your place in Court." The passion in his voice made me smile. "I knew from that moment my life would change. I waited and waited, until the day you walked into the barracks and suddenly I was there, at your side, fighting for you, with you."

"You fight for Arthur. Don't ever forget that," I said.

"As you wish." He did look at me then and things stirred inside me, deep inside. I squashed it flat. Life didn't need to be even more complicated. I also killed off any feelings for Merla. I did not want her to use me against Arthur. I'd rather die a lonely old man than threaten my King with an ill advised love affair. I paused my thoughts and corrected them, *another ill advised love affair.*

The land continued to rise all day, gradually changing from woodlands and small villages, to barren heathland. Each time we crested a rise more long rolling chalk hills with small valleys undulated for miles around us. There were few trees and the wind ripped against our skin almost as though our layers of wool were nothing but parchment. The grass waved in frantic warning about the cruelty of that wind but we rode into it nonetheless. All the horses slowed in protest and Ash's temper worsened by the step.

"We can't stay out in this all night," Arthur said. It didn't matter what he thought, we would be spending another night out in the cold before finding this sword.

The racing clouds formed a thick blanket smothering the sky and I prayed the promise of rain wouldn't be kept. It made the day darker and the afternoon hurried toward night, also sick of the wind.

We rode down, into another narrow valley and saw a small collection of huts. Tancred rode ahead to find out if they were occupied. I watched him go and found Arthur at my side.

"How are you feeling?" he asked.

"Honestly?" I said, "I have no idea. Else was the closest I've ever come to having a squire and now I have someone who will die if I order it. And he loves me," I sounded exasperated even to my own ears.

Arthur chuckled. "He certainly does."

"It's not funny, Arthur. I have no wish to hurt him and yet that's all I'm going to do if I keep him with me."

He sobered, "No, I'm sorry."

"It's hard enough preferring a man's company over a woman's, but when the object of your desire loves someone else, it's horrible." I knew exactly how that felt.

Arthur grasped my hand where it rested on my thigh. "If he makes you happy, Lancelot, I have no right to stand between you."

I looked at him in shock, my mouth hung open and my heart raced. "What?" I asked confused. I knew the end raced towards me but it didn't stop the hurt. Was he throwing me over for good already? Did he regret the previous evening? I thought we'd have a little more time now we'd made love alone for the first time in months.

"Lancelot, I can't stand between you and peace. If it's Merla you want, or Tancred, I have no choice but to accept it. Guinevere blames me for your pain over Else. She tells me I am selfish and cruel. She says you would be married and happy if I had controlled my desire for you." Arthur didn't look at me as he spoke and I knew he repeated words he should say, not words he felt were right.

I pulled Ash up and Willow stopped, Arthur turned toward me.

"Arthur, thank you for the thought, but..." I paused making certain I understood the consequences of my words. "There will only ever be room for you, especially now I've lost Eleanor de Clare. It would be a lie to force another person into my life."

"But I cannot give you the companionship you need. I don't think I can be a lover, a king, a husband and a father."

"You don't have to, Arthur, just be my friend and make certain you pay me enough for regular visits to the lovely ladies of Camelot," I said trying for a joke.

He frowned, refusing to see it, "Lancelot, please, if he can make you happy, make it happen. I cannot bear the responsibility of denying you peace. You need to be the centre of someone's world and you cannot be the centre of mine." He rode away.

"Fuck," I said into the biting wind.

Merla appeared and stared after Arthur. "That's unfortunate," she said.

"Can I keep nothing to myself?" I snapped.

"I need to keep an eye on you both. I was hoping he would lay his private life to one side while we dealt with this problem," Merla said distractedly. "My damned brother is going to ruin everything."

"It's not Tancred's fault," I said my anger with her growing.

"You and Arthur would be perfectly happy if the King did not feel threatened," Merla said, her voice as cold as the wind.

"Arthur and I can never be anything, he is King, I am his vassal," I snapped. "And we are not to be used and manipulated by the likes of you, fey witch." I suppose my temper tantrum had an inevitability about it but I didn't feel justified as I kicked Ash. He lurched forward into a disorganised gallop. We slid more than rode down the hill toward the huts. I felt dirty, confused and hurt.

I happened to hit the huts at the same moment Tancred began to investigate whether they were safe for us to use. He carefully approached the first shepherd's hut. Angry and seeking a fight, I jumped off Ash walked to the door and simply kicked it in. The wood bounced and the noise reverberated, only to be ripped away by the wind. Tancred jumped back and pulled his sword. I don't know if he feared me or the darkness more. The hut's darkness was profound but I'd been cautious enough over the last few days. I walked in, nothing attacked. I felt cheated.

"Nothing here but the stink of sheep," I announced as I walked out. These huts should be full of birthing ewes and the bleat of lambs. With spring so close they would be coming and this was the perfect venue.

Arthur and Merla arrived, she looked around. "The shepherds have no wish to be so close to places of power, not this spring. They will be herding their sheep elsewhere."

Her ability to take thoughts from my head and answer questions enraged me. "I swear to, God, I am going to rip you to shreds if you open your fucking mouth one more time," I said.

My companions stared at me, Arthur spoke into the shocked void, "Lancelot, I think that's unnecessary. Please, apologise."

I wanted to scream at him, to pull him from his horse and explain how much he'd just torn out of my soul. He used such simple words but they carved into me more than any sword, knife or arrow which had ever struck my body. I turned and walked away. I heard him call, the wind pulling the words away from me as it blasted hard into my face. I strode to the small stream in the bottom of the valley and jumped it, scrambling up the opposite hill. I knew I couldn't go far from at least half the group but damn I needed some space.

I crested the hill and stopped. The last of the dying light shot red through the racing clouds. I turned toward the sunset and watched the great blood bathed orb hover on the horizon, the only time we'd seen the sun all day. It mocked its own death with the splendid display of colour, defiant despite its decline for another night.

Ever since I'd woken from my injures at the Abbey I'd been suffering from such bewilderment and anxiety. A strange emotional vacuum kept rolling through me. Confusion and chaos its sisters filling me with dread. I needed to be rescued, nurtured, anchored in the world through desire, love, friendship, anything which held the vacuum at bay. The death I'd wrought…

Else, Guinevere, Arthur, Merla, they were all objects of my desperate floundering. Yet, they all rejected me for one reason or another and who could blame them?

I heard a noise behind me, someone's panting breath. In those arms perhaps I had a chance. A man who offered me sanctuary and peace from the tumult in my heart. Did I have the courage? I sighed.

"My Lord?" Tancred said. "I am sorry, but my sister tells me you cannot be left without fey magic to guard your mind." He knew to be cautious of my anger. I closed my eyes and tried not to think about the soft warmth of his brown eyes. He did not move, did not touch me, but I felt his presence burn into my skin.

"I wish I had magic to guard my own soul," I said as I felt the sun slip, dying into the night. I opened my eyes. The last gasp of red clawed at the clouds before following its maker into the yawning darkness.

"You should come back before it grows too dark," Tancred said. "There will be no moon."

I wanted to howl into the suffocating clouds. I wanted to rage at the sky. I wanted to scream at the stars. That rage engulfed my mind and I drowned inside it, gasping for air. The grief of days ago manifested once more. I killed and destroyed life, in return I needed someone to love me for the monster I'd become. Instead, I suffered rejection after rejection, forcing me into isolation. The ghosts of the dead the only companions I deserved.

"When will it stop hurting?" I cried brokenly. The sea-sawing emotions were making me sick in mind and body.

Tancred, more shadow than man, said, "It will hurt until you find peace, Lancelot. Your fey blood is so strong and your grief so real. I am sorry, my Lord."

I stepped toward him, my gloved hand reaching for his neck. All thoughts of maintaining his physical and emotional safety vanished. I held his throat and he remained passive in my grasp. "I have no idea what this means," I growled.

"I don't care," Tancred gasped around my hand.

I kissed him. Hard. Biting, forcing myself into his mouth. Tancred groaned and clutched at me. His lips were softer than Arthur's. His stubble hardly growing from one week to the next, his skin too young and too fey. I really didn't want to think about the consequences of this act, so I didn't stop. I wrenched myself away from his mouth and wrapped my shield arm around his hips, pulling him close to my hard body. He grunted and I released his neck only to tangle my fingers into his hair. I pulled his head to one side and bit his jaw, his neck, forcing the cloth tied around the wounds down. His hips pushed against mine forcing us off balance. It tore me away from his throat.

I looked into his face. His dark eyes were wide, scared and desperate all at once. I knew he wanted more but dare not ask. I tried to think about what I needed, not what I wanted. I tried to think about Arthur. This would hurt him, this would hurt Tancred. He felt the shift inside me and fought with his desire. He closed down. I watched the light in his eyes hide behind the mask he wore all day, every day. His hands slipped from my clothing, his body moved away from mine and the wind tore between us, jealous of our closeness. I released his hair and he turned away.

"They have a fire burning," he said, thick from emotions I had caused. "There will be food soon. I shall wait for you further down the hill that should be safe enough."

"No, stop," I said. "I'm sorry. I don't want to hurt you."

"But you belong to the King," he finished my litany.

"Yes," I said.

"Then we should get to back to him," Tancred said.

I heard the terrible sadness and felt shamed. We half walked, half slid down the hill. The evening, when I joined the others after checking Ash, remained quiet and strained. I excused myself early and lay my bedroll in the darkest corner. I rolled onto the shoulder furthest from the fire and tried to sleep.

It took hours to come. We all shared the same hut and I heard Arthur place his bed roll near enough to me to touch but he didn't lay a hand on shoulder or hip. I wanted to weep but couldn't give myself the luxury. Did he know how much he hurt me? When sleep came, so did the dreams.

I raced in the darkness, the world menacing, breathing evil and misery. I did not race alone. A Brown Wolf slightly smaller than myself, ran beside me. We were running through long grass over hills, racing against the crushing sensation of time. It felt good, reassuring, to have a pack mate matching me stride for stride in a way the Hart could not. I thought about the White Stag and suddenly his scent caught my nose. We both turned and raced to the place he waited. I slowed to a trot as his white coat blazed through the darkness and silence. He lowered his head to my muzzle and we shared our breath. The Brown Wolf lay in the grass and tucked his head down in supplication. I looked around us, we were on the edge of a lake. The stillness of the water felt threatening, brooding. I tried to see the opposite bank, the water stretched forever.

The Hart walked to the edge, his cloven hooves sinking into the mud. I followed, my paws only vanishing into the ooze a short distance. I didn't like the way it squished though the pads. It smelt bad. I watched as the mighty Stag lowered his head to the water, the crown of antlers bobbed in the inkiness. He drank a little, raised his head sharply as though he heard something I could not and continued to walk into the water. The ripples he caused the only movement around us in the dark. The Brown Wolf whined. I agreed, my feelings of fear and trepidation doubled with each step the Stag took.

I barked in distress. The Stag stopped, his great liquid eye looked into my heart and I knew I would not change his course. I began to walk into the cold water, feeling it cling to my fur and seeping toward my skin. A howl from behind me made me stop. The Brown Wolf, my pack mate, stood and paced the bank. His distress very real. He whimpered. I looked at the Stag, who continued on his own path in the darkness of the lake. I stood, my muzzle just above the waterline. I didn't know where to go, who to run with. My confusion made me whine and growl. I wanted the Hart to return. I wanted him to be safe. All I could now see were the rack of antlers and his white head as he swam away from me into the blackness. I barked, over and over, calling him back. He ignored me and I found myself swimming toward him without thinking.

I heard a short scream come from the Stag. His head jerked, the smooth swimming ceased. He vanished under the water, the tines gone in the cold and darkness. I stopped, paddling furiously and stared. The water behind me turned into foam as my companion ran and forced himself into the water as fast as he could. He pushed himself into me, forcing me back, away from the place the Stag vanished. The feeling of fear grew as something brushed my legs. I began to panic. We raced back to the shore, running out of the dark water and up the bank. Our ribs heaved. I stood, cold and wet. He'd gone, the White Hart had vanished into the lake. He suffocated in the water, that smooth calm lake from which oozed the fear causing my legs to shake. I whined. The other Wolf licked my muzzle. He wanted to leave, to run. How could I leave the Hart?

I woke, sweat dampening my clothes. "Arthur," I said as I sat, fully awake.

CHAPTER TWENTY-NINE

TANCRED STOOD OVER ME. "He's gone. The others say he and Merla left before dawn. We have to reach him, Lancelot."

I cursed almost solidly until I finished dressing. Fortunately, I'd slept in most of my clothes. Tancred only had time to put bridles on our horses. I jumped for Ash's back. He felt my urgency and didn't play games. The heat from Ash's flanks warmed my thighs.

"You know where they are?" I asked.

"I know where they might be," Tancred said.

"Good enough." We raced from the shepherd's hut, up and out of the small valley. The day had barely begun, the sky damp but the wind was gone, off to scream at others. The horses hit the crest of the hill and we turned northward, racing along the spine.

Echo did not have Ash's speed, so I fought with him to maintain stride with the smaller gelding. "Did you dream of the Wolf?" I asked as we pounded along.

"Of course, that's why I woke you. I have more control," Tancred admitted.

"What did it mean?" I asked.

He glanced at me. "It means Arthur is walking into a danger we don't fully understand. A danger he doesn't understand. The Hart walked into that water because he had faith."

"Is your sister going to hurt him?" I asked outright.

"I really bloody hope not," Tancred said. We focused on riding.

I glanced over my shoulder and watched Else and Geraint come up the hill behind us, both horses fully tacked. A good back up for whatever was to happen. We reached the long, open plain of Salisbury and raced into the dawn. I saw a lake, half a league away and pushed Ash on, leaving Echo behind. I grasped handfuls of his mane to help me remain on his back as we galloped. His pounding body raced over the ground, I felt as though we were one being.

I saw Arthur, my King, his bright golden head uncovered as he sat on his great black stallion.

"Ash, please, I need to reach Arthur," I whispered close to the horse's ear. I don't know how he did it, but bless him, Ash reached for more speed. We devoured the ground.

Arthur dismounted from Willow. I bellowed his name, but he couldn't hear me. He stepped to the bank of the great lake, Merla beside him, her arms outstretched. Willow turned his beautiful head, hearing us long before Arthur. He whinnied in welcome. My King walked, fully clothed and armoured, into the water. Ash raced past Willow, who jumped sideways into Merla's mare.

Arthur still did not turn. Merla shrieked at me as Ash and I hit the water and it cascaded around us. My horse tried to gallop for the King, but the water rose too fast, hampering his great strides. He screamed in frustration, but we were there. I reached for Arthur from the back of my horse just as he took his final step and sank below the waves. His weight pulled me sideways, Ash compensated and I felt Arthur's body bump against my leg as I lifted him by his cloak.

He came out of the water, gasping, fighting me.

"Stop, Arthur, please, God, don't fight me," I yelled as I pushed my seat backward on Ash's back and hauled Arthur over the stallion's withers.

Ash turned, almost unseating me once more and splashed for the shore. We reached the bank and my mighty warhorse stopped. He shook all over from the frantic gallop, the cold and the shock. Arthur spluttered and choked. I stared at Merla, her eyes were white, her hair wild. She pointed at me and promptly collapsed. Tancred arrived but he left his sister on the shoreline and came to me, taking Arthur.

"Are you alright?" he asked.

I nodded, trembling from the shock of events. Geraint and Else galloped toward us and I slid from Ash's back. His flanks heaved, his nostrils flared and his eyes were wild. I lay a hand on his great neck and he turned his head, his ears went back and he gnashed his teeth as though telling me – never again. I smiled at him and walked him further from the water as Tancred carried Arthur's inert body. I saw Arthur's chest rise and fall but his eyes were closed.

Tancred lay Arthur's body down and cradled his head on his lap. I knelt beside him. "What happened?" I asked

"That's what I want to know," Geraint said as he arrived, pulling Pepper up and skidding to a halt in the mud. Else took Mercury straight to Merla's inert body.

My companion looked up at Geraint. "I don't really know, my Lord. I just woke from a nightmare and I knew Arthur would be in trouble."

"Didn't you see him leave?" I asked Geraint.

He shook his head. "I saw him riding Willow up the hill with Merla but I didn't see him wake up."

I stroked Arthur's face and called his name. Else asked Geraint for help moving Merla, she remained unconscious, just as well or I'd have ripped her head off.

Arthur's eyes moved under the lids and his breathing changed. His hand grasped mine and he woke, panic vivid in his gaze. I held him as he reared out of Tancred's arms and wrapped himself around me.

"You're safe, Arthur, I have you," I told him.

"The sword," he managed. "I had to seek the sword."

"Can you tell me what happened?" I asked as I pulled back to look into his face. He lips were pale, his eyes surrounded by grey circles.

"I remember dreaming about the sword, then I woke as water rushed into my lungs and you hauled me out of the lake." His fear made me hold him close to my chest.

"You are safe now," I whispered.

"Why would she do this to me?" Arthur asked. "I thought she wanted me alive."

Tancred rose and walked to his sister, she stirred at his touch and soft voice. Whatever he said drained the last of the colour from her face. She stared at me and grabbed at her brother, as though to force him between us.

I helped Arthur stand and we made our shaky way to Merla. "Well?" the King demanded.

Her eyes were now green once more but I'd never seen them filled with such fear. "Aeddan wants the sword. I don't know how he's done it but he subverted my power. He brought us here."

"And we're supposed to believe you?" Geraint asked. His distain mirrored in Arthur.

"Give her a moment, Fitzwilliam," I said. "We've all seen how powerful this fey king is and we need to hear her out." I knelt beside her and pushed her thick hair back over her shoulder. "Tell us what happened, Merla." My temper toward her was calm now I witnessed her fear.

She reached for my hand and clutched it hard. "He took me while I slept. I guard my dreams, always have since I left the land of the fey, but he found a way through. I'm tired I suppose because I've been protecting your minds and not just my own. I woke and I knew I didn't have control, I tried to force him out but he caged me inside my own head." Tears fell into the wool of her cloak. Her voice wobbled and bobbed as she continued to speak, "I haven't felt that weak against him since we were lovers and he stole my power."

"Don't, sister," Tancred said. "Don't think about that." I glanced at him and realised whatever Aeddan did to Merla we didn't need to know.

"Tancred's right," I told her gently. "It doesn't do to dwell on past weakness."

She smiled. "You should know, Wolf." But she nodded. "He woke Arthur's body but not his mind. What he doesn't know is how Arthur's dreams are hooked into yours." She looked at me. "He also doesn't know about Tancred's ties to you. So, as Arthur dreamed of his fear, so did you, thank goodness. We rode here, Aeddan stole the spell I needed for the sword but it is a little more complex than he considered possible. Fey are a paranoid lot and I never trusted I could keep him out of my mind completely. When he couldn't make me raise the sword, he sent Arthur in after it, either way he rids himself of his human enemy."

I stared at her. "We are that vulnerable?"

"I am so sorry, Lancelot. I didn't want to endanger Arthur, I just want Aeddan stopped before he sends armies against Camelot and England is bathed in the blood of fey and man alike." She began to weep in earnest and Else took over her care.

"It changes nothing, I still need that sword to kill the bastard," Arthur said. "And frankly I'm sick of being his victim. I want the upper hand for change."

"Do you seriously think we will ever gain the upper hand over a being this powerful?" Geraint asked.

"I think we need to find his power and destroy it," Tancred said.

"You don't get a vote," Geraint snapped, "you are as bad as she is and I'm not inclined to trust you."

"I'd rather trust him than you," I muttered.

Geraint stepped toward me. "This is because of you, du Lac, so don't push your luck. Arthur is in danger because they want you on the throne."

"Fuck you," I told him.

"Stop it," Arthur snapped. "Tancred's right, maybe we attack obliquely." He rubbed his forehead. "Merla, what can give Aeddan this power?"

She stood with Else's help. "I don't know what can give him this much power in this world." She looked miserable. "In our own world he'd be hard pressed to usurp my power in a place I'd made my own, in this world it should be impossible. That's why the sword is here."

Arthur looked out over the water. Fingers from the rising sun began tearing holes in the clouds, reaching down into the lake, making the surface shine. "We need that sword," he muttered.

"Not at any cost," I pointed out as I stood next to him. "We can win these wars, Arthur, without fey magic."

"You don't believe that." He glanced at me. "You know we need that sword to stop bloodshed, or do you want all that blood on your hands?"

My breath hissed over my teeth and I thought about how damn loud the voices of the dead can be when you force more men into their ranks. I bowed my head though, accepting his wisdom.

"With you all here," Merla said, "I should be able to call the sword without danger to Arthur." With her face grey and drawn, I did wonder if she had the strength to manage such a feat. I approached her and swept her hair back from her shoulders. I held her jaw and stared into her deep green eyes. She was beautiful.

"Does he really have to have this sword? Will it really help defeat Aeddan? Can I not do this for Arthur?" I asked her.

She held my hands. "I am sorry, Wolf. Some destinies cannot be changed."

I nodded, she spoke the truth. I kissed her brow and stepped back from her side.

Merla approached the water. Arthur now stood beside her. We fanned out behind them and watched in silence as she began to speak in a foreign tongue. The words formed a perfect lyrical dance of sound, weaving into and out of each other, raising the hairs on our arms. Geraint's arm slid around Else's shoulders but I recognised the look in her eyes, the magic called to her. Tancred's eyes were unfocused and his breathing came in short gasps. I reached for his hand. I touched him and he flinched, gripping my hand as though I anchored his world. I feared for Arthur the one at the nexus of this power.

The water began to move. It wriggled and rippled, something in the centre of the lake disturbed the surface. No wind appeared to form the wavelets now soaking Arthur's boots once more. I wished he'd stepped back from that water. Merla's arms rose over her head and her hair moved in the same power which disturbed the lake. Her voice cried out. Arthur called out in the same language. I missed the first sign, but Geraint's gasp made me look over the water. From the centre of the disturbance, we watched a blade slide from the depths of the water. The sun kissed the sword and flashed bright white. I blinked, unable to focus for a moment, when my vision cleared I saw a woman rising with the weapon.

"My God," Geraint whispered.

She held the sword over her head until she rose to the surface of the water. Naked, small like Else and perfect, clothed only in hair the colour of the night she eventually lowered the sword. The woman held the sword out, flat across both hands as she walked toward us. When she drew closer I realised her eyes were as black as her hair. I didn't want her reaching Arthur with a sword in her hands but I couldn't move. I watched her draw close enough to strike his head from his shoulders and I sweated as I strained against the spell wanting to reach his side. Arthur simply dropped to his knees before her and bowed his head for a moment. When he raised his head, he raised his hands. The woman, her skin almost translucent in the sunlight, placed the sword on his open palms. She glanced at Merla and bowed low, before her eyes hit mine.

Her gaze sliced through me and I felt the weight of her power crush my mind. She bowed her head slightly before breaking the mind shattering lock she maintained. I gasped, my lungs filling with air which I'd been denied for long moments. She turned her back and returned to the centre of the lake before vanishing into the water.

Arthur rose from the lake's shore and turned toward us with the sword in his hand. I didn't hear it, but I felt the blade hum with power. He walked toward us with his eyes shining in the light caught on the blade. The light from the sword spread up his arms and over his shoulders. It caressed his hair and became a halo of gold. I dropped, my left knee squelching in the mud, my head bowed before my King. The others followed suit, including the women. The light grew and even with my head down I needed to close my eyes against the glare. I heard Arthur's breathing come in short breaths.

"Rise, all of you," he said. His voice held authority and power. The voice of my King. We all stood. The blade, the light having receded, still gave the impression of life. Ripples of frozen water kissed the metal. Runes carved into its heart gave the blade a name.

"Excalibur," Merla said with reverence. "Forged in the heart of Albion for the King of England. Our worlds are to remain separate but work in fellowship and this sword will ensure that balance is maintained."

CHAPTER THIRTY

THOSE WORDS SET US on a course. We were going to fight, kill and maim all those who stood against Arthur. I loved him but I feared the deaths of men, each one lying on our souls condemning us for our violence.

"This is the only path you can take," Tancred murmured as we broke our circle and moved to the horses. His words did not improve my mood.

"Please don't do that," I told him. "It reminds me of your sister and how bloody alien you are."

"Sorry, you just don't talk enough and I'm trying to look after your body and your mind."

"You worry about yourself," I said, grumpy with him and everyone else. I watched Arthur mount Willow, his pride at his new toy obvious. Ash's legs still trembled. I couldn't ride him without ruining him for good. I looked at Tancred and guilt nipped my heals. "I'm sorry," I said.

He smiled. "You really are a bad tempered bastard."

I took hold of Ash's bridle and walked away from the lake. Tancred walked next to me, Echo also suffering under the hard ride but not as badly as Ash.

I looked at Tancred's dark hair, his pale skin, his handsome oval face as he fussed with Echo's nose. My chest constricted and I realised something utterly terrifying. I suddenly saw my future. If we survived this insanity, I wanted to spend time with Tancred, real time. I lay a hand on his neck. He looked at me startled.

"Thank you for helping me today," I said.

"You are my lord, it is my duty and," he looked away, "my passion."

"I am glad," I said.

He glanced up at me, trying to understand the context. I smiled and allowed my gloved hand to brush his jaw. His eyes lit with a joy that warmed my whole world. I laughed aloud and we bumped shoulders as we walked behind the others.

I didn't notice instantly, but Arthur led us away from the shepherds' huts. We headed into the great plain.

"Arthur, where are we going?" I asked, handing Tancred my reins and jogging to catch him up,

His face contained peace, smoothing his brow and calming his blue eyes. He looked like an angel. He smiled, a benediction, a gift for me. "We are going to face Aeddan and I will defeat him."

"We are going straight to the henge?" I asked. "Don't you think it would be a good idea to discuss a plan?"

"I have a plan," he said. "I have the sword, Excalibur." His hand fondled the pommel.

"Arthur, we will stop Aeddan, not the sword. The sword is a tool not the answer, we need to talk about how we are to use the sword." I looked up at him, dread filling my heart.

"You worry too much," he said. "Have some faith in your King."

I wanted to tear the sword from his hip and cast it back into the lake. This boded ill, if Merlin was correct, if this sword bonded with Arthur and took his common sense in the process, we were in deep trouble. Until I could think of something else to bring Arthur to his senses, I merely bowed my head. "As, your Majesty, wishes." I stood still and waited until Tancred caught me up.

"What the fuck is going on with this blade?" I asked, still watching Arthur.

"What are you talking about?"

"Don't give me that bollocks," I snapped. "What fey tricks are in that sword? They are turning Arthur into an idiot."

"Oh." His face twisted and he glanced at his sister's back. He sighed, "It will settle, the sword is kind of whispering in his head, making him feel indestructible. It sings of its joy at being with the King of England at last. I can hear it." He didn't look happy at the prospect.

"Arthur will make mistakes if he doesn't start using his head," I said frowning hard, trying not to become cross with Merla and Tancred for making this foolishness real.

"You have to hope the sword blends with him quickly but Arthur will be forever under its influence."

"What does that mean?" I asked.

"Nothing sinister. The sword will call to him, will take him into the fight, has become a living weapon much like Ash or Willow. He will make decisions because of the sword, in the same way you decide who to fight because of the direction Ash is facing."

I understood that, a sword becomes an extension of my body. It finds its own way as I fight, but essentially it is an inanimate object. Riding and fighting is like fighting with another being, independent of your thoughts but blended with them. There is a level of trust between us, I know Ash will find enemies I miss and he knows I will protect him as he takes me into battle. To have a semi sentient sword as well as a horse would make Arthur a fearsome warrior.

I grunted at the thought causing Tancred to say, "What is it?"

"I suppose I worry too much about Arthur. If this sword is able to help save his life then I should be grateful to Merla," I conceded.

We slumped into silence and walked behind the others. Ash's legs gradually stopped wobbling and he began nipping my fingers. He obviously felt better. The great plain stretched for miles around us. There were few trees to break up the vast stretches of grassland and the moody day changed the colours in the landscape. The sun dazzled and bejewelled the wet grass one moment, then clouds plunged the world into murky gloom the next, sucking the colour from the land. I could see for leagues and watched rain hit the ground over a day's ride away. The air smelt of cold rain but blew more softly, no longer torturing what trees there were and forcing them into twisted shapes. I wished we did not have to walk into another fight. Facing Aeddan did not raise my battle madness. It simply filled me with dread.

The grass soon made my legs soaking wet and cold. The leather and wool clung to my skin. Arthur had changed clothes and Else wiped his armour after his ducking but I was not so comfortable. Tancred laughed as I tried to wring out the bottom of my cloak.

"We could double up with Else and Merla," he said.

I considered either option far too complicated. Both women caused my loins to tighten and I needed to consider the implications of my desire for Tancred. I wanted to think with more than my balls for once. "I'd rather walk through snow drifts thanks, but feel free to ask."

"What is wrong with you?" Tancred asked. "You feel all twisted up." He made some vague corkscrew movement with his hand.

"I have a lot to think about," I mumbled. Then realised I'd have to come up with something to think about to which I willing admit. "Aeddan has proved to be both powerful, relentless and dangerous. He wants Arthur dead and yet

Merla thinks she can call him to heel for Arthur to dispatch. I don't think either of them are considering all the options. Such as, where is he getting so much power?" The frustration in my voice made me realise these things confused me as much as my ridiculous emotional life.

"Merla is strong at the henge, she has been a part of its history for a long time," Tancred admitted.

I peered at him. "How old are you?" I asked.

He half smiled. "Don't worry, although we are siblings things are different in Albion. We share the same parents but I really am as old as I seem. Merla stole me and brought me into the world of men when I was barely more than a child. In this world I live a normal mortal lifespan because my magic is dormant, in Albion as full fey I'd live longer if I prove powerful enough. I am young and untested. I don't really know anything other than the life I have in Camelot. I don't know if I am as strong as Merla or just another normal fey, hardly any different to a plain mortal human."

"You could be as powerful as a goddess?" I asked shocked.

Tancred laughed. "Not really. It's different. I don't plan on being worshipped by mortals for centuries. Primarily Merla is a healer, which can also mean she ushers men's souls to the land of dead. Hence her connection to battlefields. She helps those who cannot be helped any other way. I hope that one day I might be able to heal, but few fey are born with that kind of power in these times. We've become too corrupt and grown too distant from our world."

"That's all very diverting," I said, trying hard to stay on track, "but that doesn't help me protect Arthur."

"With luck you won't have to and Merla will be able to contain Aeddan in the henge. It is a mighty place."

"Gives me the bloody creeps," I complained. I'd ridden past it several times over the years and always opted to travel on rather than stop and have a nose about. It struck me the place didn't invite casual visitors.

"You just feel its call," he said. "It hums like the sword, only louder and those who are fey feel the power."

"Oh, good," I said not hiding my unhappiness.

"Try not to worry about Arthur," Tancred said. "I'm certain we will have victory."

"But at what price, my friend?" I asked him. We slumped back into silence. At midday we stopped and ate. Else, somehow responsible for my horse, declared I could ride for the afternoon but we needed to stay at a walk. Arthur chaffed, he wanted to reach the henge long before nightfall. The longer we took the happier I'd be if I were honest. He felt so far away from me, whenever he spoke it took effort not to drop to one knee and say, *'Yes, Sire, whatever you wish.'* Not something our relationship had suffered from since my return to England.

Tancred and I changed into almost dry clothing and mounted the horses. I forced myself to ride next to Arthur. We had to plan the next move. He however, did not want to talk about Aeddan. He had a plan and everything would be fine. He wanted to talk about his future son. I listened to his parental twittering for most of the afternoon, my temper growing blacker and blacker. Around the time they would be calling the monks in for nones and the afternoon light threw new shadows over the rolling landscape, the mighty stone henge came into view.

The enormous, hewn stones towered over the landscape, but they were also dwarfed by the barren expanse. A strange optical illusion. There were no trees nearby, just scrubby bushes and mounds scattered around the place. The circle sat still. We sat still. It seemed as though the stones watched us with the same wariness we watched them.

"I really fucking hate this place," I muttered.

"Amen, brother," Geraint said. The first words we'd shared without argument all day. We shared a moment and I knew our friendship would survive his marriage if we were both careful. He smiled, grateful.

"We are staring at victory," Arthur announced.

"If you want my advice, Sire –" Geraint tried.

"If I wanted your advice, I'd request it, my Lord Fitzwilliam," Arthur interrupted. Again, Geraint and I shared a look. We both knew Arthur far too well, he was on a mission and we were not going to stand in the way of his charging ambition.

"Can you at least let us in on the plan?" I asked.

"We place some of your blood on the altar stone in the circle, Merla calls your blood to Aeddan's and he appears. We fight, I defeat him with Excalibur, we go home to Camelot and do not have to leave again to go to war," Arthur announced.

"My blood?" I asked, unhappy at the prospect.

"It won't be much," Merla said. I looked at her. Her eyes were bright and very green. I glanced at Else, her eyes were amber in the afternoon light and contained that same distance they had the first time we'd approached Avalon.

"Can we not leave this until tomorrow?" I asked.

"We have to do it before the moonrise tonight," Merla said. "The time is close for the best possible outcome."

I glanced at Tancred. His skin appeared waxy as though he fought the pull of the magic calling to the girls. I had to admit I didn't like the sickness I'd begun to feel. I wanted to turn Ash and run him into the ground in an attempt to escape this place.

Tancred tried to clarify Merla's words, "The moon is dark, it gives her power and saps it from Aeddan, there is a perfect aliment between the moon, the sun and other planets. In theory she can call more power to her hands on a night like this."

"In theory?"

"She hasn't done anything this big in a very long time," he said looking at Merla as though to remind her she lived the life of a mortal woman, not a goddess.

"It's the same as riding a horse," she said, dismissing him with a wave of her hand. "I cannot forget the song of my land and how to use it."

"This is too much for me," Geraint said. "I cannot take part in some mystical ceremony I don't understand." I heard his panic. He didn't understand this any more than I did, but his pure mortal blood must be screaming at him to run.

"Fine, then wait here," Else told her husband as she nudged Mercury forward along with Merla and Arthur.

Geraint looked to me for support. I almost laughed at the irony. "You are very much on your own with that problem. You married her, you learn to manage her and I wish you luck," I said feeling smug.

We rode the decline toward the massive stones. Ash began to react to my tension, thinking we headed toward an enemy. I wished I could explain we did, but he couldn't help me fight this one.

"Lancelot," Tancred said, interrupting my grim thoughts. "I need to tell you something."

"What?" I asked instantly suspicious and ready to race after Arthur to save his life.

His eyes, so perfectly brown I could find nothing in nature with which to draw a comparison, were filled with pain. "Whatever happens in that place." He nodded toward the henge and I realised Arthur and the others were among the stones. "Please, remember me with fondness and know I love you."

I stopped Ash. "What's wrong?" I asked. I found his honesty about how he felt exhilarating.

He rubbed his chest, over his heart. "Just tell me you will never forget me, my Lord."

"Tancred..." I'd seen him ride into battle beside me. He did not suffer from the vapours over a scrap. I lay a hand on his thigh. "You mean more to me that even I understand right now. I will never forget you, I promise you that and I promise we will talk more about this when we have time."

He nodded, almost pacified, but I could see his remaining unhappiness. It made my own double. We rode into the circle together, both disturbed.

CHAPTER THIRTY-ONE

THE GAP BETWEEN THE two stones we chose to ride through made certain we arrived as far from the altar stone as possible. The sun headed toward the horizon, mocking me and only visible through the great gate type structure behind the altar. The cold made me shiver.

"Come, Lancelot, I need you," Arthur said.

I dismounted from Ash, who vanished from inside the circle of stone. I almost followed him until Arthur called me. I walked to my King and dropped once more to my knee. "I am yours to command, Sire," I said. Somehow we'd become vassal and lord in my head. I suppose, because Arthur did not want to listen to me, the distance was inevitable.

His hand brushed my damp hair. "I know you don't approve, Lancelot, but this is the best path."

I looked up at him. Majesty clothed his shoulders. "It is not my place to question you, my King," I said, but I knew my eyes begged for a different response from him.

He smiled. "Are you changing on me suddenly, Wolf?"

"Perhaps, your Majesty." My heart ached with the familiar nickname.

His smile faded and his voice hardened, "Very well. Right now, I just need your left arm and a sharp knife. I also need the rest of you to take places by the stones."

I felt movement behind me but didn't react because Arthur's eyes remained passive.

Geraint spoke, "Arthur, please, don't do this. This feels wrong. I know I'm as thick as a plank when it comes to fey shenanigans, but you have trusted my judgement many times over the years. Please, don't use Lancelot like this, we have to find another way." The stress in my friend's voice chased shivers over my flesh.

"I have listened to you, my Lord," Arthur said, with deceptive mildness. "But you are wrong. There is one way to do this and my Wolf will help me."

"I was once your sword," I said very quietly. "Let me become that blade once more, rather than your Wolf. Give Excalibur back, Arthur. Release yourself from its power. Do this without magic. Rely on us, your real strength."

He ran his thumb over my bottom lip as he caressed my jaw. "Rise, Sir Lancelot du Lac and serve your King."

I did, inevitably. I would consent to this because Arthur is, was and always would be the centre of my universe but in that moment, I craved a freedom I knew I would never possess.

Merla approached, took my hand and led me to the altar stone. "Lives have never been taken in this place but the dead walk among the stones and blood calls to blood. I need your blood to call to Aeddan." She rolled up my left sleeve. "Heart's blood," she said as she took out an ancient looking knife. I watched as she placed the knife at an angle against my forearm. She sliced down, the edge so keen it took a moment for the sting to register. The cut was not deep but because of the diagonal slice it bled freely. She held my arm over the stone and my blood flowed onto the stone, splashing the ancient lichen.

Her voice began to intone a chant deeper and harder than the one she'd used by the lake. Power built around us, making my skin itch and stomach roil in unhappy unison to her words. More blood flowed, now trickling from the stone and onto the grass by my feet. I started to worry about the amount. Merla's voice rose along with the wind. It ripped through the stones, which screamed with deafening in harmony. I tried to cover my ears but she grabbed my arm and raised it high over our heads. Blood flowed down her hand and wrist. Light struck the altar stone and made my blood glisten. Merla screamed into the sky and a huge shockwave sent me stumbling away from her, ripping me free of her bone snapping grasp.

I found myself on my knees in the centre of the stone circle. The others held the hewn rocks to remain upright. Arthur clasped Excalibur. The horses had vanished over the hill. I faced Else, her eyes were wide with fear but she did not look at me, she looked behind me. Dread, the same dread which hounded my dreams, made me rise, turn and draw my blade all in one smooth movement. Aeddan, my father, stood far too close.

He smiled as I pointed my weapon at his throat. I held the sword as steady as the rocks surrounding us. The wind died, so did the screaming in the stones.

Merla slumped against the altar. Tancred moved to her side but kept his eyes on me.

"My son," Aeddan said. It sounded as though he was trying the phrase out to see if he liked the sound it made.

"I am not your son," I said.

"But my presence here denies that." He gestured to Merla. "Do you think she would have the power to call me without using my son's blood?" He took a step forward.

I took a step back. "You may have lain with my mother and you might have given her your seed to create me, but I am not your son, Aeddan. I belong to no one, I have no father, the relationship is moot. You have no power over me through those ties."

His mouth twitched in amusement. "If you say so." He grinned. "After all, I don't believe you called me here for a family reunion." His dark eyes, so much like my own, focused on Arthur. "I see you have your new toy despite my efforts."

Merla, pale but obviously stronger, walked to Arthur's side. "Surrender England to Arthur, Aeddan. Return to Albion and lead us into a new era without our dependence on humanity." Her words were formal, controlled, legal somehow, as though this ceremony had to be completed in a particular way.

"My beautiful lover," Aeddan said. His lust became thick on my tongue, I gagged. Aeddan stepped toward Merla. His power grew and images flashed through my mind. Merla in ropes, being used by Aeddan. My body wanted to react to his sexual depravity.

Tancred stumbled forward. "Don't let him touch her," he gasped as he struggled to fight Aeddan's magic.

Arthur raised Excalibur and stepped toward Aeddan blade pointed outward. Aeddan stopped just as the weapon kissed the ties on his shirt. "Release the power you've placed on my people," Arthur ordered.

The wash of lust vanished. Replaced by something purer, cleaner. Geraint sank to his knees. Else drew in sharp breaths and stared at me a little too hard. I helped Tancred stand, he shivered at my touch.

Aeddan's arms opened. "I have done as you asked, Pendragon. Now, I ask something of you. Leave Camelot to me and you, your wife and son, and your lover can leave England alive. If you stay, they will all die, starting with Lancelot."

Nothing moved but I felt a band around my heart and pain shoot through my chest. Blood rushed in my ears and my head pounded. My vision blurred and I reached for Tancred. He held my arm, I heard my name but the band in my chest tightened until I couldn't breathe. My knees gave way. I was going to die, my bastard father was killing me with magic. I only knew one thing. I would not allow that to happen. I reached for the Black Wolf and kicked it awake inside me. The power and strength of that wild, sentient beast rushed through me, filling my limbs with his grace. I glanced at Tancred, his brown eyes shot to amber, the same colour as his Wolf and he growled. The pain in my chest receded. Aeddan had no power over my Wolf.

The fey king's eyes widened in surprise. I looked to Arthur. A slight nod from my King made me rush towards Aeddan. I yelled a battle cry. A sword materialised in the fey king's hand and he deflected my attack, just as I intended. Arthur came in on my left and before anyone thought to say different we attacked the king together. I felt Excalibur's joy and I felt its power fill Arthur. He fought with a grace I'd never seen in him before, we were a perfect match for the first time, then he reached beyond my level of skill. He took the fight himself and I dropped back. Even that short time under Aeddan's mighty blows were enough to make my arms ache and my chest heave. The Wolf begged to be set loose, but Arthur fought with magic and I could no longer equal his perfection.

The two kings filled the centre of the stone circle, making it their private arena. Back and forth played their mighty battle, blows raining down and the dull chime of metal on metal filled the dusk. The first time Arthur lost a perfect parry and Aeddan's blade nicked his arm, I rushed forward, only to be stopped by Merla.

"No, this has to be them, Arthur has to win alone," she hissed

"Arthur has never been alone," I cried out.

"It is his time, Wolf, not yours," she told me pushing backward.

This was not the only injury suffered by my King, but he inflicted his own on his enemy. Aeddan bled and the grass turned black where his blood lay on the earth. The two men fought for the right to a kingdom and the battle proved to be worthy of the prize. I lost count of the strikes and marvelled at Arthur's stamina. Finally, the sun set and the sky lit up with its farewell.

"At last," Aeddan cried out, "now you are mine." He backed up from Arthur and raced to the altar stone, jumping onto its surface.

Merla cried out, "Arthur, stop him!" Too late, the last of the sun's rays hit

Aeddan and power crashed through the circle. Vast, crushing, chaotic power smashed into us. I heard screams of agony. It might even have been my own, before darkness hit me like a smith's hammer.

The stink filled my head. Horribly familiar. Stale, rotting straw that sat on cold damp stone. The next sensation – metal, cold hard metal bound my wrists and ankles. I tried not to move as I came around, just in case the enemy were watching. I heard weeping though and Else's voice calling Geraint's name. The pain in her voice made my body jerk and the chains rattle. My eyes tried to blink away the darkness and managed to an extent. I saw her huddled over a large figure in the corner furthest from me. I struggled to sit up.

"Lancelot?" she called.

"Else, is he alive?" My guts twisted at the thought of my friend lying dead. I remembered that feeling all too well when we faced Nimue.

"He won't wake up," she cried.

"But has he a pulse?" I asked slowly.

"Yes, but it's weak," she replied.

"Then he is alive," I said. "Calm down and try to help me with this. Is anyone else here? Wherever the fuck here is."

I ached all over and struggled to move from my side. I needed to sit upright. I might ache but my body informed me I'd not been beaten. My shackles were tight and forced my body into uncomfortable positions. My feet and hands were chained to the wall. I could not reach Else. Looking around I saw other slumped forms. My heart calmed when I recognised Arthur's blonde curls and Tancred's dark head. Of Merla, I could see no sign.

"We are the only ones to wake so far," Else said. "I think we are in a dungeon controlled by Stephen." I heard her fear. I felt it too. What had gone so wrong? How were we here? Where was Aeddan? Were we magically transported north to Chester and Stephen's stronghold, or were we being held somewhere close to the henge? In which case, Arthur had another traitor in his court.

"What makes you think we are under Stephen's control?" I asked, trying to remain calm.

"The voices I heard, the accents were northern and I think I heard reference to their rightful king. As their rightful king is in their dungeon I assumed they meant Stephen."

Or me, I thought, but didn't say. "Are you hurt?" I asked her.

"No, and I can't find any wounds on Geraint," she sounded calmer now she knew she wasn't alone.

"He'll be fine, Else. He has a thicker skull than mine." My heart ached for her fear, she loved her husband and I wanted to protect that love.

I heard a groan to my left, Tancred moved. He'd been chained like myself, with at least some room to manoeuvre. I wriggled, making my chains clank dully. I turned onto my knees and shuffled as far as my chains would allow. I could reach his leg and hand. His head came up as he felt my fingers grasp his limp fingers.

"Lancelot," he whispered.

"Hey, good to see you awake," I said. It did feel good too. A part of my soul relaxed as soon as he uttered my name. His chains slid, screeching when he moved.

"Where is Merla?" he asked, panic clear.

"I don't know, Else?" I asked the opposite corner.

"She wasn't here when I woke, which must have been around midday." She looked up at the narrow barred window far over our heads. The day now looked old and dull.

I explained what we knew and as I finished, Arthur stirred. He'd been chained tighter to the wall, I couldn't reach him. He cursed violently and fought his chains. I tried to tell him it was wasted energy, I'd been chained in dungeons far too often, I knew this game. He did however wake Geraint, so at least Else was happy.

"Arthur, Arthur, please, calm down," I shouted over his noise. "I need to know if you are hurt. Aeddan cut you several times."

"I don't give a fuck," Arthur yelled.

"I understand that but it doesn't change the fact that you could bleed to death and I can hardly see your face," I said.

He slumped against the wall, a lumpy shadow more than a man. "I think they've all been dressed," he muttered. "So, when the bastard traitor takes my head I'll be in one piece."

"I'm so cold," Tancred said. I peered through the gloom at him and he looked terrible. His lips were white against his drawn skin and I felt him shivering.

"What's wrong?" I asked. The dungeon might be cold but it was not that bad.

"I think the iron in the bonds is hurting me," he mumbled just as his head dropped to his chest.

"Tancred?" I fought my chains and dragged his body into my arms, cradling him to my chest. "Tancred, please, wake up." Nothing. "Else, what the hell is going on?"

"He's right, he is full fey, the high iron content is draining his strength. Steel he could cope with but not these bonds." She rattled her own chains. "Being half breeds we aren't affected."

"Will it kill him?" I asked. My chest constricted.

"Possibly, eventually," she said. "If we find a way to insulate his skin from the iron it might help."

'Might' was good enough for me. I struggled to pull layers of clothing up and began tearing strips off my shirt. I heard Else explain to a groggy Geraint and more tearing cloth. After some careful juggling, I managed to grab the roughly made bandages from the others and I stuffed the cloth under Tancred's bonds. I heard his breathing change as I rubbed sore skin. I raced against the dying light. Arthur sat, unable to move and now silent.

"He means a great deal to you," he stated quietly at one point.

"Yes, I am responsible for him, Arthur. He's sworn allegiance to me," I spoke in a distracted way, not really considering the implications.

"Do you love him?" Arthur asked.

I paused, I caught the tone, a thread of danger. "Don't over think this, Arthur, I'm not." But I did care. I cared a great deal. These sensations were far too new to be classified as a definitive emotion but I knew it would hurt beyond endurance if he were killed.

"I just want an honest answer," he said.

My first instinct made me want to snap that it had nothing to do with him. After all, he didn't need me anymore. I paused, fortunately, "You have your honest answer, Sire."

I stuffed the last of the fabric under Tancred's ankle cuff. He stirred and his eyes fluttered open. Relief swept through me and I began to calm. He lay on me and I made certain nothing iron touched his skin. I watched him sleep as the last of the day vanished and we were plunged into darkness. He seemed so young, so fragile and yet I'd seen him hack men to death to defend his comrades, including me. I held his hand, strong like my own and remembered that one brief kiss we'd shared. I wanted this man, I really wanted to hold him and protect him. I wanted to share my life with him. I wanted a future with him. Whether as friends or lovers I didn't yet know or understand but there must be more to life than bleak future I feared at Arthur's side. I stroked his long dark hair.

I discussed briefly what we knew with the others and whether we could escape. It didn't take long. We'd just have to wait. Arthur shifted as his limbs grew numb. I tried to tell him how to endure the pain, how to exercise muscles held still but he grew too agitated to listen. I wondered if his separation from Excalibur hurt him more than the chains.

I must have dozed off for a few moments because I didn't hear anything until a key opened in a lock. Else whimpered, Geraint hushed her and wrapped his arms around her tightly. He held her, the same way I held Tancred. The door opened, torchlight flared and blinded me for a moment. I blinked and heard Geraint curse. A figure, dark against the light, descended followed by others.

"Get the boy," came a thick voice.

Boy meant Tancred. My heart raced. "Who are you?" I asked. "Where are we and why have you imprisoned us?"

Arthur shifted. "You will not take any of us, you will release us, I demand –" his voice broke off as he cried out in pain. I heard a thud and an audible crack.

"You don't give me orders, scum," the voice snarled.

Two men reached for Tancred. I lashed out as they came within striking distance. My chains hampered me but I realised I hit something solid.

"Fuck, bastard, pervert," someone snapped.

"Just fucking hit him," his companion muttered.

"Try it," I barked, pushing Tancred off my lap and rising. They did. I learned something that night. You cannot defend yourself against three men when you are chained to a wall. I heard Else screaming my name as the last kick made darkness take over.

CHAPTER THIRTY-TWO

THE COLD WOKE ME, that and the pain. I groaned as I came round.

"Thank, God," Else cried out as I moaned and moved. "Lancelot, please, tell me you're alright."

"Fuck," I managed while trying not to move my jaw or lips. I couldn't open one eye and my ribs were killing me. "Tancred."

"Gone," Arthur said. "You've been out for hours." His voice sounded so dull, lifeless.

"Are you hurt?" I asked, my voice thick and words slurred.

"Ribs are broken but I'm better than you," he said.

A scream from somewhere else in the underground hell which contained us ripped into my heart. Else wept.

"What..?" I asked.

Geraint answered, "It's Tancred. I am sorry, Lancelot."

I lay, unable to breathe as the sound penetrated my soul. He screamed over and over, endlessly, while I found myself weeping into the mouldy straw, curled around his pain, my own a pale echo. It stopped, which was worse.

"Lancelot," Arthur's voice coaxed. "Please, please, I need you to be strong, my Wolf."

"If it weren't for you none of this would have happened," Else actually screamed. "Lancelot would be happy and be with him, if it weren't for you, selfish bastard."

The door above us opened, stopping us all from either agreeing or disagreeing with her brutal words. Once more, the torch blinded us but by this time a long line of men with drawn swords filled our cell. My eyes took too long to adjust.

"Unlock the prisoners," came a much smoother voice from the door of the cell. Someone reached for the lock attaching my chains to the wall and released them but the chains remained on my cuffs, which remained on my wrists. I tried to rise under my own steam but didn't manage it fast enough. The man who held my chains laughed as he yanked and I grunted. Pain shot through every bruise and fracture in my body. I'd taken beatings before but this one hit way too many sensitive spots. His florid, pox marked face and toothless grin marked him in my mind. He'd die when I found myself free.

Arthur struggled as much as I. His face remained undamaged in the torchlight but his ribs were in a far worse state. His chains meant he'd had no protection at all from his beating. His breathing came in short gasps and I saw blood on his lips.

I found myself being dragged forward behind Geraint, when we were in the corridor I saw the man who'd given the orders. Henry Wallington, a man of rank. His hazel eyes were cold as they assessed me. I spat at his feet, more blood than anything else.

"You will die traitor," I promised him.

He smiled. "I've supported Stephen a long time, now is no different. It's just that victory is finally in my grasp." I stared into his eyes and realised he meant it, he had no doubt that Stephen, not Arthur should sit on the throne of Camelot. We held no common ground. I did not understand anyone who threw their lives away on a usurper's cause. He joined the list of waiting dead in my mind.

I stumbled as I tried to move with the chains. Geraint caught me and held me. The guards hurried us through the dungeon area of a huge keep. I realised we were not in Salisbury, we were in Chester, Stephen's stronghold. How had magic brought us to this place or had we been controlled for weeks?

"Can you fight?" Geraint whispered.

"I can kill," I informed him, wondering if my hands were actually broken or just bruised.

I'd only been to this place once before, many years ago. Arthur sent me soon after his marriage. I'd volunteered to travel anywhere at the time. I'd come to present Stephen with a gift, a fine horse for some trade agreement he'd arranged with the Irish over the water. I remembered it as a brutal, cold place, old and built from Roman stone taken from ruins long empty. The path we took remained dark, lit by the occasional smoky torch. We were ushered through great doors into a large hall. Else held Arthur upright behind us and Geraint stopped me rushing headlong into a battle, when the men surrounding us dispersed to take up duties around the walls.

The hall, more or less square, contained two huge fireplaces, one on my left, one on my right. Firelight, almost the only radiance in the room, made it hot and sooty. The walls were covered in dark tapestries. The hall floor looked filthy under the fresh reeds thrown at random to cover the worst of the putrid substances. I could barely breathe through the smoky air and my eyes smarted. This place was no Camelot. I didn't see any grace, light, culture. Just rough stone and squalor.

Before us, on a raised rectangular platform sat three huge dark wooden chairs, meant to represent thrones. A woman sat very still. Her pale skin appeared waxy and her eyes glazed with horrors too deep to share, she wore a simple gold band around her hair. She did not look at any of us. Stephen's wife. Young and beautiful once, now torn and weary in soul. I saw her pain, weak red tendrils floated about her head and chest.

I saw other colours surrounding people in the room. Wisps of darkness crept from the men, their hunger for violence like waves feeding the hate in my own soul. I felt their joy at our pain.

A bundle before the platform caused my knees to tremble. I stepped out of line and Geraint tried to stop me. He held me back, forcing me to stillness.

His beautiful face lay toward me, his eyes closed, his lips blood stained. He did not have chains binding his wrists and ankles, one arm and leg were clearly shattered. He stayed so very still.

The Black Wolf howled its agony and I screamed my loss. Sounds of animal pain ripped through the great hall and cascaded back into me. Hands held me, strong hands wrapped around my body. Geraint fought me, encircled me, Else moved to help him. They forced me down onto my knees and she kissed my broken face until the first wave of pain receded. Arthur did not move. He just stared at Tancred's body.

"I am glad it hurt, you perverted sodomite," a tortured voice, barely human, cut through my grief. I raised my eyes from Tancred and realised the two other chairs were now filled. I had not noticed my enemy in my grief. I would not be making that mistake again. I wanted blood.

Stephen de Clare sat in the centre. The damage to his face was not hidden by shadows and firelight. The wounds I'd inflicted just a few weeks before were horrendous. The knife left a scar which meant his mouth would never close properly.

Arthur stepped forward, stealing my view of Tancred. "Stephen, release us," he said as a token. I heard the weary tone. Arthur already thought us lost.

Stephen laughed, a terrible cackling sound. "Arthur, you are a gift from my ally. I don't think I'd like to throw you away."

Arthur shifted and I caught sight of the other chair, Aeddan sat clothed in silver and gold. Merla stood, her dress torn, her mouth swollen with bruises and an iron collar around her neck with a chain to Aeddan's gloved hands. She stared at the body of her brother on the floor in front of Aeddan's chair. Excalibur leaned against the wooden throne, close to his left hand.

"Merla," I whispered. Her green eyes, filled with hate and shame, turned to me where I crouched on the floor. Her eyes swam with tears. I ached for her agony. Arthur's back stiffened.

"What do you want?" Arthur asked Stephen. I couldn't stand the dull defeat in his voice.

I watched Tancred as I struggled to my feet. If I couldn't save him, I could save Merla. I would not leave her with Aeddan. I zoned out of Arthur's wordplay with Stephen, I needed to think about how to win a fight. I shifted closer to Geraint, with Else making the third of our triangle. It brought me nearer to Tancred, only by a foot or so, but I saw something to make my heart scream with silent joy. His back moved as he breathed. His eyes fluttered. I focused on his face and watched as he struggled to find something he recognised. I moved my feet. His dark eyes caught it and rose upward. When he looked into my face, the relief and faith in his gaze made my heart leap. I smiled for him and he tried to smile in return, but the pain clearly overwhelmed him. I heard him whimper.

"My little catamite is awake," Aeddan said brightly. Merla's eyes widened in fear.

"Leave him, my Lord," she said as all eyes turned to Aeddan. "You have me."

She reached out for the fey king's sleeve. He back fisted her with casual brutality, knocking her to her knees. I stepped forward, until Arthur and Geraint caught hold of me.

"You are a fine fuck, Merla dear, always have been, but the boy you tried to hide is so much better," Aeddan looked at me. "Don't you agree, son?"

I felt sick. I couldn't say anything. I didn't trust myself to speak. I'd never seen or heard anything so cruel and depraved. If these men took Camelot, England would die. I had to stop this, I had to kill Stephen, rid Arthur of his presence. Then I must kill Aeddan and spend the rest of my life caring for Tancred. These were things I simply had to do, so my body obeyed.

The pain from the beating receded far into the distance. The weight of my iron bonds became irrelevant. I moved from my companions toward the dais. Arthur called my name. I needed Excalibur to kill Aeddan but he lifted the blade as soldiers rushed forward. I held most of the chain in my hands and it became a living ribbon of death. The world moved into stark colourlessness. Except for the blood. It rained down like water, the only colour left in a world so cold and empty.

I heard him, for the first time I heard his true song just as clearly as I saw the blood. Death whispered benedictions in my ears while I carved through the attacking men. The sound was sweet and the harmonies caressed my mind giving me great strength. I heard the screams and yells for reinforcements. I worked diligently until I reached the steps of the low dais. Stephen and Aeddan stood there with swords drawn. I swept up a fallen blade and walked toward them both. Arthur and Geraint were engaged in their own fights, trying to protect my back. Merla knelt by her brother. I felt Death move into me offering to help me swell his ranks, welcoming me at last. My true father perhaps?

I now held the sword by both chained hands. I swept it over my head as I came into Stephen. I smashed his blade, just as before in Avalon. The added weight of the chain making all the difference. I turned in the same movement and engaged Aeddan, forcing him back, before once more returning to Stephen. I wanted to see his blood more than anyone else's. Death laughed. I laughed. The blade took Stephen. One stroke, almost before I'd prepared myself for the satisfaction. Just one stroke is all it took in the end. In the uncertain flickering light his eyes died. Blood poured over my hands. Bright with a life now fleeing the body of a man I never needed to endure again. I'd carved into his chest by going through his collarbone and shoulder. I tugged the weapon but it wouldn't come free. I'd done it. I'd killed Stephen de Clare. He'd never even had a chance to torment his sister. I'd avenged Guinevere and stopped a war.

I turned to Aeddan. My new focus for vengeance and Death crowed in delight. The fey are long lived and Aeddan had cheated Death of the final dance for too long. The fey king had left the dais. I searched for him and caught a flash of gold at the edge of my vision snagged my attention before it vanished behind me. The connections were made too late. The kiss of a blade at my throat brought my simple world, that of killing for Death's favour, to an end.

"Everyone, stop," Aeddan said. His magic enhanced the simple words, they reverberated enough to make the dust fall from the tapestries.

He held me. Excalibur lay across my neck, the blade warmer than my soul in that long lonely moment. His fingers were tight in my hair and he forced me to my knees. I focused on Tancred. He lay in Merla's arms. Else stood over them with a sword in her trembling hands. Blood dripped from the end.

"Stop, Arthur, or your pet dies," Aeddan repeated. The sword cut my throat just a little but Arthur froze. The song from the blade twisted, confused by the taste of my blood and man in control of its dance.

"What do you want, Aeddan?" my King asked.

"I want you off the throne of Camelot but my people will not allow me to take it from your dead hands and my son has just murdered my best hope. At least for now. You've also killed most of de Clare's men between you, so for the moment I suppose I'm just looking for a way out," he didn't sound bothered. "My power is weak after bringing you all here so quickly. Stephen never did have patience. It's all rush, rush, rush with you mortals," he sighed. My eyes remained on Tancred. He breathed as he watched me in return.

"Get to the point," Arthur snapped.

"You take Lancelot, I have them," I felt him move his head but I couldn't see him. I did see the effect on my small tableau. Merla gasped a soft 'No'. Tancred looked at me frantic horror and Else turned her blade to Aeddan. He wanted my family. He wanted Merla and Tancred.

I threw a frantic glance at Arthur. He stared at me a long time before speaking, "You give me Excalibur and Lancelot for Merla and Tancred."

"Arthur, don't," I called, finding my own voice for the first time. "I beg you don't. I love him, don't." I hadn't realised, I didn't know, but I wanted Tancred to live, I wanted a chance to find out if I could make it work.

"You hear that, son?" Aeddan hissed close to my ear. "He's giving away the last chance you will ever have for love." Aeddan chuckled. "Why not, it'll even the odds and make the next round all the more exciting. Done, Arthur Pendragon. I hope you can live with the consequences."

"Arthur, please," I begged. Aeddan's hand twisted in my hair trying to force my head back so I could not look at Arthur. But I could speak, "I am your sword, my King, you don't need Excalibur." I knew if I had Tancred, he would help me rescue Merla. I could save them both if only Arthur would trust me and give up that damned weapon.

The whispering song from Excalibur rippled outward from Aeddan. I heard the questing sound, pale silver blue inside my head, it touched all those standing until it reached Arthur. When it felt him, it caressed him. Danced around him. His dark blue eyes widened and a slight smile kissed his lips. Arthur remained silent. I didn't need to see his face. I knew he would not rescind his agreement.

I screamed my grief and Aeddan laughed. I lunged for Tancred, his dark eyes full of fear, hope and love. Blinding white light filled the room.

When I opened my eyes, we were on Salisbury Plain, inside the stone henge. Darkness surrounded us but a moon rode low in the sky. My body felt torn in a thousand places. I raised my hands, the shackles had gone but the blood remained. Dead men's blood covered me. I sat, staring up at the sky, clear, bright, cold, perfect stars. So, cold. Cold, like my heart, my soul.

"Lancelot?" Arthur's voice, his arms around my shoulders, his breathing ragged in my ears. "I am sorry, I am so sorry, but I had no choice. I can never give you up, never sacrifice you. They are not you, my Wolf. You saved us. You are the mightiest of us and I love you for that." His voice sounded so far away and it slid off a shell which now covered my soul. He told me he loved me and I felt nothing. I didn't need these words. I needed other words from someone else.

The golden boy I'd once loved did not live inside this man. I wondered briefly who did. I felt Death inside my mind chuckling. Did someone live inside Arthur? Is that why he chose the sword over..?

I didn't finish the thought, it made my heart cramp tight. Arthur continued to touch me and speak words of justification.

I heard quiet tears and realised Else wept in Geraint's arms. They stood near us. I stood. I pushed Arthur off and walked out of the stone circle. I thought about Tancred's brown eyes and light, mocking smile. My legs stopped working and I sat heavily in the wet grass. I lay back in the damp winter grass and stared up at the sky. A small hand found mine.

"You alright?" Else whispered.

I squeezed her fingers. "No, no, I don't think I am."

"You love him?" she asked gently.

"I never had a chance to find out and with everything that happened between us..." I left the sentence hanging. She could make of it what she wished. Her thumb rubbed my knuckles in a frightening familiar way. All this was so new. A deep and terrible wound on top of barely healing scabs and at the centre, Arthur. A canker deep inside the wound, festering inside me, robbing me of everything. Each time I tried to strive for a love, for a peace, outside of Arthur, he tore it down, blocked it, changed it, stole it. And now,

now, Tancred would pay with his life and Merla would be raped and beaten and I would remain with Arthur, forever.

"I can't do this," I said suddenly. I rose, and with difficulty, but only because my rib ends rubbed against each other. I should feel pain, great pain, but nothing registered. I looked to the east and realised Ash stood on the horizon. I whistled and his head shot up. He whinnied and began trotting toward me.

I heard Arthur calling my name. I heard Geraint trying to stop him coming after me. Geraint recognised the grief.

It took a long time but I reached Ash. He knelt when I couldn't lift my leg to mount up. I climbed onto his back, my breathing ragged and sharp. The pain began to build, a relief at last to feel something normal, human, real. I turned Ash and I grabbed Echo on the way.

We walked into the rising sun.

Excerpt from

Lancelot and the Grail

Book Three
The Knights of Camelot

PROLOGUE

THE MOON SHONE DOWN on a tall broad man, turning his golden hair silver. A beautifully crafted sword hung from his left hip and his hand flexed on the pommel. He stood on the highest point of the wall surrounding his city, Camelot. An army spread out over the valley, cutting off supplies from the land and the sea, bringing anger to his spirit that he turned inward. Thousands of men camped down there, the lights from the fires, mirroring the stars in the night sky.

The people of Camelot were beginning to starve. The war machines, trebuchet mainly, loomed dark and silent in the night, but their devastation during the day made widows and orphans of his people.

"Arthur," Geraint said, his voice tentative.

"What is it?" Arthur asked. He fought for a neutral tone.

"You need to sleep, Sire," Geraint said, placing a hand on his King's shoulder. "Staring at them won't make them go away."

The tension in Arthur's shoulders fled and his back seemed to collapse. The proud man became broken in the space of a single breath.

"Come, you are exhausted, you need to rest." Geraint turned his King away from the vision before them.

"My people cannot rest with this army on our doorstep," Arthur said.

"No, but they don't have to make the decisions you do and they don't hold the lives you do, so you need to rest. Killing yourself through exhaustion won't help any of us survive. Eleanor has a draft of something which will help you sleep without dreams." Geraint guided Arthur into the main keep.

"You drugging your King?" Arthur asked.

"Whatever it takes," Geraint said.

"I don't know what to do," Arthur admitted.

"I know."

Geraint led his King into his apartment. Sparse candles flickered but barely held back the night. Everything was now rationed.

"We have to survive," Arthur said while Geraint unbuckled Excalibur.

"We will, Arthur."

"How?" the King asked.

Geraint paused. Only one other man in the world had these conversations with their Sovereign, but now it all lay at Geraint's door. "Right now, I don't know," Geraint said. "But we will survive, Arthur, because we have to and this is Camelot. Lean on your Knights, Sire. We can help you with this burden."

"I fear there is just one man I can lean on," Arthur muttered. Geraint didn't reply.

CHAPTER ONE

WE LEANED OUT. "COME on, ducky, quack, quack," we coaxed in a whisper. We thought about wriggling off the bank further but all our muscles ached from the tension of holding still for so long. Our fingers brushed the soft feathers of the duck's tail. "Dinner ducky, come on, dinner ducky," we muttered almost silent.

"Hello?" said a loud burning voice.

Our arm jolted and hit the duck hard. We grabbed but the thing squawked, flapped and shot off her nest into the water. Ducky gone. We lost the ducky but we tried to reach anyway.

I overbalanced and slid off the bank. If the water gave me a nasty shock, the loud people voice behind me shocked me more. I caught sight of a man, deep in the shadows of the summer trees.

We'd been playing with the ducks too much, we'd let a nasty man thing catch up with us.

I swam into the river, turned onto my back and floated with the current. I'd join the fish for a short time.

We liked fishy. We liked to eat fishy. Maybe we'd catch fishy tomorrow.

I'd go hungry unless my rabbit traps did something useful.

The water held us in its cold embrace.

I knew how far I could travel down it before finding myself caught up in the rapids. The trees were beautiful in their summer clothes, full green and reaching over the river, sheltering the banks.

We stayed in the centre of the river for a long time, the sun warm on our face.

I knew the winter would be harsh, last year's nearly finished me off, so I ought to be gathering more stores.

We liked the sun though and in this moment, we were all happy, so long as we didn't remember about the nasty loud voice. We tipped ourselves over and began to swim through the river.

But the event swam with me and I ended up thinking about the voice. How had it found me? I lived so far away from any of the villages and the roads. Occasionally, I went into the smallest of the villages which scratched a living from the forest, but not often and none of them knew where I lived.

We didn't like being found, we didn't want to be found. It made us angry to think we were found. We needed to build a wall between us and the rest of the world. We lived in our den, safe, warm, we didn't want anything else.

I came out of the water, pulling my naked body effortlessly from the river's embrace. My hair dripped water and tickled the top of my backside. I grabbed the mess and wrung it out, shaking water from my beard before leaving the riverbank.

We ran through the forest, trying to leave the fear and anger behind. We often ran from the fear and anger. It made us sick.

I found the world so hard to deal with, the last thing I needed was interference.

Our anxiety receded and we found a nice fat rabbit in a trap for supper. We cleaned it, cooked it and lay the skin out to scrape and dry. It would help keep us warm this winter.

I watched the sky through the tree canopy and thought about my friend, the Brown Wolf.

Sucking on a leg bone, we tried to remember what it was like to run with a pack mate. The memories were a long way away and they made us feel prickly and made us feel restless. We ran from those thoughts, we were alone and we were together, we'd stay like that forever.

I nodded my head at the stars as though sealing a pact between us, no more thoughts about that voice. No more thoughts about the past.

We found the next few days were busy. We collected more dry wood and hid it in the back of the cave. That spring had been blowy so many of the trees shed their branches for us to use, we often said thank you. We also tripped over a stag when hunting for bird meat.

I rose from the forest floor as I took aim with my simple hunting bow and he turned his mighty head toward me. His great liquid brown eye stared right into me and I found tears coursing down my cheeks. He shook his head and took off, long before I managed to focus well enough to shoot.

We did find some nice fat birdies though so it turned into a good hunt.

On a wet day, we don't like wet days, we sat in our den eating day old meat and picking at sorrel. We watched the slithery rain fill our river, when something caught our eye. A shadow flickered in the wind, hanging from our favourite oak tree.

I squinted and pushed hair off my face. Something black? Why would there be something black hanging from my oak tree?

We thought we knew and it made us squirmy inside. We thought we knew and it made our skin itch bad. We didn't want to know, we didn't want to think about the nasty voice which made us remember.

I rose from my nest of fur and fern inside a shallow cave. The rain felt cold on my bare skin, though the wind wasn't sharp, just a dull kind of effortless affair. The place I called home, a dell inside the mighty forest, lay cluttered with my belongings.

Furs were left out to dry on stretching frames, arranged around a large fire pit, and carvings were scattered about, which I made when I grew sated with hunting. I crossed the hollow and walked up the bank at the front of my home. I squatted down, making a smaller target for whatever fluttered in my oak tree.

We didn't want this, we wanted to run, please let us run from this. It's a nasty bad itchy squirmy horrible fluttery thing. It will haunt us; you do know that, it will haunt our nightmares. You hate nightmares. They come all the time. When was the last time we slept through a night?

My heart raced and my body sweated even as I sat in the rain. I, we, rarely connected so succinctly. Even as we did, I knew my sickness would grow worse if I went to the tree and retrieved the black cloth. I knew what it was; I saw the silver reflect the light. I saw the emblem on the chest. A wolf's head surrounded by oak leaves.

We ran. We vanished into the trees for days. We lived away from our den. Its disturbance made us nervous of return. Someone knew we were here and that meant trouble. If they found us, they wanted us and they only ever wanted us for one thing. We whined. They wanted us for Death. He chuckled. Only ever Death. He laughed. We hunted people so Death could feed once more on our soul. That's what people wanted.

Nights and days moved and He lost interest once more. Soon, when the moon became a slither of newness, we returned to our home.

I approached slowly, wary of potential visitors. I came in from the east, so I could pass the oak tree before approaching my home.

We sniffed the air, letting it roll over our tongue to see if we caught something extra.

No rain had fallen since the day I'd found the cloth on the tree and I sensed nothing stirred in the area but birds and squirrels. The black cloth remained on the oak tree. I stared in disbelief, having half convinced myself that my sickness made the thing real.

We also saw something else. A gift? A large wooden barrel hung from the tree. It had a tap in the bottom. A trap maybe? An ale barrel, hung from our favourite tree. Perhaps they were gifts and we'd been worried for all the wrong reasons. Gifts from the forest rather than warnings from Him.

"Why would the forest give you gifts?" I muttered aloud. The first true sound I'd made since the last full moon took more of my grief from my soul.

The voice was rough, deep, horrible. We didn't like it, we shook our head, we needed to find a new home. We keened in fear. We liked this den we'd been in it a long time. We were safe until now. But now we had ale. We thought for a long time. In the end we chose to climb the ash which grew near the oak. We climbed high and moved carefully into the oak. If it were a trap, it would be on the floor because the nasties were not clever. They did not know we could climb. We scrambled down the oak's trunk, checking the ground all the time for the nasties to appear. Nothing happened. So, slowly we reached the branch with the ale. And the cloth.

I reached out, stretched along the branch and pulled at the rope holding the ale. The barrel came up, as did the black cloth. There was the trap. I could not have one without the other. I considered dropping the ale but it had been so long since I'd had a drink, my mouth watered at the thought. I could throw the cloth away once I'd taken the ale. I'd do that, throw it into Sister River. I nodded vigorously.

I caught the ale up in rough hands and pulled the black cloth off the branch. With my arms full, I almost fell out of the tree but slowly wriggled backward onto the hollow created by several branches in which I slept some afternoons. The black cloth felt soft and smelt good, despite it being outside for days. The silver twinkled in the light making me smile.

We held up the ale barrel and opened the tap. Warm amber liquid filled our mouth up. We choked at the strange taste but swallowed in glee. When we finished guzzling, we switched it off and lay back to watch the sun. The nice fuzzy feeling in our head made our limbs tingle and tongue go numb. We giggled, surprising us with the sound.

I drifted, lying in the arms of my tree. I found the cloth, the black and silver tabard lay over my chest and I stroked it, tracing the embroidery of the wolf's head.

Nothing else happened for several more days. I finished the ale, having fallen into the water twice after imbibing said brew and burnt the barrel. I meant to burn the cloth to but it felt so soft.

We decided we could keep it if we didn't look at the wolf's head.

It made the nightmares easier when I woke sobbing because as I held it to my chest and buried my face in its softness. It reminded me of strong arms protecting me.

After a day picking berries, a long way from the den, I returned to find a haunch of meat hanging over my fire dripping fat into flames I hadn't created. I stopped, stunned and just watched the deer cook. Something, someone, wanted my attention.

We stepped into shadows and lay our berries down. Our beard felt sticky from juice as we tugged on it and our fingers were stained red. We smelt the meat when the wind changed direction. We were so hungry and here was free food. We shifted from one foot to another trying to figure out the game the nasties were playing. We heard a whine and realised we made the noise. As we watched, the fire died and the meat stopped cooking. A figure, dressed in green with dark brown hair and pale skin came out of another set of shadows to our left and approached the fire. It placed more branches in the flames and fed the monster so it would cook the deer. Then it vanished back into the trees.

The man held no knife or sword at his belt. He held no bow and did not acknowledge my presence in the trees, though he knew I watched. He now stood closer to my den than I, which meant he owned it, unless I killed him.

NO! We screamed altogether. WE DO NOT KILL THE NASTIES. The voices screamed so loudly we covered our ears and hid our eyes so we didn't have to listen.

They calmed as I reassured them I would not kill the invader, merely watch and wait. The day grew old and a fine summer dusk coloured the sky. The fat dripped into the fire and soon the flames completed their work, a cooked meal with berries for afters sounded so nice. The man only moved to tend the fire and the meat. He did not touch my things or touch my black cloth, which sat in the front of my cave to say hello to the sunshine. He did leave a barrel of ale by the fire though. A barrel of ale and a haunch and my berries.

When the meat finished cooking, the nasty sat on a log, not ours, its own, and began eating. It pulled strips off with its fingers and we heard it sucking the juice. We crept forward with the roughly woven basket in one arm, full of berries. We smelt the air. We crept closer. Our stomach growled so loudly the nasty froze having heard us behind its back. It didn't stay still for long, it kept eating, just more slowly. We realised half the meat sat by our log. We circled the campfire and came up behind it, remaining aware. It didn't look at us. We sat on our log and picked up the hot juicy meat.

The man and I ate. He used his foot to push the ale closer to me. I used mine to push my berries closer to him. I didn't look at his face. I didn't want to know. I wanted him gone but having him here made things feel different. Odd. Scary but nice. It made my chest hurt in a funny way. He and I shared the meal, until full dark came.

He finally stood up and wiped his fingers on his leather clothes. I wiped mine on my naked thighs.

"I hope I'll be welcome tomorrow, Lancelot," he said, with a soft voice. He walked away from the camp. I watched him vanish into the night and realised I wept again.

Find Sarah Luddington on <ins>Facebook</ins> and <ins>http://romanticadventures.net</ins>

AND

Welcome to the Newsletter
of Sarah Luddington's Romantic Adventure Books

Sign up for the newsletter and you will receive every month, author news, competitions and free downloads!
I promise on Lancelot's honour I will NOT spam you, sell your email address, become a monster troll and I will make sure you don't regret committing to my strange new worlds.

<ins>www.romanticadventures.net/newsletter/</ins>

And if you enjoyed this story, or even if you didn't, could I trouble you for a review? I know it can be annoying but they are the life blood of authors and they matter, they really matter.
Many thanks.